"I am accustomed to getting what I want," he said softly.

Was she dreaming, Sylvia wondered, or was that a thinly veiled threat that referred to much more than the painting? She laughed shortly, angry that this man could be so sure of her capitulation. "Then your heart has misled you, my lord, and you had best prepare yourself for disappointment. That painting is not for sale." Nor is anything else you may have set your heart on, she added to herself.

He grinned at her, a devilish, catlike grin. Had he read her thoughts? "I offered you the chance to contribute to the art collection in the Long Gallery at Longueville, my dear. A singular honor, I might add. My mother is anxious to add my likeness to the family heirlooms. You are my choice, Lady Sylvia."

She blushed and glanced towards the cliffs. The prospect of hours of intimacy with this man, alone in her studio, unnerved her. . . .

SIGNET REGENCY ROMANCE
Coming in March 1999

Melinda McRae
The Unrepentant Rake

Margaret Summerville
Gentleman Jack

Martha Kirkland
To Catch a Scoundrel

The Lady in Gray

Patricia Oliver

A SIGNET BOOK

SIGNET
Published by the Penguin Group
Penguin Putnam Inc., 375 Hudson Street,
New York, New York 10014, U.S.A.
Penguin Books Ltd, 27 Wrights Lane,
London W8 5TZ, England
Penguin Books Australia Ltd,
Ringwood, Victoria, Australia
Penguin Books Canada Ltd, 10 Alcorn Avenue,
Toronto, Ontario, Canada M4V 3B2
Penguin Books (N.Z.) Ltd, 182–190 Wairau Road,
Auckland 10, New Zealand

Penguin Books Ltd, Registered Offices:
Harmondsworth, Middlesex, England

First published by Signet, an imprint of Dutton NAL,
a member of Penguin Putnam Inc.

First Printing, February, 1999
10 9 8 7 6 5 4 3 2 1

CONTENTS

Prologue

The Betrayal

Weston Abbey, Horsham, Sussex
October 1804

"Cornwall?"

Lady Sylvia heard the quiver of hysteria in her voice and fought to control it. "Oh, Papa, I *hate* Cornwall. Please, oh *please,* do not send me there."

The Earl of Weston glowered at his youngest daughter, shaggy eyebrows crunched together over his large patriarchal nose.

"You should have thought of that before you shamed us all, my girl," he growled. After a short, pregnant pause he added somberly, "You leave at dawn tomorrow."

There was a finality about her father's tone that frightened her. For the first time Lady Sylvia began to realize that her latest escapade—which even she had to admit made her regular peccadilloes pale by comparison—had driven her doting parent beyond the limits of his endurance.

The silence in the earl's study became oppressive, pressing in upon her until Lady Sylvia imagined herself shrinking, compressed by the weight of disapproval that hung in the air.

She was not accustomed to disapproval. Indeed, Lady Sylvia had been confident that when her dear papa realized how set she was against the match he had arranged for her, he would indulge her. As he had so many times before.

She had been dreadfully wrong.

When the news reached Lord Weston that his daughter had—

civilly and with all the respect due to an aging marquess—declined
Lord Warburton's obliging offer, the earl's bellows of rage had
been clearly audible down at the gatehouse.

Lady Sylvia had been ordered to present herself instantly in her
father's study—a summons she considered wise to obey with more
than her usual alacrity—where she was subjected to a tongue-
lashing such as she had never before experienced from her mild-
mannered parent. The outcome of this unpleasant encounter was
not open to dispute, her father informed her grimly. The rejected
marquess had graciously agreed to renew his offer, overlooking
what Lord Weston chose to excuse as an attack of modesty in a
young lady unaccustomed to such an honor. Lady Sylvia would
behave like any self-respecting, obedient daughter and accept her
father's choice of husband without further protest.

"But, Papa, I cannot *love* Lord Warburton," she remembered
blurting out, hoping against hope that her indulgent parent would
grasp the impossibility of the match he proposed. "Besides, he has
grown sons older than I am."

It had been the wrong thing to say.

"Love?" the earl had shouted, his face turning an even deeper
shade of purple. "Love has nothing to do with the matter, you silly
little fool. This is what comes of reading that insidious, romantical
nonsense from the lending library, child. I warned your mother
how it would be. A good marriage is founded on trust, obedience,
and duty. Love is for fools and those damned poets who have nothing better to do than spout rubbish to fossilized half-wits at so-
called literary soirées."

Daunted but not deterred by this plain speaking, Lady Sylvia
had held her piece, and had finally been dispatched to her room to
ponder the error of her ways. It took her less than twenty minutes
to determine that her dear papa was mistaken; love had everything
to do with her choice of husbands. Once this was firmly established in her mind as irrefutable logic, Lady Sylvia had dashed off
an impetuous note to Sir Matthew Farnaby, whose protestations of
undying devotion—couched in that very poetic form maligned by
her father—had become so convincingly insistent of late that
Sylvia had been swept off her feet.

Sir Matthew had instantly understood her dilemma and come to
her rescue quite in the manner of one of Mrs. Radcliffe's romantical heroes. Lady Sylvia had been dazzled at the baronet's suggestion that she throw a few things into a bandbox and meet him down

by the gatehouse at midnight. She had been less enthusiastic at his insistence that she leave her abigail behind. Molly had been with her since childhood, and Sylvia had flung herself into the abigail's plump arms and wept when the moment came to mount Sir Matthew's traveling chaise and depart her father's house, perhaps forever.

Ten days later, looking back on that magical midnight moment when she had taken that momentous step from which there was no turning back, Sylvia still found it impossible to believe that she was not the respectable married lady Sir Matthew had vowed to make her. Had she not the marriage lines to prove it?

Lady Sylvia fidgeted restlessly under her father's accusing gaze. Her eyes fastened on the crumpled paper Lord Weston had tossed contemptuously on his desk at the start of this painful interview. Marriage lines did not lie, she reminded herself firmly, clinging to the one piece of evidence that could save her from utter disaster. If only her father would admit that he no longer had the authority to send her to Cornwall or anywhere else. She must remind him of that fact, instead of pleading with him as if she had no loving husband to protect her.

"Tomorrow at d-dawn?" Her voice sounded decidedly unsteady to her own ears. "That will be impossible, Papa. I must pack my trunks and be ready when my husband comes to escort me to my new home in Bath."

"What husband, you silly chit?" Lord Weston demanded, his voice thunderous. "When will it penetrate that addle-pated head of yours that you have no husband, Sylvia? You have been led down the garden path like some ignorant scullery maid."

Sylvia flushed at this unkind cut. "Oh, no, Papa. You are mistaken. I have the marriage lines to prove it." She gestured weakly towards the crumpled document on the desk.

"Marriage lines, indeed?" he exclaimed, his voice heavy with disgust. "Poppycock! How any daughter of mine could be such a nodcock as to believe that Banbury tale is beyond me. Rest assured that Town Tulip will not dare show his face around here again. Doubtless he is back in London enjoying a good laugh at our expense."

The specter her father's words conjured up caused Sylvia to wince. Ever since Sir Matthew had made his precipitous retreat from that poky little chamber at the Blue Duck Inn in Dover moments before her father's arrival, Sylvia had found any number of explanations for her new husband's continued absence from her side. Her father's cynical conclusion had never, until that moment, been one of them.

Now she was not sure what to believe.

The fact remained that her dear Matthew had disappeared from the inn, leaving her to face an irate Lord Weston alone. Her father had not ceased to repeat this indisputable truth during the entire journey back to Weston Abbey. Matthew could not have abandoned her, Sylvia kept telling herself, but her excuses for his prolonged absence were becoming less and less convincing.

Sylvia felt a lump in her throat, and blinked back the tears that clouded her eyes. She had promised herself she would not dissolve into a watering-pot. Up until now she had held firmly to the belief that as soon as Matthew came to claim his bride—acknowledging before her father and the world the validity of those precious days and nights they had shared at the Blue Duck Inn—her life would miraculously fall into place again. She would be feted and celebrated as the new bride she felt herself to be.

Perhaps her dear papa might be persuaded to hold a Public Day on the grounds of Weston Abbey as he had when her sister Margaret had wed Viscount Scovell several years ago. At the very least he would insist on a church ceremony in the ancient Saxon chapel attached to Weston Abbey, with old Reverend Martin—his jolly red face wreathed in smiles of approbation—banishing any lurking hint of scandal from the match.

She sighed. None of this could happen unless the elusive bridegroom put in an appearance, of course. And as the hours dragged by, Lady Sylvia found her dream of wedded bliss slipping from her grasp. How inconsiderate of Matthew to leave her alone at a time like this.

As her father's carriage left Dover in the pre-dawn hours to return posthaste to the Abbey, she had expected to hear the rattle of Matthew's traveling chaise behind them on the coastal road. But she had evidently expected too much of her new husband. Even the slovenly serving wench at the Blue Duck had known of Sir Matthew's defection. A most mortifying revelation, Sylvia recalled. The girl had informed her with a smirk—after taking Sylvia's proffered shilling—that it was pointless to send *billet-doux* to the handsome dandy, because his nibs had left in a bang not ten minutes since, springing his horses as though the bailiffs

were on his heels. Which—the saucy minx had the audacity to suggest—like as not they were, since he had not paid his shot.

Lady Sylvia had pooh-poohed this uncharitable notion, although
she had wondered why her darling Matthew had chosen such an
out-of-the-way, ramshackled inn for their wedding night instead of
the elegant Turk's Head in the center of town. She had been so nervous at the time that she had scarce paid heed to his explanation.
And afterwards, Sylvia recalled—with a faint blush at the memory
of her unsuspected wantonness—it had hardly mattered where
they spent that and the following delirious nights, as long as they
were together.

Looking back at those few blissful days, Sylvia wondered why
she had not thought to ask why the passage to France—where
Matthew had promised her the wedding trip of her dreams—had
taken so long to arrange. But she had known nothing of France, of
ferries, of wedding trips, of men. She was a novice at love, a
stranger to betrayal.

And if Sir Matthew Farnaby had betrayed her, as her father was
suggesting, and those marriage lines were counterfeit, then Lady
Sylvia Sutherland was indeed ruined beyond repair. What did it
matter, she thought miserably, whether she lived in the wilds of
Cornwall, the faraway hills of Ireland, or the bleakest moors of
Scotland? She could not stay here. Here at Weston Abbey, where
everyone knew her shame. Where everyone she had ever loved
would look at her as her father did now. With pity and sorrow,
ashamed of her.

The sudden wetness on her cheeks seemed to signal the end of
her resistance. Now that it was too late for tears, Sylvia realized
that her father had been right. Love did not guarantee happiness.
In her case, it had brought profound misery. Perhaps it had no
place in marriage, after all, she thought sadly. Perhaps such delightful interludes only occurred between the covers of library
books. She would never know, of course. No one was likely to
marry her now. Even the assiduous Marquess of Warburton had
departed for his estates in Kent, washing his hands of a female who
had thrown herself away on a charming philanderer and disgraced
her family name forever.

She glanced at her father's stern face.

"Tomorrow at dawn?" she repeated. "That is so terribly soon,
Papa. May I not wait until after my birthday on Sunday?"

Sylvia's heart lifted at the uncertainty she saw in her father's eyes. Perhaps he would relent if only she might celebrate her eighteenth birthday at the Abbey. Perhaps he would forgive . . .

"No," he said heavily, and her heart cried out at the pain in his voice. "Tomorrow at dawn. There will be no more birthdays for you here, lass. You have brought too much shame upon this house. It is only fitting that you go to your Aunt Marguerite. After all . . ."

Lord Weston sounded as though he would say more, but he stopped abruptly. Then he waved dismissively.

"Go and pack, child. Your brother will escort you down to Whitecliffs in the morning."

Chapter One

~

Mystery Cove

A cool, wet nose burrowing under her arm caused Lady Sylvia Sutherland to pause in her careful application of cerulean blue to the canvas before her. She glanced down into two pools of liquid umber and smiled.

"Time to find out what Cook has packed for us today, is it, Rufus?" she asked, her fingers automatically reaching for the dog's sleek head.

"Woof!" the collie responded obligingly, feathery tail confirming his readiness to interrupt his morning exploration of rabbit warrens for a more rewarding occupation.

Her brush still poised over the clear blue sky in the seascape she was completing, Lady Sylvia let her eyes slide over the scene before her with a deft proficiency gained from years as a successful artist. She was pleased with her rendering of the strangely desolate subject she had chosen.

The rocky coastline was broken at this point by a tiny cove indented into the sheer cliffs, as though some hungry sea monster of long ago had stuck his snout into the rocks in search of lurking eels. The darker green water in the cove promised depth and safety for small craft seeking a place to beach. Sylvia wondered how many storm-pressed vessels had found a brief respite from the rock-infested waters of the coastline in that hidden inlet. It was clear to her—from the warped, sun-bleached shapes huddled against the foot of the cliffs—that many had not been so fortunate.

The weather-beaten stone shanty clinging to a ledge in the steep incline just above the reaches of all but the highest tides appeared, at first glance, to be part of the cliff itself. Sylvia had come across it quite by accident during her first weeks of banishment in Cornwall, and had been charmed by the rugged tenacity of the primitive little hut. She had sketched it many times, but this was her first attempt at a full-scale likeness in oils. She was more than satisfied with the results.

When she had first come to Whitecliffs at eighteen, full of bitterness and regret at the blow fate had dealt her, Sylvia had taken up her childhood hobby of dabbling with sketchpad and paint as a means of blocking out painful memories. As time passed, however, she had grown tired of reproducing endless pictures of gulls, and farmyard animals, and her aunt's gray tabby cat, Jonas, and turned her hand first to portraits of the reclusive inhabitants of the wild Cornish coast, and then to the ever changing sea.

Leery at first of the intrusion, the local fishermen had kept out of her way, averting their eyes or mumbling incomprehensibly when they chanced to cross her path on the lonely cliff tops. Gradually, however, and particularly after Sylvia had the brilliant notion of offering a few coppers to a tow-headed lad with more cheek than his fellows, she was able to acquire all the subjects she could handle.

But it was the sea and everything connected with it that presently held her attention. Sylvia found the little gray hut on the cliff side especially fascinating, and had amused herself during those long wintry evenings at Whitecliffs imagining all manner of mysterious explanations for its presence there. Even now, in the warmth of the bright June sunlight, her mind drifted to the tragic circumstances—Sylvia knew in her bones the history of the stark hut had to be tragic—surrounding the half-hidden stone structure that occupied a prominent place on her canvas.

Perhaps little Timmy Collins, the cheeky lad who figured so often in her sketches, was right about it being haunted, she mused, dipping her drying brush in the jelly-jar of turpentine she always carried with her. Perhaps . . .

The damp nose under her arm gave an impatient jerk, interrupting her ruminations on the past. There was nothing like a dog to keep one's mind firmly on immediate concerns, she thought wryly, and Rufus's mind was clearly set on food.

"All right, old boy," she murmured, getting to her feet and stretching, "let us explore Cook's basket and see if we can find something to take the edge off your appetite, shall we?"

Followed by the ecstatic collie, Lady Sylvia ambled over to the stunted clump of gorse bushes that huddled, like a troop of bedraggled survivors of a particularly vicious military encounter, beside the faintly rutted path that led down to the cliff. Sylvia had often speculated on the unknown feet that must have worn that track into the tough Cornish grasses. Her vivid imagination had led her to speculate on marauding Vikings from long ago, putting ashore to kill and plunder, making off with female captives and meager livestock. More recently she preferred to visualize hunched figures of smugglers trudging along beneath the weight of French brandy in the waning moonlight, furtive glances on the lookout for excise men from nearby Falmouth.

Her favorite fantasy, one that incorporated all the elements of one of Mrs. Radcliffe's more lurid novels—if Timmy's occasional bursts of confidence held any truth to them—appeared to be shared by the local inhabitants. Perhaps because Sylvia could see herself in the love-bewitched lady whose white-clad figure had been seen—according to Timmy's highly embellished version—flitting along the cliff path under the full moon, she had been fascinated by the tale. Not that she believed it, of course, smacking as it did of ignorance and superstition, and even of the fairy lore so dear to the hearts of country folk everywhere. But the image of the lonely lady seeking her lover intrigued her, and she had made many sketches of the imaginary scene, fully intending to create a full-sized portrait of the ghost-like figure on the cliff top.

The unpretentious little trap Sylvia occasionally used to transport her canvases stood beside the gorse bushes where she had left it that morning. Puffin, the shaggy pony whom she had learned to harness to the cart herself if she wished to get out of the stable-yard at a reasonable hour, stood nearby, flicking his long tail languidly, eyes closed drowsily.

"Still not awake, Puffin?" she remarked companionably to the animal. Sylvia could have sworn that the pony came fully conscious only on the way home, when the prospect of stable and oats loomed into sight.

Rufus whined, reminding her that it was well past their usual refreshment hour. Sylvia smiled to herself as she plucked the covered wicker basket from the trap, marveling once again at the changes she had undergone since her arrival at Whitecliffs ten years ago. Had anyone told her that she would spend a significant portion of her days out on the cliffs and desolate moors in the company of a rabbit-obsessed dog and a sleep-walking pony, she would have scoffed at the notion.

Settling herself on the plaid rug she used to protect herself from the tough, blade-sharp grasses, Sylvia removed the linen serviette from the basket and peered inside. Predictably, Rufus's bone lay on top, and Sylvia had learned not to dally in presenting it to him. After that small but vital ritual was taken care of, she could enjoy her own meal, although her mind soon drifted back to the mysterious moonlight wanderer.

By mid-afternoon, when the slanting shadows had caused the stony cliff hut to recede once again into the rocky background, Sylvia had long since pronounced the painting complete and washed out her brushes. As she sat on enjoying the waning sunshine, the notion came to her that perhaps it was time to tackle the subject of that lonely lady in white.

An anxious growl from Rufus interrupted these pleasant thoughts. Thinking it was young Timmy come to help her harness the somnolent Puffin, as he often did, Sylvia paid no heed. It was the harsh voice that followed closely on the dog's warning that made her whirl around, spilling the jelly-jar of turpentine on the hem of her skirt.

"Who gave you permission to trespass on my land?"

Raising her annoyed gaze from the oily stain spreading over the pale gray muslin of her gown, Sylvia was prepared to blister the intruder for his rudeness.

The sight of the man glowering down at her made the tart retort die in her throat.

She had never seen the gentleman before. Nor had she ever heard that the stretch of land between her aunt's manor house, on the outskirts of the village of Cury Cross, and the sea belonged to any of the isolated estates of the local gentry.

"I beg your pardon, sir," she said, her voice icy. "I do not believe we have met."

The gentleman—his attire if not his manners proclaimed him as one—smiled grimly. At least Sylvia deduced the grimace that twisted his harsh features was intended as a smile.

"A dull-witted, superfluous observation," he snapped. "Of

course we have not met. I do not favor redheaded ape-leaders of dubious breeding. All of which does not alter the fact that you are trespassing on my land, madam, and I must insist you leave instantly."

The quite monstrous incivility of this response deprived Sylvia momentarily of breath. Never in her life had she been addressed in such deliberately offensive terms. Dubious breeding indeed! While it was certainly true that her muslin gown was several years out of fashion and a little the worse for wear, it was not the sort of garment worn by females existing in that unenviable state of genteel poverty. Or was it? she wondered, never having considered the matter before.

Ape-leader she would have to admit to, of course, but it was unpardonably rude of him to mention a lady's advanced years. And of course, there was no denying the flamboyant color of her hair. Sylvia had always considered it her crowning glory, and had been accustomed to having it greatly admired by the gentlemen of her acquaintance—before she fell from grace, she reminded herself quickly. It did not surprise her to hear this oafish rudesby malign it; he obviously lacked both discrimination and good taste.

Her first impulse was to give the jackstraw the blistering setdown he deserved, but a quick glance at the deserted cliffs reminded Sylvia that she was quite alone with a creature who was at best deranged, and quite possibly dangerous.

She forced herself to smile as at a contentious child.

"You are quite correct, sir," she said sweetly, gathering her artist's paraphernalia into its box. "I shall take your advice instantly." She glanced up at the sky. "It must be nearly tea-time in any case," she could not resist adding, just to show him that she had better things to do.

Sylvia was quite sure that Puffin was still dozing by the time she had him harnessed to the trap and turned towards Cury Cross. He stumbled once or twice on the rough terrain, but as soon as he realized they were on their way homewards, he blew the dust from his nostrils and put one hoof before the other in a purposeful manner.

The surly gentleman made no attempt to offer assistance, and Sylvia did not so much as glance at him.

Climbing into the little cart, she whistled to Rufus and gave Puffin a vigorous slap with the reins.

Glad to have escaped with nothing but a display of rudeness from the stranger, she did not once look back.

Nicholas Morley watched the little cart rattle away down the grass track towards the village. Not once did the fiery-haired occupant, her back rigid with indignation, glance behind her. Only the dog, perhaps sensing the man's hostility, stopped to express his disapproval with a warning bark.

Long after the unknown artist had disappeared into the dip where the cliff track joined the main lane from the little port of Mullion to the village of Cury Cross, Nicholas stood rooted to the spot, his mind flooding with memories he had thought buried by years of exile.

He had not intended to come up here to the cliff this afternoon. Nicholas could not explain the morbid fascination that had directed his steps to the one place on his estate that he most wished to avoid. Perhaps the unresolved mystery of what had happened here still haunted him, he thought. Perhaps he had hoped to discover—looking back with clearer, wiser eyes at that horrifying event that had changed his life forever—the answers that had eluded him, eluded them all, on that summer evening long ago.

If truth be told, he had not wanted to return to Longueville Castle at all. Had not his mother, her health failing in the harsh climate in Calcutta, begun to talk with nostalgia of joining her husband in the family cemetery, Nicholas might still be in India.

He had thrived there, expanding, with an acumen he had not known he possessed, the small trading company he had established in Falmouth on a youthful wager long before he inherited his title. The risk of being ostracized by the *haut monde* for his association with Trade deterred Nicholas not a whit. On the contrary, the tainted nature of dabbling in such ventures increased their allure for a bored young buck whose generous allowance seemed to be perpetually incapable of covering his needs. Besides which, the knowledge that his father would be livid if he discovered his heir rubbing elbows with the merchant class gave an unholy piquancy to the adventure.

With a sigh the earl turned back towards the coast. He had left his horse at the Pirate's Cove inn at Mullion early that afternoon, and on impulse struck out along the cliff towards the hidden cove from which the inn derived its name. Now he wished he had accepted old Bill Bates's offer of a tankard of local ale instead. He would have been spared the shock and unpleasantness of his meeting with the red-haired female.

His behavior had been execrable. The virulence of his response to the strange female had surprised him, and Nicholas was relieved when she chose not to argue with him, but took off in a flurry of outrage, wisps of red hair escaping from beneath her wide-brimmed straw hat. Her parting remark about it being tea-time was a deft set-down, he realized belatedly. A reminder that there was somewhere else she would rather be.

It was the kind of remark Angelica had been so fond of using.

Nicholas was thankful he had not seen it sooner; he might well have compounded his inexplicable rudeness with physical violence. The thought alarmed him. Was he indeed capable of such violence against a female? All those years ago people had seemed to think so. His neighbors, his tenants, his London friends, his relatives, the local magistrate, and most certainly the villagers. All but his mother had believed him capable—although none had dared to say so openly—of the most violent physical crime a man might commit against his wife.

In spite of the warm sun on his bare head, Nicholas shuddered. He had thought those soul-wrenching doubts overcome and buried in his past, together with the bitter memories of betrayal and heartache. But the sight of that lone female figure sitting on the cliff before the familiar easel had resurrected every one. For one agonizing moment the past had crowded into his consciousness—that solitary artist had become *her.* His heart had leaped into his throat, and he experienced a nostalgic joy that evaporated before it was fully formed.

Before he could control it, the violence set in. As he strode towards the solitary figure, Nicholas felt his hands curl into fists, his fingers itch to coil around that slender white neck, his heart fill with fury and bitterness at *her* betrayal. When he had come up behind her and seen the infamous stone hut depicted so blatantly on the canvas, he had felt his control slipping, his latent violence roiling inside him.

Then he had seen the red hair.

The sight of the hair had abruptly diffused his anger, leaving him confused, hostile, needing to lash out to relieve the tightness in his chest. So he had taken refuse in rudeness, in unspeakable, uncharacteristic remarks that he regretted now that it was too late to retrieve them.

Unable to stop himself, Nicholas walked to the edge of the cliff and gazed down the steep, rocky steps at the stone hut. It had not changed in the years he had been away. Still squat and menacing, it clung to the cliff like an evil excrescence, a canker that had eaten away at the heart of his marriage, destroyed *her* just as surely as he himself had been destroyed by the events that had occurred here.

Impatiently, the earl swung away from the cliff and strode in the direction of Mullion. He would retrieve Arion from the Pirate's Cove and go home. Home? Nicholas wondered if Longueville Castle would ever seem like home again. Perhaps if he never came this way again. Perhaps if he could forget this whole unfortunate incident when, for a devastating moment, he had thought *she* had come back to haunt him.

The notion of being haunted was patently ridiculous, of course, but he had already heard rumors—spread by the superstitious villagers no doubt—of a wandering figure on the cliff tops. He would have to put a stop to such nonsense immediately, he told himself. The only wandering figure he would acknowledge was the female in gray with red hair. And he had effectively banished her from interfering in his life.

Much later, as he came in sight of the church spires of Helston outlined against the late afternoon sky, it occurred to Nicholas that perhaps he owed the lady in gray an apology. After all, she had, momentarily at least, chased that other spectral wanderer from his mind.

Chapter Two

~

The Lady in Gray

The open landau creaked ominously as it swung between the stone pillars that guarded the entrance to Whitecliffs, the Tudor manor house inherited by its present owner, Lady Marguerite Sutherland, from her grandmother. The pillars, topped by weather-beaten lions staring out fiercely at the distant sea, reminded Nicholas of his childhood. How many times, he wondered nostalgically, had he hesitated in the lane before urging his pony through the gates at breakneck speed to avoid the fulminating glare of those hard gray eyes?

"When we go up to London in October, Nicholas, you must see about ordering a new carriage from Hatchett's," his mother remarked as the landau bowled unsteadily up the driveway, lined with ancient lime trees. "This poor thing was old in your grandmother's time."

The earl's attention shifted abruptly back to the present. "Are we going to London in October?" he drawled, recognizing his mother's favorite gambit for introducing plans she knew he would dislike. "That is the first I hear of it, Mama. I was under the impression that we had only recently returned home from India."

The Dowager Countess of Longueville glanced up at him coyly from beneath her elegant parasol and smiled sweetly, seemingly unaffected by the earl's gentle sarcasm. "I am well aware of that, my dear boy," she said. "After so many weeks cooped up in that stuffy cabin, I am grateful to be able to breathe fresh Cornish air again. But we must not disregard the future, Nicholas. Your aunt and I have decided it is high time you took your place in society again." The dowager cast an encouraging glance at the third occupant of the carriage, "Is that not so, Lydia?"

Mrs. Lydia Hargate nodded vigorously in agreement, as Nicholas had anticipated. In the six years since the death of her second husband, his amiable, self-effacing aunt had never, to his knowledge, contradicted her more assertive relative in anything. The earl had always found this passivity mildly annoying, because he had long ago recognized that his Aunt Lydia was possessed of far more common sense than his mother. She might be counted upon to take charge, quietly but efficiently, in any disaster.

As she had with Angelica. With his brother Stephen, lost at Talavera. And still further into the tragic past, with the sudden death of her own eldest son, his cousin Luke. It was no coincidence that, after being widowed for a second time, his aunt had joined the Morleys in India at the earl's urging. "You belong with us, Aunt," he had told her and meant it. What he had not confessed was that she seemed to be the only one able to hold what was left of his crumbling family together. He needed her quiet strength more than he cared to admit. He always had.

It was to Aunt Lydia he had appealed, close to tears, the evening before his mother's thirtieth birthday, he remembered. He still recalled the overwhelming grief he had felt when he discovered the small brooch, painstakingly chosen and secretly purchased at Falmouth, missing from its hiding place. His unflappable aunt had clasped him to her ample bosom and suggested that the gift was merely misplaced, not lost. Nicholas had believed her, as he always had.

After the family had retired, Aunt Lydia appeared in his room with the missing brooch. He had come to her room before dinner to show off his prize; did he not remember? she explained in her matter-of-fact voice.

Nicholas had believed her again. Why should he not? It was years later, long after the incident should have been forgotten, that it dawned upon him that the missing brooch was perhaps the first in an endless list of peccadilloes—he had not called them anything stronger until much later—that could be traced directly to his cousin Matthew.

The earl had not consciously thought of his cousin in years. There were too many unanswered questions about Matthew Farnaby that did not bear close examination. Unfortunately, one of the disadvantages of returning home to England was that Nicholas would eventually have to face his flamboyant, debonair cousin again. For the present, however, he preferred to ignore the existence of Sir Matthew Farnaby.

He turned to smile at his aunt. "Am I to believe that you are anxious to spend a fortune on fripperies and throw yourself into the social whirl of London, Aunt?" he demanded teasingly. "I never would have guessed it."

"You are being absurd, as usual, Nicholas," his aunt replied with her characteristic calm. "When have you seen me pining for the delights of the *haut monde,* such as they are? 'Tis true I enjoy the theater, and musical soirées can be relaxing, but—"

"Do not pretend you did not like visiting the silk bazaars in Calcutta, my dear Lydia," the dowager interrupted, as she invariably did whenever she felt herself excluded from the center of the conversation. "I fail to understand why you would only pack two bolts of silk for your own use. Heaven knows when we shall ever see Calcutta again."

"I thought you could not wait to shake the dust of India from your feet, Mama," the earl remarked mendaciously. "I distinctly remember you saying that—"

"Do not, I beg you, Nicholas, be constantly reminding me of what I said," the dowager interrupted pettishly. "How am I supposed to remember? And besides, have I not the right to change my mind? You must admit that those silk bazaars are fascinating places. I never could make up my mind which colors suited me best."

"So you bought one of each, no doubt," the earl mocked her gently, fully aware of his mother's weakness for clothes.

"And what if I did?" the dowager retorted. "Some of them are for gifts, of course." She gestured to the parcel on the seat beside her. "I have chosen a green shot silk for Marguerite that will complement that red hair of hers."

She paused as if an unpleasant thought had crossed her mind. "I do trust she still has red hair," she added. "It has been so long since I saw her, she may be gray by now." Her gloved hand touched her own chestnut curls self-consciously, as if to convince herself— Nicholas knew exactly the way his mother's mind worked—that her own hair still maintained its natural color.

"You may count upon it, Dorothea," Mrs. Hargate said. "All those redheaded Sutherlands keep their color long past their prime. Only remember Marguerite's grandmother, the Lady Giselda. She was seventy if she was a day, and I have heard tales of her riding into Helston on her big roan gelding with that wild red hair flying all over the place."

His aunt's description of their late, lamented neighbor nudged the earl's memory. He still retained childhood recollections of the flamboyant Countess Giselda Weston before she was carried off one winter with a severe attack of the colic brought on by an overindulgence in raw oysters. She had been a female who lived on the edge of propriety—as did her granddaughter, Lady Marguerite, whose open liaison with an Italian artist had scandalized the countryside years ago.

"I wonder if that sculptor is still in residence at Whitecliffs," he remarked, more interested in scandalizing the two ladies in the carriage than in any real interest in Lady Marguerite's *amours*. "What was his name? Giovanni Patorno . . . Paterno?"

His mother blushed a bright pink, but Aunt Lydia merely smiled tolerantly. "Petorno. You may count upon it, Nicholas," she replied, when it became obvious that the dowager had pretended not to hear the question. "And it appears that Marguerite now has a niece staying with her. I would not be surprised to learn that the Sutherlands have produced yet another black sheep. The men in that family are steady enough, but the females seem to kick over their traces with alarming frequency. I would not mind a small wager that the girl has red hair."

The vision of a tall female in shabby gray muslin and wisps of red curls dancing about her angry face flashed through the earl's mind. Yes, indeed, he thought wryly. It would be just his luck to have mortally offended a relative of Lady Marguerite's. Not that he greatly cared for himself, but his mother counted their scandalous neighbor among her dearest friends, an incongruity he had long ago ceased to marvel at.

"Oh, how lovely!" the dowager exclaimed as the carriage emerged from beneath the lime trees and approached the entrance to the manor house. "I do believe that sunken garden is a vast improvement over those terraced beds of peonies dear Marguerite used to have in front of her door. I never did like peonies; they are so very . . . well, so flamboyant and *lewd*, if you know what I mean."

"Lewd?" Nicholas gazed at his mother in astonishment. "Flowers cannot be lewd, Mama," he argued. "People are lewd. Or art perhaps, but not flowers. Now, if you had complained about that statue"—he gestured to the lightly draped figure pouring a stream of water from a Greek amphora into the rippling surface of an artificial pool—"I might have understood your objections. Not agreed, of course," he added with a laugh, "for the statue is quite lovely."

"I must agree, Nicholas," Aunt Lydia said. "I have always admired the classical Greek style. I would not be surprised if Marguerite herself had posed for it. She is capable of every bizarre extravagance, as we all know."

"Shameless extravagance, I trust you mean, Lydia," the dowager interrupted huffily, averting her eyes from the offending statue. "I shall insist that she remove it," she muttered under her breath as she allowed the earl to assist her out of the carriage. "It is quite beyond the pale to have one's park dotted with nude females."

Nicholas raised an eyebrow and winked at his aunt. "I must agree with you, Mama. If the park were indeed dotted with nude females, it would be a sight for sore eyes," he remarked, hard put to keep the amusement from his voice. "I, for one, would be a constant visitor. Lady Sutherland would become sorely vexed at me, I imagine."

Mrs. Hargate chuckled. "Try not to tease your dear mama, Nicholas," she cautioned. They mounted the steps in the wake of the dowager, and Nicholas noted that his mother was vainly attempting to pretend she had not heard his outrageous remark. Her rigid back told him otherwise, and he knew that he had indeed ruffled her sensibilities a trifle too roughly.

The front door swung open before the earl could think of a mollifying rejoinder, and the dowager swept in with a regal nod at Hobson, the ancient Sutherland butler.

"Welcome back to England, milady," the butler remarked in a tone calculated to convey the message that he had been holding his breath for the past ten years in anticipation of the dowager's return. Giving Mrs. Hargate the merest nod, Hobson turned to the earl with something approaching a smile on his wizened countenance.

"Welcome, milord," he said, taking the earl's tall beaver and malacca cane. "It is indeed good to see your lordship back home again. Her ladyship is awaiting you in the Italian Saloon," the butler added stiffly, turning to lead the party up the marble staircase to the first-floor apartments.

Nicholas was about to follow the ladies when his attention was caught by a full-length portrait in a gold-leaf frame hanging in what was obviously a place of honor facing the entrance.

The gray eyes that gazed down upon him reflected a secret, mischievous amusement rather than outrage. The mouth, which he had last seen drawn into a thin line of repressed fury, had softened into a sweet, mysterious smile that gave the face such a glow of confident loveliness that Nicholas felt his breath catch briefly in his throat. The wide-brimmed straw bonnet, embellished with a single large pink rose, full-blown and voluptuous, was a far cry from the shapeless hat she had worn on the cliff two days ago. The red hair was unchanged: less riotous perhaps, but still escaping—a wisp here, a wayward curl there—from the severe clusters of ringlets that framed her face.

Her gown, a simple, shimmering gray silk, was nothing like the old-fashioned gray muslin he remembered. The effect was the same, however, giving her a ghostly, untouchable aura found only in truly exceptional females. Her sculpted arms, covered by the palest of pink gloves, buttoned modestly from wrist to elbow, held a bouquet of pink roses carelessly against the rich gray silk.

Ignoring his mother's voice, and the sound of footsteps ascending the stairs behind him, Nicholas felt himself drawn towards the luminous female in the painting. Leaning forward, he read the small brass plaque fastened to the center of the gilt frame.

The Lady in Gray.

Nicholas looked up into the amused gray eyes and smiled wryly. So, he thought, playing coy, are we? In a few minutes he would be called upon to tender this same mysterious female in gray an apology—an abject apology if his memory of their first encounter was anywhere as uncouth as he remembered it.

He shrugged and turned his back on the portrait, wishing he had not come.

Lady Sylvia glanced critically at her latest canvas. The afternoon sunshine pouring in through the high, domed windows of her studio offered another two hours of prime working conditions that she was reluctant to squander. She wished she might have stayed in the village that morning, and taken her midday meal with the family of the two elfin-faced girls whose wide eyes stared at her from the unfinished painting.

She sighed and turned to put away her brushes. Taking tea with her Aunt Marguerite and Giovanni inevitably developed into lively discussions on some aspect of the art world that often lasted until dinner time. Only yesterday she had slipped away, leaving Lady

Marguerite heatedly defending the style of a relatively unknown artist, one of her aunt's numerous protégés, whose work was presently displayed at one of London's galleries.

This particular afternoon Sylvia had been summoned to meet the Morleys, one of the neighborhood's principal landowners, recently returned after a lengthy sojourn in India. It had been futile to assure her aunt that she had no interest whatsoever in the Morleys. Or in any other of the landed gentry who all too frequently descended upon Whitecliffs to make the obligatory morning calls.

Privately, Sylvia considered these social calls nothing but endeavors to embellish the scandalous rumors that had followed her into Cornwall ten years ago. Aunt Marguerite had originally put it about that her niece's health was the cause of her prolonged sojourn in the south. But it was not long before wildly exaggerated versions of the truth began to filter down from Sussex. Both ladies had derived much amusement from these indiscreet attempts to ferret out what locals began to refer to as Lady Sylvia's peccadillo. Now they simply ignored all such impertinences.

As she trod down the stairs to the Italian Saloon—so named in honor of her aunt's companion—Sylvia wondered which of the Morleys would be the first to probe her past. She wished people would accept her at face value, judging her not on her past mistake—and Sylvia freely admitted that she had committed a major error in judgment in trusting the word of a charming blackguard—but on her growing reputation as an artist.

Hobson was waiting on the landing, ready to usher her into the saloon with his unbending formality, a carry-over from the days of Sylvia's great-grandmother, the flamboyant Giselda, Dowager Countess of Weston. The ancient butler had been but a stripling in those days, an under-footman, but the years had passed slowly in the old man's life, leaving him embedded in traditions that sat oddly in the informality of an artist's household.

Lady Sylvia smiled warmly. "I see I am late again, Hobson," she remarked. "I only hope these Morleys are worth the interruption in my work."

Barely acknowledging this breach of decorum with an imperceptible nod, Hobson threw open the doors of the Italian Saloon with his usual flourish.

Sylvia stepped inside reluctantly. She did not relish spending the next half hour talking about the unseasonably warm weather, or the lack of rain that threatened the apple crop, or the fate of the

young poacher caught in Squire Robinson's wood the week before. None of these subjects interested her as vitally as the two
elfin faces waiting for her up in the sunny studio.

As Sylvia paused on the threshold, she intercepted Lady Marguerite's smile from across the room. The two ladies sitting with
her aunt could not have been more different, and with her artist's
eye Sylvia easily distinguished the elegant Dowager Countess of
Longueville from the comfortable-looking lady in drab green bom-
bazine.

She trod resolutely across the room and sketched a curtsy to the
dowager, who acknowledged her with a brief nod. Sylvia was conscious of the hint of disapproval in the pale blue eyes taking their
toll of her plain gray afternoon gown. Accustomed to disapproval,
curiosity, disdain, and other ignoble sentiments from callers of all
stations, Sylvia gritted her teeth and forced herself to smile.

"My aunt tells me you have recently returned from India, my
lady," she remarked. "I do so envy you the experience. I understand the colorful pageantry quite dazzles the senses."

When the dowager stared at her without responding, the plump
lady reclining in one of the blue satin chairs—whom her aunt had
introduced as Mrs. Hargate—chuckled. "If colors, sights, sounds,
and smells intrigue you, my dear," she remarked kindly, "Calcutta
is the place to be. It is beyond anything amazing to one accustomed, as I was, to the quiet English countryside near Bath."

"You are too kind, Lydia," the dowager protested. "I declare I
never did become accustomed to the noise and filth. I was just
telling my dear Marguerite that the streets were so full of beggars,
and cows, and stray dogs, that one dared not venture out without a
carriage." The dowager wrinkled her nose as if the smells had followed her into the drawing room.

"It sounds like an artist's paradise," Lady Marguerite said with
a hint of laughter in her rich contralto voice. "I am tempted to pack
my palette and brushes and depart tomorrow. I wonder if we could
persuade Giovanni to accompany us?"

There was a slight, uncomfortable pause, and Sylvia knew that
her aunt had mentioned Giovanni, her longtime paramour, quite
deliberately.

Lady Marguerite had never been one to live in the shadows. Her
nature was open and spontaneous, and she despised hypocrisy in
any form. When Sylvia had first come to make her home at Whitecliffs, her sensibilities had been severely shocked at her aunt's pas-

sionate relationship with Giovanni Petorno, the Italian sculptor who had, according to local gossip, debauched and ruined Lady Marguerite Sutherland as a young girl.

Hounded by fantasies of depraved goings-on in her aunt's opulent bedchamber every night, Sylvia had locked herself in her room and avoided any contact whatsoever with the foreign lecher. A week later, Lady Marguerite had taken her by the hand, and the two had walked for hours through the riotous flower beds of the estate.

Sylvia had learned her first lessons in true passion from her aunt. She realized that, contrary to her earlier belief, the romantical haze she had taken for love and that had carried her straight to ruin in that poky little inn in Dover was a beautiful but dangerous illusion.

"Gentlemen—although too many of them do not deserve to be so named—" her aunt had said, "are all too often driven by desires that have little or nothing to do with the heart. You and I, my dear Sylvia, have clear evidence of this lamentable fact. As do far more unfortunate females than I care to consider," she added calmly.

Sylvia blushed painfully at this vivid reminder of her recent experience of the perversity of a certain gentleman.

"He promised . . ." she began, her voice choked with tears.

Her aunt put a comforting arm around her shoulders and guided her down a brick path shaded by a riot of climbing pink roses. "I know, my love. They will all make promises. But promises are like so many candles in the wind. Some will hold steady through every storm; others will flicker and die at the least sign of adversity. I am lucky to have known both in my lifetime."

"Lucky?" Sylvia had exclaimed, incapable of following her aunt's logic. "How can you say so, Aunt? I have been disgraced forever." She paused, her attention caught by her aunt's last words. "You have known both . . . ?"

Lady Marguerite smiled, a beautiful, contented smile, Sylvia thought.

"Yes, love. And contrary to what you will hear from the local gossipmongers, Giovanni is not the villain in my life."

This had become increasingly obvious to Sylvia as the months and years went by. The Italian artist was a permanent and essential part of her aunt's life at Whitecliffs. It was not long before he had become a valued companion and critic to Sylvia as well.

"Where *is* Giovanni?" she demanded, following a perverse impulse to emphasize the Italian's place in her aunt's household. "It is not like him to miss Mrs. Riley's lemon tarts."

Sylvia caught the amused glance that flickered across Lady Marguerite's face. "Oh, you know Giovanni, my love. He is forever puffing up your landscapes to anyone who will listen to him." Her aunt's gaze wandered to the far end of the long saloon, and Sylvia suddenly became aware of the murmur of male voices.

She whirled around, her eyes settling not on the familiar slim figure of the sculptor but on the taller, broad-shouldered gentleman standing beside him. The stranger seemed absorbed in her latest attempt to capture the somber turrets and towers of Longueville Castle, perched in lofty isolation on the cliffs south of Helston, as it had since the eleventh century.

Even as she stared, Sylvia felt a prickle of apprehension.

Longueville Castle had always been one of her favorite subjects. The threatening power implied in its medieval presence, the hint of violence within its massive walls, had been impossible to resist. But most of all the legend of that pale rider on the cliffs above the lonely stone hut had aroused her artist's imagination to fever pitch. She had not been able to stay away.

The two men turned, and as they sauntered towards the group of ladies around the tea-table, Sylvia could not help remarking on the striking difference between them.

Giovanni Petorno radiated elegance and supreme self-confidence. His power was internal, springing—as Sylvia well knew—from his achievements and reputation as an artist. His gaze was relaxed and affectionate as it locked with hers across the room.

The man beside him, taller, broader, his deeply tanned countenance suggesting an inner darkness of the soul that Sylvia could only guess at, struck her as a medieval Goliath next to Giovanni's slender David. This man's power was there for all to see, resembling nothing so much as the massive stone fortress on the cliff top that had spawned him. For this could be none other but the Earl of Longueville, the man villagers held responsible for the tragedy behind the legend of that pale rider on the cliffs.

And unlike the urbane Italian, the earl had, by local report, been the villain in that poor lady's life.

If the legend had any truth in it whatsoever.

Sylvia had not really believed it. She did not want to believe it now, but as the men approached, she could not blame the local fishermen for casting this dour man in that violent role.

He certainly looked the part, and he had acted it with her two days ago on the cliff. His rage had been palpable. The coldness in his dark eyes was palpable now.

With an effort Sylvia repressed a shudder and forced herself to smile. She had put her own particular villain behind her years ago, and refused to allow a cold, arrogant stranger to disturb her peace of mind.

Chapter Three

~

Echoes from the Past

The earl had not expected the Lady in Gray to receive him with any degree of pleasure. He had treated her with extraordinary rudeness up there on the cliff, and was prepared to apologize profusely. But as their eyes locked across Lady Sutherland's drawing room, Nicholas was startled at the open hostility he detected in the lady's gaze.

As a result, his apology was not as polished or sincere as he had intended, and the lady's acknowledgment of it far from gracious.

"Why did you not tell us you were already acquainted with Lady Marguerite's niece, my dear?" the dowager asked him, her tone tinged with reproach.

"His lordship did not make himself known to me," Lady Sylvia offered in a flat voice. "At least not directly," she added, and Nicholas did not miss the ironic inflection in her voice.

The dowager glared at her as though she had committed a social gaffe. "Who else could he have been?" she demanded impatiently, as though the earl's very presence were sufficient to establish his identity.

Lady Sylvia laughed shortly at that pompous remark, and Nicholas did not like the sound of it at all. He braced himself for the set-down he guessed was coming.

"I rather thought his lordship was a madman."

His mother gasped at this unflattering remark, but Mrs. Hargate broke the sudden tension with her easy laugh. "Nicholas did mention meeting an artist on the cliffs a day or two ago, Dorothea," she remarked. "I should have guessed that it was you, my dear," she added, turning her smile to the slim figure in gray still standing beside the tea-table, "since he is well known to your aunt."

"Indeed he is," Lady Marguerite agreed, "as is my dear Dotty. I do not want to think how many years it has been since we attended Miss Harris's Academy for Young Ladies in Bath together, dear. Do you remember that divine dancing master? What was his name? You were quite taken with him yourself, as I recall. It seems only yesterday that the old harridan caught us—"

"Oh, Marguerite!" the dowager interrupted in obvious agitation. "I forbid you to remind me of all the foolish things we did in those days. It is quite unkind of you to bring up our little peccadilloes at all."

The earl watched his mother's growing confusion with amusement. If his memory was correct, it was at that same Bath Academy that Lady Marguerite Sutherland first encountered the impecunious gentleman who later enticed her to throw discretion to the winds and run off to Italy with him.

The daughter of the Earl of Weston was reported to have cut off her glorious red hair, masqueraded as a boy, and ridden all the way to Dover on the open road. When the romantic swain—who by all accounts had hoped to be bought off by an enraged father—discovered that his lady had every intention of holding him to his promise of Italy, he cut his losses and bolted back to Bath to spread vastly exaggerated accounts of his exploits.

Lady Marguerite laughed, and Nicholas noticed that, unlike her niece, her eyes were more hazel than gray. The hair was the same vivid, blatant red, and escaped from her casual chignon with the same abandon as Lady Sylvia's undisciplined curls.

"I would hardly call our peccadilloes *little,* Dotty," Lady Marguerite remarked innocently, and the earl sensed his hostess was on the brink of making an outrageous confession. The dowager must have thought so, too, for she turned a bright pink and wrung her hands pathetically.

Unexpectedly, it was Lady Sylvia who came to the rescue.

"I am sure we all know that anything you undertake could never be *little,* Aunt. You have always lived as you have painted, in the Grand Style. But I cannot see her ladyship indulging in anything improper. After all, that appears to be the prerogative of the Sutherlands, does it not?"

The lady's oblique but unmistakable reference to her own reputation startled Nicholas, who was accustomed to the dowager's rigid suppression of anything vaguely associated with the scandal in his family's past.

Nicholas preferred it that way.

Any reference to that summer evening when his life had crumbled around him had to be—indeed, had been—ruthlessly suppressed if he was to maintain his sanity. The recent encounter with Lady Sylvia on the site of that tragedy had jolted old memories that he had thought carefully buried years ago. The vision of that female figure, sitting as *she* had so often sat, dabbling at her watercolors, had broken down that tenuous wall he had constructed for himself over the years.

There was no other place to hide. He wished he might have stayed away in India, but that had seemed cowardly and selfish, in view of his mother's failing health. There were definite disadvantages to being the only surviving male in a family as ancient and tradition-bound as the Morleys of Longueville. There were certain responsibilities that must be placed above his own inclinations.

Nicholas thought with sudden regret of his brother Stephen, whose death at Talavera had left a chasm, both emotional and physical, in his life. With Stephen gone, the earl had been the only one left to carry on the line. They had long since ceased to look to his uncle, Colonel Lord Peter Morley, and his comfortable wife, Agnes, to contribute a presumptive heir to the title, and that left only Matthew.

The idea of Longueville going to his cousin Matthew by default had finally brought Nicholas back from India.

His mother had been right, he reminded himself as the Longueville party rose to take their leave. It was long past time for him to take a second wife and start his nursery.

Sylvia breathed a sigh of relief when the dowager countess rose to signal the end of the visit. It was not that she found the lady uncivil, although her manner often verged on the condescending. She seemed genuinely fond of Lady Marguerite, and Sylvia knew her aunt well enough to know that Marguerite was equally attached to the starched-up dowager.

Mrs. Hargate appeared less eager to leave, and Sylvia would have welcomed a chance to further her acquaintance with the lady. Upon Mrs. Hargate expressing similar inclinations, it was agreed that the earl would convey his aunt to Whitecliffs the following afternoon to take a tour of the West Gallery, where many of the paintings hung.

"I never was any good with watercolors," Mrs. Hargate admitted ruefully, "but I do so admire those artists who create beauty or tragedy that touches our souls."

"Paintings should reflect only the beauty of the world," cut in the dowager, turning to glare at her companion. "I cannot imagine why you would wish to have ugliness staring at you from the walls, Lydia, when there is quite enough of it all around us."

"Tragedy is an inescapable part of life, my lady," Sylvia could not help remarking. Her thoughts flew to the ghostly figure said to roam the cliffs by the stone hut. There was undoubtedly some tragedy attached to the legend. Mere death alone—and the lady had reportedly died mysteriously on the cliff, that much was true—would hardly be sufficient to cause the villagers to sublimate the death of a young countess into a quasi-romantic legend of lost love.

"Tragedy is all around us," Sylvia continued, intrigued at the sudden pallor that invaded the dowager's smooth cheeks. "Who was it who said that we each carry our own death within us?"

The dowager flinched visibly. "Rubbish!" she exclaimed angrily. "One of your idle poets or philosophers, no doubt, who have nothing better to do than spout platitudes that they hope will pass as wit."

Sylvia caught the earl's eye and was startled to see a gleam of amusement there. Her first impression of the gentleman two days ago had been anything but pleasant, and this afternoon Lord Longueville had shown little evidence of enjoying the company at Whitecliffs.

"I agree with you, my lady," she heard herself saying smoothly. "Too many of our young poets place wit upon a pedestal and disregard good taste and common sense."

Alarmed to hear herself agreeing with a female she suspected of lacking rudimentary tolerance towards art in any form, Sylvia was relieved when the doors of the Italian Saloon swung open, and Hobson ushered in another visitor.

Sir Geoffrey Huntsville was not one of her favorite gentlemen, but his arrival could be counted upon to change the tone of any gathering he happened to grace with his presence. He was jovial, gregarious to a fault, and considered himself to be a poet of no small merit.

After a perfunctory greeting for his hostess, the baronet turned a beaming countenance on the dowager.

"My dear Lady Longueville," he gushed in a stirring baritone that served him well in the choir at the chapel every Sunday, "I am enchanted to have this unexpected opportunity to welcome you home again."

Sylvia guessed this to be a bouncer of major proportions. Sir Geoffrey's household staff, like that of all neighboring gentry, was largely local, and gossip was no less the chief entertainment of servants in Cornwall than in the rest of England. She suspected that Sir Geoffrey had known to the minute when the party from Longueville intended to visit Whitecliffs.

"You have been sorely missed, my lady, let me tell you," the baronet continued in his caressing voice. "The yearly bazaars at Helston have been dull affairs indeed without your inspired patronage. And the glitter of our social gatherings has diminished to the point of becoming a mere flicker of what it was when your ladyship presided over them."

At that moment he appeared to notice the earl, standing quietly beside Mrs. Hargate.

"Longueville!" the baronet exclaimed warmly, stepping forward to pump the earl's hand energetically. "How provident that your lordship is back among us once again. The Castle has languished far too long in the shadows. My dear Martha was remarking to me only this morning over the breakfast table that she despairs of ever attending another of your famous Public Days. I trust I may relieve her mind on this score, my lord. No doubt you will wish to restore Longueville to its former glory. How well we all remember those summers when the Castle was filled with guests from London, and music, and laughter."

An uncomfortable silence followed this tactless remark, and Sylvia wondered whether the baronet had not thrown it out deliberately to stir up painful memories. She recalled Aunt Marguerite mentioning that Sir Geoffrey had rather fancied himself as the young countess's cicisbeo during that first—and last—summer of her marriage to Longueville. As had a number of other young gentlemen who flocked to Cornwall to enjoy the earl's hospitality. According to her aunt, the new countess had seemed to attract and relish the male attention. Perhaps beyond the bounds of what was entirely proper, Sylvia had guessed, given the rare note of censure in Lady Marguerite's tone.

"I do not believe you have met my aunt, Mrs. Hargate," the earl cut in coldly, breaking the tension that had settled over the group. "She visits Cornwall infrequently, and I hope to encourage her to make her home here."

Sir Geoffrey transferred his attention briefly to Mrs. Hargate, but Sylvia suspected that he saw nothing of interest in the short, plain-faced widow, for after a few perfunctory remarks he turned back to the dowager.

"I trust your ladyship will condescend to dine at Huntington Hall next week," he said. "My dear Martha has planned a small, select dinner party to celebrate the publication of my latest volume of poetry, and I know she would consider the occasion incomplete without your presence, my lady."

There was another pregnant pause after this announcement, which Sir Geoffrey appeared not to notice, for he continued to elaborate on the favorable reviews his little book—as he chose to call it—had received in such prestigious journals as the *Edinburgh Review.*

Sylvia had read these reviews, and could not for the life of her find anything remotely favorable in them. Perhaps they were not as scathing as some that appeared in that prestigious journal, she reasoned, and had refrained from comment, unwilling to incur Sir Geoffrey's wrath.

"We shall have to see, Sir Geoffrey," she heard the dowager saying with an aplomb that Sylvia envied. "We have not yet unpacked our trunks, and as you can imagine, Longueville has almost ten years of estate matters to catch up with. I must congratulate you on your marriage, however, even though I am sadly late in doing so. I remember Martha Grenville as a very sweet and biddable girl."

"Oh, indeed she is, your ladyship," Sir Geoffrey gushed, evidently gratified at the dowager's condescension in remembering his personal affairs. "And one who knows her duty as well, I might add. My dear Martha has already presented me with four lovely daughters, and is even now in hopes of adding a son to make me the happiest man in Cornwall."

With his uncanny knack for broaching topics calculated to stir up controversy, Sir Geoffrey again managed to create another awkward pause in the conversation.

Sylvia noticed that the earl's face had turned rigid and that he cast a stern glance at the dowager, who abruptly took her leave of Lady Marguerite and swept out of the room.

On the whole, Sylvia had to agree with her aunt after the earl and Mrs. Hargate had followed the dowager's lead, the visit had not been an overwhelming success.

The ride back to the Castle was fraught with uncomfortable undercurrents. After listening to the dowager disparage, at great length and with obvious relish, the Sutherland females for their deplorable lack of propriety, the earl lost his patience.

"If our neighbors are so distasteful to you, Mother, I wonder that you encourage the connection," he remarked shortly.

The dowager glanced at him in amazement. "And I wonder how you can ask such a thing, Nicholas," she said reprovingly. "Marguerite is my oldest and dearest friend. Her letters sustained me through those long years in India. And I cannot begin to tell you how much her friendship meant to me during our time together at Miss Harris's Academy. Marguerite was absolutely fearless. She actually laughed at the old dragon's threat to tell your grandfather about that dancing master. . . ." Her words tapered off, as though the dowager had suddenly realized her slip.

"And what was there to tell about that dancing jack?" the earl could not resist asking innocently. His imagination boggled at the notion that his mother, always a stickler for propriety and decorum, might have strayed from the path of virtue by so much as a hairsbreadth. But women, he had found to his own sorrow, were not always what they appeared. Had he not been roundly deceived by his own wife, like some inexperienced rudesby?

"Nicholas!" his aunt exclaimed sharply, although the earl caught a tremor of amusement in her voice. "How can you tease your poor mother so? Do you see any dancing masters installed at the Castle, my dear boy? Shame on you!"

The dowager looked genuinely distressed, and Nicholas regretted his cavalier attitude.

"Oh, Lydia," she wailed, her hands fluttering nervously at her throat, "how can you say such a thing? I never did enjoy dancing above half, as even Marguerite will tell you. I cannot imagine what inspired her to bring up that man at all, unless she wished to tease me."

*   *   *

As Nicholas made his way upstairs to change for dinner, it struck him that the enigmatic lady an gray had once again intruded upon his thoughts. He shook his head impatiently, but by the time his valet had teased his cravat into in intricate version of the Mathematical, Nicholas realized that between Lady Sylvia herself, the wind-tousled apparition she had presented on the cliff, and *The Lady in Gray* staring down at him from the walls of Whitecliffs, his imagination had been stimulated to a degree he found unsettling, to say the least.

It was the dowager, however, who gave the earl the first clue to the possible nature of his dilemma.

"I think we should remove to London as soon as possible, Nicholas," she remarked, quite out of the blue, over the baked salmon with buttered turnips at dinner that evening. "I do not believe I am quite up to the tedious round of country soirées and insipid dinners that pass for entertainment here in Cornwall. Sir Geoffrey has grown more pompous with age, and I fear his literary endeavors may reflect this deplorable folly. Then there is Morley Court to be refurbished before I can feel comfortable receiving our friends in Town."

"London in July!" Mrs. Hargate exclaimed, her blue eyes round with astonishment. "Surely you are jesting, Dorothea. The Metropolis is entirely devoid of company in the summer, besides being unhealthy. I trust I misunderstood you, dear."

"You may count upon it, Aunt," the earl responded calmly. "My dear mama is exaggerating, of course. And in any case, there is no way I can get away before October at the earliest. I intend to spend another month or two here with Gates; then I have arranged to visit Falmouth. Ned Barker writes that two of our ships are due in September, and I want to be there when they dock. Particularly since Jason Ransome is the master of one of them. You remember Jason, Mama? That red-haired rogue who allowed you to beat him at whist every time you played?"

"He did nothing of the sort," the dowager snapped. "I count myself a superior player, and Captain Ransome has graciously admitted it any number of times. A charming rascal, of course, but why the son of a marquess should fritter away his life as a common sailor I shall never understand."

"He is making his fortune, as we all are in the shipping business," the earl answered tersely. "Jason's ambition is to own a fleet of his own, as it was mine. He will do it, too, before he is much older."

The dowager motioned to a footman to fill her glass and glanced reprovingly at her son. "You have led the poor boy astray, Nicholas," she protested. "His mother, the marchioness, is a dear friend of mine, as you know, and Lucy tells me that Jason received a tidy inheritance from her brother, so he could have spent his days in England living like a gentleman instead of roaming the world like some scruffy pirate. How he ever expects to find a suitable wife and settle down is beyond me. Poor Lucy has quite washed her hands of him."

Nicholas grinned at his aunt, who had listened to this tirade with her usual patience. They both knew that the dowager would always find fault with any scion of a noble family who sullied his hands in Trade. She had never forgiven Nicholas for his astonishing success in establishing a shipping route to India, although she seemed to have no qualms about spending the money brought into the family coffers by such despised activities.

"I trust you will invite Captain Ransome to stay at Longueville when he arrives, Nicholas. It has been too long since I enjoyed a challenging game of whist."

"As you say, Dorothea, the captain is a charming rascal," Mrs. Hargate remarked. "His presence would be a welcome addition to our party."

"Then I shall most certainly invite him," Nicholas said, rising to accompany the ladies into the drawing room.

Later that evening, long after Digby had eased the blue superfine coat from his master's broad shoulders and loosened the starched cravat, Nicholas flung himself into his favorite chair beside the empty hearth, full glass in hand, a brandy decanter within easy reach, and let his mind slide back to that glorious summer ten years ago when he had considered himself the most fortunate of men in England.

Chapter Four

~

Angelica

Longueville Castle, Cornwall
Summer 1804

Nicholas listened to the soft breathing of the girl in bed beside him. In the flickering glow of the gutted candles, he could see her breasts rising and falling in the gentle rhythm of sleep. His fingers ached to reach out to caress her, but he restrained his intemperate urges, forcing himself to ignore the now familiar tightening of his groin every time he contemplated his wife for any length of time.

His wife!

The Countess of Longueville. Nicholas marveled at the sound of it ringing in his head, and grinned foolishly down at the sleeping girl. He still thought of Angelica as a girl, although he had discovered on their wedding night that she was as eager and uninhibited as any woman he had ever bedded.

Or so it had seemed to a bridegroom rather more in his cups than was proper.

It had been the wedding of the Season. That Nicholas did remember clearly.

St. George's in Hanover Square had been unable to accommodate the crush of London's elite who came in record numbers to witness the leg-shackling of one of England's most eligible bachelors. His euphoria had been so intense that even the most ribald of jests from his circle of friends had failed to shake the quiet certainty Nicholas had felt that he had stepped into a fairy wonderland of delight and undeserved joy.

Even the wild coach ride along the London-Bath Road to Farnaby Hall, his uncle's estate on the outskirts of Bath, could not dim his joy. Accompanied by a roisterous cavalcade of those same ribald friends, who had set themselves up as his unofficial escort, Nicholas had accepted his Aunt Lydia's invitation to break his journey back to Cornwall at Farnaby Hall. His cousin Matthew, ever ready for a lark, had helped persuade the new bride to forgo a quiet wedding night at Morley Court in London for an adventure by moonlight on the King's highway.

Angelica had been more than willing to be persuaded by his handsome cousin, and the noisy procession of coaches and riders had set out at midnight, after the sumptuous bridal feast, laid out with meticulous care by the Dowager Countess, had been demolished and the musicians sent home to their well-earned beds.

This was yet another side to his new bride that charmed the earl. She was ever ready to override what she called stuffy conventions if they stood in the way of her pleasure. In this the new countess was like his cousin, although in Matthew the pursuit of pleasure had already acquired a reckless edge that his mother, Lady Lydia Farnaby, privately deplored.

Nicholas was not surprised when his mother bitterly protested what she termed a vulgar display of ramshackled manners better suited to London street sweepers than a peer of the realm. In any other circumstance, Nicholas might have agreed with the dowager, but Angelica declared the scheme a famous lark, and one glance at her sweetly pouting lips was all it took to convince the earl that no possible harm could come of the adventure.

He had not counted on the frequent stops at posting houses along the Bath Road, nor the increasing quantity of local ale consumed by his boisterous escort. By the time the party pulled into the Black Swan in Melksham, ten miles short of their destination, Nicholas was feeling the effects of the innumerable toasts he had been obliged to drink to his bride.

He glanced down again at the girl who had brought him so much happiness.

Angelica.

She was well named, he thought. Seeing her lying there so vulnerable and trusting, her spun-gold hair spread on the silk pillow in a halo around her delicate face, Nicholas knew that *angelic* was the only word that truly caught the essence of his wife.

He really should go back to his own bed. It was unseemly for a husband, however infatuated, to take advantage of his wife's sense of duty to satisfy his own unquenchable desires. Once should be enough. Or perhaps twice, he thought wryly, since once would never be enough with Angelica.

And what was this farradiddle about sense of duty? One of the things he most admired about his wife was that she lacked the dowager's rigid adherence to protocol and tradition. Her nonchalant attitude towards his title and fortune had both shocked and amused him. And what might be termed duty in other wives was nothing so conventional in Angelica. Had he not intended, night after night, to leave her at a decent hour, only to be sweetly detained by two white arms flung impetuously about his neck? And two soft lips begging to be kissed? And a warm, seductive voice whispering deliciously erotic nothings in his ear?

How was a man expected to resist such temptation?

His wife sighed, and her eyelids fluttered. The little minx was awake, he thought. When her lips twitched into a smile, Nicholas knew he had guessed correctly. Throwing caution to the winds, he leaned down and brushed one last kiss on that tantalizing mouth.

He should leave now, he told himself, but knew he would not when her arms slipped round his neck and drew him down on top of her.

"Do not leave me yet, love," she murmured against his ear. "Surely it is no more than midnight."

"The clock downstairs has struck three, sweetheart," Nicholas said, breathing in the exotic perfume that his mother had declared more appropriate for a second-rate opera singer than a countess.

Nicholas liked it. There was something vaguely wanton about it that never failed to arouse him.

He was aroused now. The warmth of her arms about his neck and the hot pressure of her lips against his ear chased any thought of retiring to his own bed out of his mind. And then his wife whispered something so outrageous that he raised his head and stared at her in disbelief.

"What did you say, love?"

A gurgle of mocking laughter told him he had not misunderstood her. "I forbid you to be stuffy, Nicholas," she murmured, gazing up at him through half-closed eyes.

There was a moment's silence while Nicholas digested his wife's new fantasy.

"Did you actually ask me to . . . ?"

Angelica pouted prettily. "Of course I did," she said, a touch impatiently. "I asked you to rip my night rail off and ravish me. What is so unusual about that?"

If truth be told, Nicholas considered his wife's request highly unusual, particularly in the marriage bed, but he knew better than to say so. Only last week she had begged him to put her across his knee, pull up her night rail, and smack her like a naughty child. When he flatly denied her, she had banished him from her bed and refused to speak to him for an entire day.

That had been almost too much to bear. Nicholas did not wish to repeat the anguish of falling out of his wife's good graces. Neither did he wish to behave like a brute with the woman he loved beyond reason.

"Are you sure you wish to destroy that bewitching night rail, my sweet?" he ventured, hoping he could deflect this aberrant request with more practical considerations.

"Of course not, silly," she retorted pettishly. "I want *you* to destroy it, Nicky. So do not disappoint me, darling. You know what happens when you do that."

The words were spoken seductively, and his wife's hands caressed his hair and trailed suggestively down the length of his naked back, but Nicholas could not fail to hear the threat echoing in the background. He would be banished again, he thought, and that was unthinkable.

Angelica grasped his hand and brought it up to the lacy neckline of the night rail. Instinctively, Nicholas grasped the fragile silk, his senses already aroused by the implications of what she demanded of him.

"Go on, Nicholas," she urged, her back already arched in anticipation. "Do not be a slow-top, dearest. Surely you have played these love games with your amourettes. Do not pretend you are an innocent. I am the innocent here, sweet, and I expect you to teach me all you know about pleasure."

She smiled up at him, her eyes glimmering hotly through half-closed lids; her lips moist and parted, her breath already shallow with desire.

Nicholas felt his resistance dissolving.

In vain he reminded himself that he had—or so he thought—taught Angelica all about pleasure. At least as much as was proper for a wife to know. The notion of extending that education into the realms frequented by the more experienced courtesans of his acquaintance disturbed him. Perhaps he was a slow-top, he thought wryly. Perhaps his notions of what was proper behavior in a wife was, as Angelica claimed, stuffy and old-fashioned.

"Well?" his wife demanded, impatience making her voice sharp. "What are you waiting for, love?"

"You wish me to tear your clothes off? Seriously?"

"Of course," she purred. "And do not tease me, Nicholas. You know I hate to be teased."

He grasped the silk more firmly and sensed that it would be child's play to rip the garment in two. All it required was determination.

"Do it, dearest," his wife murmured in a passion-heavy voice. "Pretend I am an unprotected female you simply must have and ravish me. Do it, Nicholas. Please do it."

Much later, back in his own bed at last, Nicholas could find no way to justify the violence he had perpetrated on the body of the woman he loved. Violence had never been his way. His weakness in acquiescing to Angelica's demands for rough games disgusted him.

The sound of ripping silk followed him into what remained of the night, and for many nights to come.

Chapter Five

~

Unanswered Questions

"Are you actually suggesting there is any truth to those old rumors about the earl's role in his wife's death, Mrs. Rawson?" Lady Sylvia replaced the delicate porcelain cup in its saucer and shot a skeptical glance at Lady Marguerite.

She had joined her aunt and Giovanni for tea in the Italian Saloon, where they were entertaining the vicar's garrulous wife, Mrs. Violet Rawson, and her widowed sister, Mrs. Rose Downy. Predictably, the conversation of the two elder ladies had veered towards the recent return of the master of Longueville Castle, which they had pronounced unwise in the extreme.

Mrs. Rawson—who prided herself on being able to recite the entire family history of every last one of her husband's parishioners—fixed her sharp agate eyes on Sylvia and smiled condescendingly.

"Where there is smoke, there is usually fire," she murmured, falling back on popular wisdom, which she invariably did at the slightest hint of opposition. "And let me assure you, my dear Lady Sylvia, that there was plenty of smoke on the moors and cliffs in these parts when her ladyship came to her untimely end."

"I have always maintained that the mystery of the countess's accident was vastly exaggerated by the locals," Lady Marguerite remarked, motioning to Hobson to add hot water to the silver tea-pot. "Do try these watercress sandwiches, Mrs. Downy; the cress is particularly tasty this year."

Sylvia watched her aunt offer the plate to her guest, and realized that Lady Marguerite was heartily tired of the topic introduced by every visitor who had set foot in Whitecliffs since the return of the Morleys to Longueville Castle. She was becoming more than a little tired of it herself, although certain aspects of the young bride's sudden death seemed to defy explanation.

"But you will admit there was a mystery surrounding the event, my lady," Mrs. Downy insisted, helping herself to one of the delicate cress sandwiches, "and that it was never explained why her ladyship ventured down to the cliffs by moonlight. All alone, too, if what the magistrate said was true."

Her sister gave a snort of derision. "That one was not alone, you can take my word for it," the vicar's wife cut in with what Sylvia considered a deplorable lack of Christian charity. "Birds of a feather, you know," she added darkly. "And as for that mealy-mouthed magistrate, we all know Sir Gerald was hand in glove with the earl to put a good light on the affair."

"I daresay there was enough evidence to support the verdict of accidental death," Lady Marguerite remarked evenly, ignoring the unflattering allegation of Sir Gerald Littlefield's handling of the affair. "The young countess was rash to a fault, perhaps, but everyone knows those cliffs can be treacherous."

"If it was an accident, as you claim, my lady," the vicar's wife insisted pugnaciously, "why did her ladyship leave a suicide note? And what exactly did that note say?"

"We do not know it was a suicide note," Lady Marguerite cut in sharply. "It may have had no bearing on the tragedy at all."

"Besides," Sylvia added, anxious, for some inexplicable reason, to divert the accusations from the earl, "I understand that Lord Longueville denied the note was written in his wife's hand."

Mrs. Rawson looked at her pityingly. "Of course he would deny it, my dear. He did not wish the poor child to be banned from hallowed ground. But Mr. Rawson confided to me that the note was definitely written by her ladyship."

Her sister shook her head vigorously. "So you have told us many a time, Violet," she said. "But how do you explain the rumor, still current in the village, that the note was from a gentleman?"

Lady Marguerite put her cup down with more force than necessary, and Sylvia saw that her aunt had finally lost patience with this pointless gossip about the unfortunate countess.

"I do believe this is a moot point, ladies," she said coldly. "How the countess died and why is no longer our concern. It was settled ten years ago by Sir Gerald, and I suggest we allow the poor child to rest in peace."

She looked pointedly at the handsome gilt clock on the mantel-piece, indicating that the visit was over.

Mrs. Rawson opened her mouth to protest, but she evidently thought better of it, for she smiled ingratiatingly at her hostess and turned to her sister. "I believe we have taken up enough of her la-dyship's hospitality, Rose. And remember we have promised to stop in at old Mrs. Jones's to ask after her daughter."

She leveled her agate stare on Lady Sylvia, who wondered what new piece of vicious gossip the old Tabby was about to regurgi-tate.

"Have you heard that Lila Jones is finally riveted to that rogue who led her into a fool's paradise last spring, my lady?" The smile that accompanied this arch pronouncement was deceptively mild. "Thanks to my dear Mr. Rawson's intervention, of course, that Daly lad finally made an honest woman of the lass. Mrs. Jones is in alt over the happy ending to what might have been an ugly scan-dal. What with the baby expected around Christmastime and all."

The smile, which had definitely become a smirk, did not reach the woman's eyes, and Sylvia suddenly realized that the tid-bit of gossip had been expressly intended to remind her of her own fall from grace. With a Herculean effort, she kept her face expression-less. Not for the world would she give this old harridan the satis-faction of knowing she had hit her mark.

"What delightful news," Sylvia heard herself gush insincerely. "I do hope Lila is happy with the match. I have heard Tom Daly is a bit of a scoundrel."

"Never you doubt it, my lady," Mrs. Downy remarked, and at least her smile appeared genuine, Sylvia noted. "Young Tom may be a bit of a devil with the lasses, but now that poor Lila has a ring on her finger, she is respectable again."

"Poor Lila!" Sylvia exploded, after the two gossips had de-parted. "What a hypocrite that woman is. Poor Lila will live to re-gret throwing in her lot with that jackstraw, unless I am very much mistaken. And as for a marriage ring making her respectable again . . . Bah! What humbug!"

Giovanni spoke for the first time since the subject of the count-ess's mysterious death had been introduced by Mrs. Rawson. "There is at least some truth to it, my dear Sylvia," he said gently.

"To the ignorant mind, marriage is the cure for all kinds of sins. Another much abused concept, of course," he added hastily as Lady Marguerite threw him a dark look.

"Are you actually endorsing that dreadful woman's misguided illusion that Sylvia and I are sinners, my dear Giovanni?" she inquired with deceptive sweetness.

Sylvia glanced at her aunt's Italian paramour and saw him smile—a tender, sensuous smile he reserved solely for Lady Marguerite—a smile so full of love and devotion that it had shocked Sylvia when first she witnessed it. She had been brought up to believe that gentlemen never, not even in their most intimate moments, entertained what her father had always referred to as uncouth emotions, much less displayed them as frankly as Giovanni did. She had since learned that Lord Weston had misled her into believing that all gentlemen were equally reticent about the expression of their feelings.

Watching the Italian's smile deepen, and his eyes turn a warmer shade of velvety brown, Sylvia reflected, as she had many times before, that her aunt was the luckiest woman she knew. To command the love and loyalty of such a man had become, over the years she had spent in Cornwall, one of Sylvia's secret fantasies. But eligible gentlemen were as scarce as hen's teeth in this remote part of England, and had there been any, not one of them—if her father's dire prediction was true—would have looked at her with anything but contempt.

Eligible, indeed! Sylvia had soon discovered that in one respect, at least, Lord Weston had predicted correctly. She was herself ineligible. As if it was not revealing enough for a young, unmarried female to take up residence in a household as notoriously debauched as Lady Marguerite's was reputed to be, local gossip endlessly speculated on the truth of Sylvia's disgrace.

She should have been prepared, of course, and her aunt had warned Sylvia that she would have to endure a period of open disdain from some of the more narrow-minded gentry. Particularly the females. As for the gentlemen, Sylvia had been pleasantly surprised at how accepting they had appeared. Several of the younger men had become assiduous callers at Whitecliffs, but it had been Sir Geoffrey Huntsville who had opened Sylvia's eyes to the true nature of this masculine interest.

The baronet's entirely unexpected offer to become more than her platonic admirer had been delivered with all the pompous assurance of one who had no doubt of her grateful acceptance. Sylvia could now smile at the memory of Sir Geoffrey's outraged expression when he heard her disdainful set-down, but the experience had disabused her of any notion of finding a gentleman as understanding and loyal as her aunt's paramour.

"Doucement, ma petite," Sylvia heard Giovanni murmur caressingly. "You mistake the matter, love. Do you not know your Giovanni better than to think such calumny? Besides, *peccato* is a relative term, is it not? For some—like your poor Mrs. Rawson, for instance—sin is an unpardonable transgression, a matter for the Devil himself; for others—"

"Such as yourself, I suppose," his lady cut in with a laugh. "Tell us, you rogue. What is sin to you?"

"Certainly nothing that you are capable of, *palomita mia,*" he replied soothingly. "But if you are uneasy on that score, I am sure the Reverend Rawson would be more than ready to oblige us if you were to decide—"

"To become respectable? Oh, no, you sly fox," her aunt interrupted, hazel eyes dancing with amusement. "I will not listen to another of your homilies on the advantages of the married state. You are getting as tiresome as old Mrs. Rawson. Besides, after so many years of defying the local moralists, have we not earned the right to live as we choose, *amor mio?*"

"Précisament, cherie. And if we choose to become—as your quaint Mrs. Rawson puts it—respectable in the eyes of the world, who will say us nay?"

Giovanni reinforced this teasing remark by carrying his inamorata's fingers to his lips and bestowing upon them a kiss so blatantly amorous that Sylvia averted her eyes.

Sylvia had witnessed this scene played out any number of times over the years she had been at Whitecliffs, but recently it seemed to her that the Italian sculptor had become increasingly serious in his desire to formalize his relationship with Lady Marguerite. Her aunt remained adamant in her refusal to cater to the gossips. Unnecessarily so, Sylvia had always thought.

She herself would have jumped at the chance to become respectable again. In truth, she often found herself wishing that Sir Matthew Farnaby had never appeared that fateful day at her father's shooting party to beguile his daughter with false promises of love and never-ending happiness.

Sylvia wondered idly whether the handsome rogue had found

some other heiress to mend his fortunes. Was he at this very moment surrounded by a doting wife and a loving family of little ones?

The picture was painful, and Sylvia brushed it aside impatiently.

At a staid eight-and-twenty, her lot was to lead apes to Hell, she reminded herself philosophically. Her work would sustain her. And was not the growing notice she had achieved in the London art world more precious to her than the uncertain loyalty of a husband?

For the first time in several years, the answer to that question did not sound as convincing as it usually did.

There was a light tap on the study door, and the earl glanced up, curious to hear his mother's latest argument in favor of an early departure for London. His stern expression softened when his aunt's rosy face peeped apprehensively into the room.

"I do not mean to disturb you, Nicholas," she said, "but I promised to call at Whitecliffs this afternoon and wondered if I might ask John Coachman to drive me. Your dear mama has developed a megrim and has begged off."

Nicholas laid down his quill and smiled. His Aunt Lydia was one of his favorite females and, he suspected, understood him far better than his own mother.

"I shall do better than that, Aunt," he replied, suddenly glad of the chance to escape from the tedium of poring over estate ledgers with his agent. "I shall drive you over to Whitecliffs myself. I am in urgent need of fresh air since, thanks to Tom Gates, I missed my ride this morning."

His aunt's homely face lit up instantly. "That would be splendid, my boy, but I would not wish to put you to such a bother."

"No bother at all, Aunt," he said, rising to his feet and closing the heavy ledger. "Gates has abandoned me to ride up to Falmouth with a message for Ned Barker, my man of business. It appears Barker has received information that the *Voyageur* is to be put on the block next month, and is offering me first choice."

"Yet another ship, Nicholas?" his aunt exclaimed, her eyes twinkling with amusement. "Now, can you tell me what you need with so many of those expensive toys? I would be hesitant to invest so much in a vessel that might sink at the merest quirk of fortune."

Nicholas laughed. He enjoyed talking Trade with his aunt. Despite her seemingly frivolous remarks, Mrs. Hargate was as sharp as she could hold together. Nicholas had found over the years that her suggestions for the disposal of her substantial fortune—which the earl had managed since her second husband had passed on, leaving her unexpectedly well provided for—were surprisingly astute.

"We lost the *Intrepid* off the coast of Africa only last year, Aunt, and Jason has been urging me to replace her for months now. If she is sound, the *Voyageur* might meet Jason's standards. Of course, I would want him to test her mettle first, so I hope he is not dawdling in some French port drinking cheap wine and getting into fisticuffs with the local thugs."

"If I know anything about Jason Ransome, he will not be anywhere near cheap wine, my dear," his aunt said. "I believe his tastes are rather more expensive. Which reminds me, Nicholas," she added, veering suddenly to another topic as she often did, "there is something of importance I wish to discuss with you."

From her tone of voice the earl guessed that the subject on his aunt's mind was in one way or another related to her only remaining son, his notorious Cousin Matthew. He had received a disturbing note from Barker two days ago containing a detailed list of his cousin's debts, which the careful solicitor had refused to settle.

He was not mistaken. No sooner had the earl's curricle swept past the Longueville gatehouse and turned south towards Cury Cross and the Sutherland manor than his aunt poured out her latest tale of his cousin's infamy.

"I fear my poor Matthew is in the suds again, Nicholas," she confirmed in a serious voice. "I received a letter from him yesterday claiming that Mr. Barker has refused to advance him his monthly allowance, and has turned a deaf ear on Matthew's repeated requests to increase the amount. He demands that I apply to you to override Barker's stinginess unless I wish to see my son in Debtors' Prison."

The earl felt his pleasure in the fine morning dissipate. He had not laid eyes on Sir Matthew Farnaby for nearly ten years, but the indelible memory of their violent encounter in his study after Angelica's funeral stirred simmering anger and bitterness in Nicholas's heart.

The wretch had had the audacity to insinuate that Angelica was no more than a common slut.

Nicholas was better off without her, his cousin had said, a sneer marring the classic beauty of his face, as it all too often did when things did not go his way. There was no telling what dark scandals lurked in the future for a man saddled with an unpredictable, hot-headed female like the young Countess of Longueville. Unbridled passion was all well and good in a man's mistress, but in a wife it boded only chaos and dishonor to the family.

Far better the lady had removed that threat of scandal by taking her own life, Matthew had remarked in that cold, callous way of his. Or that some particularly thoughtful friend had removed it for her, he had added, a sly, knowing smile twisting his shapely mouth into an ugly grimace.

Rumors that his wife's mysterious death had been neither suicide nor accident were already rampant in the neighborhood, Nicholas remembered. He and Sir Gerald Littlefield, magistrate from the adjacent borough and lifelong friend, had been hard pressed to convince the obdurate vicar that Angelica had every right to be interred in sacred ground.

He had been able to override local superstition, however, although not suppress it. But what had upset his peace of mind forever was his own cousin's spiteful confirmation of a nagging doubt that had lodged in his mind ever since the dowager had complained to him that his new bride's flirtatious ways went beyond the pale.

Unbridled passion? His cousin's words had caused a deep and lasting laceration in his soul. How would Matthew *know* that Angelica's passion was indeed unbridled, bordering on debauched?

Had his licentious cousin been in a position to know such intimate details about the countess? Angelica had undeniably flirted with Matthew. Quite shamelessly, as he recalled. But she had behaved with hardly less restraint with all the other gentlemen at Longueville that summer of 1804, single or married. With Jason Ransome, his best man. With Sir Geoffrey Huntsville, who fawned on her like the veriest spaniel. With the Brodley brothers, fresh down from Oxford and still bashful in the presence of a beautiful woman. With the Earl of St. Aubyn, who was very clearly absorbed with his own lovely countess. With that consummate rake, the Viscount Hammond, who had demonstrated admirable restraint with his friend's new bride. Even with the genteel Mr. George Connan, the garrulous Mrs. Violet Rawson's nephew, who had recently taken over the small bookshop in Helston left to him by his parents.

And all the others whose names escaped him.

"You are wool-gathering, Nicholas," his aunt protested indignantly as the curricle turned into the gate guarded by the two stone lions. "While here I am facing the prospect of seeing my only son cast into prison for debt."

The earl pulled his uneasy thoughts back from the past.

"It will hardly get to that, Aunt," he assured her with more confidence than he felt. "I shall talk to Barker and see what we can work out. But remember that you promised not to squander another penny of your own on Farnaby. He has run through his father's fortune, and he will run through yours if you give him half a chance. That I will not permit, Aunt, take my word on that."

His aunt was silent for several minutes. When she spoke again, she broached a subject the earl had rather left undisturbed.

"Matthew is in Falmouth, you know. So close by. He wants to see me and begs me to visit him there." She paused, then continued hesitantly. "Unless of course, dear, you might be persuaded to lift your ban on his visits to Longueville."

When the earl made no response, she insisted. "Would you do so, my dear Nicholas? If I asked it of you?"

"No," the earl replied harshly. "I would not. I am sorry to disoblige you, Aunt," he added tersely, "but some things are best left buried."

His choice of words was unfortunate, Nicholas realized, but also full of perverse irony. Angelica was indeed buried and, in spite of his almost obsessive infatuation with her during their brief marriage, he had—over the years—come to agree with his cousin's conclusion that the passionate creature he had wed would one day bring disgrace to all of them.

She had done so already, he thought bitterly. Only yesterday he had heard the word *murderer* whispered behind his back in the village.

Ten years in India had not been enough to erase that stigma.

Chapter Six

~

Summer Beauties

The scene that greeted the visitors as Hobson led them down the shallow terrace steps and through the crisscrossed brick pathways might well have been recorded on canvas as *Summer Beauties*. The roses, growing in exuberant clumps of pinks and brilliant reds rather than the regimented rows of carefully pruned bushes Nicholas was accustomed to seeing in the manicured gardens at Longueville Castle, took the breath away.

He heard his aunt's gasp of pleasure and surprise as the riot of color opened up before them. Nicholas could detect no recognizable pattern to the design of Lady Marguerite's rose-garden, which appeared to have been scattered haphazardly like gaily tinted butterflies on the green turf.

"How enchanting!" his aunt murmured in an awed voice.

"The gardeners were surely in their cups when they laid out this planting," the earl remarked dampeningly. "There is no hint of symmetry that I can ascertain."

"Symmetry! Pooh!" his aunt exclaimed disdainfully. "Must you always insist on restraint and control, Nicholas? Even in the garden? Cannot you feel the harmony here? The freedom of it fairly vibrates in the air. Unlike those stiff rows of repressed rose-bushes one sees in too many gardens that look so uncomfortable in their conformity that one can only feel for them."

The earl felt obliged to correct this fanciful female nonsense. "Since when can roses feel uncomfortable, Aunt?" he said, guiding her around a pot-bellied tub in the shape of a naked Cupid, overflowing with pink geraniums.

Mrs. Hargate ignored this indecorous intrusion of Eros into an English garden, and her attention had shifted to the group gathered around a particularly unruly cascade of startling pink blossoms.

"Oh, dear," she said, "I do believe we are interrupting a sitting, my dear boy. Perhaps we should make our apologies and return another day."

Nicholas had to agree with his aunt, although he had no intention of retreating. The notorious couple, composed of Lady Marguerite and the Italian, whose presence at Whitecliffs still caused averted glances in the village even after twenty years, was arranged in a charmingly innocent pose on a wooden bench beneath a cascade of pink roses. Privately, Nicholas considered the pose more appropriate to young lovers than to a middle-aged couple whose obvious infatuation he found faintly embarrassing.

"What a very charming picture you do make," he heard his aunt gush as they approached the party. "And what a rare treat to surprise the artist at work."

The artist, whom the earl had instantly recognized by the pale gray of her simple gown, turned with obvious reluctance from the canvas before her and glanced over her shoulder.

Unaware that he had been holding his breath, the earl let it out slowly as the gray eyes slid over him and settled upon his aunt. Then she smiled, and the sweetness of it transformed Lady Sylvia's guarded expression into one of genuine welcome.

"My dear Mrs. Hargate," she said, moving across the grass to greet his aunt and draw her into the group beside the arching rosebushes. "I am so glad you were able to come. My lord," she added less enthusiastically, but without the hostility of their previous encounters. She glanced behind them, as if expecting to see the dowager emerge from the open French windows.

"My mother sends her regrets," Nicholas felt obliged to explain. "She is still exhausted from the sea voyage."

Lady Sylvia looked into his eyes from beneath the floppy brim of her faded pink straw bonnet and smiled enigmatically. It was quite as though she had read his mind, Nicholas thought, and divined the real reason for the dowager's absence. The notion that a mere female might find him so transparent annoyed him.

He frowned, and she looked away, the smile still on her lips.

"I trust we are not interrupting your work, my lady." As usual his aunt appeared completely at home in the odd assembly.

"Nothing of the kind," Lady Sylvia replied brightly. "My aunt has been fidgeting for the past twenty minutes, which is an un-equivocal sign that it is time for tea."

"Yes, indeed," Lady Marguerite agreed, "Sylvia is a demanding taskmaster. If we left it to her, we would still be sitting here when the moon comes up. Hobson," she added, turning to the butler, "you may have the tea-tray sent out, if you please. It is too glorious an afternoon to waste indoors." She glanced at her companion. "Do you not agree, *caro mio*?"

For answer the Italian ran a knuckle down the lady's cheek, a gesture Nicholas found uncomfortably intimate. "Anything you say, *bella,*" he said in the seductively low voice he invariably used with Lady Marguerite.

His hostess smiled meltingly up at her lover, and Nicholas wondered what it might be like to live twenty years with the same woman and still be able to kindle that spark of unabashed adoration in her eyes.

He felt the old bitterness swell up within him. Ten years ago he had seen a similar adoration in another woman's eyes—or imagined he had—and that illusion had cost him dearly. Even today Nicholas had difficulty admitting that the delicate beauty of Angelica DeJardin was but an innocent facade behind which lurked the creature of unbridled passion his cousin had spoken of. A creature he himself had discovered in the privacy of her bedchamber.

"Are you ready for more tea, my lord?"

The earl dragged his thoughts back to the present to find Lady Sylvia regarding him quizzically. He had no recollection of having consumed any tea at all, but he passed his empty cup to her without comment.

As he watched her lift the ornate silver tea-pot and refill his cup, Nicholas briefly wondered what it might be like to sit across the breakfast table from such a vibrant female as this. Or better still, to share his bed with her. An absurd notion, of course, since the lady was clearly cut from the same cloth as her more flamboyant aunt. True, Lady Sylvia did not have a lover in residence as her aunt did, but there must have been one in the shadowy recesses of her past, if persistent rumors of her disgrace could be believed. Why else would a female of obvious breeding, fortune, and beauty live as a recluse in the wilds of Cornwall?

Oddly enough, the lady's less than pristine reputation made Lady Sylvia more attractive to the earl than a chit of unimpeachable honor. Not as a mother for his children, naturally. That was out of the question, given her tarnished standing in the *ton*. But there were other, less formal arrangements that might be worth exploring.

Nicholas found himself smiling at the thought.

His eyes rested on her face as she refilled his aunt's cup. A beautiful face, he thought, lovely in a restful, unself-conscious way. He had an unexpected urge to run his knuckles down her cheek, as the Italian had done to Lady Marguerite. A gesture of affection And possession.

Nicholas felt his body respond to the eroticism of this fantasy.

He withdrew his gaze and found himself under the scrutiny of a pair of hazel eyes. Lady Marguerite appeared amused, and her generous mouth was curled in a half smile.

"What do you think of my niece's latest portrait, my lord?" she inquired. "I do believe she has flattered me quite outrageously."

"Not at all, *cara*," Giovanni cut in before the earl could think of a polite response to the lady's leading question. "Sylvia's painting is but a poor rendition of your beauty—"

"Thank you for that kind remark, Giovanni," Lady Sylvia remarked acerbically. "Remind me to include every single one of your blemishes before I conclude the sitting this afternoon."

"The sitting is already concluded, my dear Sylvia," the Italian retorted. "Have you forgotten that Lord Hazelworth is coming down from Bodmin to choose a statue for his new folly?" He glanced toward the house. "I am surprised he is not already here."

As if on cue, Hobson sedately stepped out onto the terrace, followed by a tall, broad-shouldered gentleman in his forties.

The earl watched as Hazelworth bowed gracefully over Lady Marguerite's fingers and nodded to Petorno.

"Longueville." He acknowledged the earl with a careful smile. "What a pleasure to see you again. I trust you have come back to stay. The company around these parts has been sadly dull without the summer festivities at the Castle."

The earl extended his hand, which the baron shook with a heartiness belied by the flicker of unease in his bold blue eyes.

"So I have been told," Nicholas replied dryly.

"And how is your lady mother, Longueville?"

"Her ladyship is in good health, but glad to be back in England," he answered briefly.

The baron did not pursue the issue, but turned instead to the last member of the party.

"And my dear Lady Sylvia," Hazelworth said, and Nicholas became aware of a subtle softening in the baron's tone. "What a delight to find you as dazzling as ever. You quite put the roses to shame, my dear." The gallantry of this remark sounded rather forced, and the earl sensed a sudden tension in his hostess.

Nicholas could not see the baron's face, but he caught a flicker of annoyance in the lady's eyes. Had he imagined it, he wondered, or could it be that Lady Sylvia was less than enthralled at Hazelworth's visit?

"You are much too kind, my lord," she said coolly. "May I offer you a cup of tea?"

The awkward moment passed as the conversation turned to the sculpture Hazelworth had commissioned from Signor Petorno. But Nicholas could not forget the brief annoyance—or was it disgust?—in Lady Sylvia's eyes.

Was it possible, he mused, as the lively conversation flowed around him, that this consummate lecher had designs on the lovely artist? Or perhaps there had been an understanding between them that had run its course, as such affairs invariably did with Baron Hazelworth?

For some inexplicable reason the vision of Hazelworth's hands exploring the intimate secrets of Lady Sylvia's lovely person brought the earl's blood to a sudden boil. He experienced the unnerving urge to throttle the life out of his erstwhile friend and neighbor.

As quickly as his rage had surfaced, however, it subsided, leaving him with the uncomfortable feeling that he was no less contemptible than Hazelworth.

Had he not, that very afternoon, lusted after the lovely Sylvia himself?

The arrival of Baron Hazelworth disconcerted Sylvia. Had she remembered that he was riding down from Bodmin this afternoon, she thought, wincing at the touch of his lips on her fingertips, she would have remained in her studio.

The marked attention of the handsome baron had begun shortly after her arrival at Whitecliffs ten years ago, long before Lady Hazelworth had been carried off by influenza. His address was so polished that at first Sylvia—unaware of the existence of a mistress at Hazelworth Hall—had been flattered.

She was still smarting from her father's blunt dismissal of her chances of ever becoming a wife and mother, and the baron's admiration had eased her loneliness.

"You must resign yourself, child," her father had said during that last dreadful interview in his study. "No decent man will have you now. You are ruined, Sylvia. A blot on our family name as black as any your Aunt Marguerite inflicted upon us with her wild ways."

Sylvia had refrained from reminding her irate parent that the streak of wildness in the Sutherland women could be traced much farther back than Aunt Marguerite. The earl's own grandmother, Lady Giselda, who had brought the Cornwall estate as her dowry when she wed the second Earl of Weston, had been known to gallop along the cliffs on her big roan gelding, her red hair loose and streaming in the wind.

Sylvia looked with distaste at the baron's sleek black head bent over her fingers. She had been eager to believe the comforting words that flowed so smoothly from his smiling lips. How naive she had been, Sylvia recalled, returning the baron's appraising stare as he straightened and raked her with a covert glance. That innocence had been brutally shattered when she discovered the existence of Lady Hazelworth, and lost forever when the libertine had offered her a carte blanche in her aunt's drawing-room.

Lady Sylvia looked away only to meet the earl's interested gaze. Was it possible, she reflected wryly, that she had attracted the interest of yet another lecher? The glint of admiration in Longueville's dark eyes had been unmistakable. Sylvia had seen it before. In Baron Hazelworth's. In Sir Geoffrey Huntsville's, who continued to ogle her although she had attended his wedding several years ago. And most memorably, in the man she had thought to wed, Sir Matthew Farnaby.

So, she mused with a flash of humor, her father had been right. Her admirers had improved in rank and fortune, from mere baronet to earl, but none of them would give her the future she had yearned for at seventeen.

After tea, her aunt and Giovanni bore Lord Hazelworth off to view the Italian's latest sculpture, and Sylvia was left to entertain Mrs. Hargate and the earl. Perversely—or so it appeared to Sylvia—Lord Longueville showed no sign of wishing to view statues of Greek goddesses in déshabillé, and followed the two ladies into the house.

As they passed through the Italian Saloon, the earl paused before one of Lady Sylvia's latest landscapes, which she had called *Longueville Castle at Twilight.*

"You have captured both the majesty and the mystery of the place," Mrs. Hargate remarked reverently. "One can still sense the strength of the Morleys stretching back into history. The Castle was originally a fortress, you know, my lady, built to defend the shores of England from pirates and other rascally invaders."

The earl glanced down at his aunt, a wry smile on his face. "You are incurably romantic, Aunt," he said, and Sylvia was surprised at the affection in his voice. "The Castle was a barracks, cold and drafty. It still is, of course, and were it not for the improvements my grandfather added, it would be impossible to live there."

"Oh, Nicholas!" Mrs. Hargate exclaimed in a shocked voice. "Never say you are not proud of your lineage, my boy."

"I said no such thing, Aunt," the earl replied gently. "But you are right about the majesty and mystery. Lady Sylvia has an uncanny knack of evoking the historical atmosphere, of drawing it out of the past and immersing us in it." He paused for a moment, then added, "It should be hanging in the Great Hall at the Castle. How much will you take for it, my lady?"

Sylvia was no stranger to selling her work, but Lord Longueville's interest surprised her. The vivid memory of the earl interrupting her work on the cliff hut and ordering her off his land flashed into her head. His rudeness still rankled, and she felt no desire to let him have the painting at any price.

"That particular painting happens to be one of my favorites, my lord," she responded.

"That does not answer my question." He spoke as though he understood her resentment. "I am prepared to meet any price you name."

Sylvia found the arrogance of the earl's tone offensive. "The portrait is not for sale, my lord," she said firmly and turned away.

"A thousand pounds? I believe that is a fair price."

And indeed it was, Sylvia thought, much more than fair. But she would not allow herself to be bullied into changing her mind.

"Two thousand?"

She turned and stared at him. His expression was veiled, but she knew he was baiting her. The sum he mentioned was preposterous on all accounts, and she finally laughed. "Are you always so extravagant, my lord?" she murmured. "I wonder that you are not under the hatches. And no, the picture is still not for sale."

"Are you merely being obstinate, or is there another reason why you will not sell to me?"

Sylvia hesitated briefly, then decided that she should not be afraid to tell the truth. "That is my last portrait of Longueville," she began. "I treasure it for that reason."

"Your last, my lady?" Mrs. Hargate exclaimed in surprise. "Surely you jest, my dear?"

Sylvia laughed. "I wish I was. But your nephew has forbidden me to set up my easel on Longueville land, so I must go farther afield for historical subjects."

"Nonsense," Mrs. Hargate replied sharply. "Tell me this is not so, Nicholas."

When the earl made no answer, Lady Sylvia smiled and turned once more towards the stairs.

"Perhaps I was a little hasty," she heard the earl admit grudgingly. "I withdraw the ban, my lady. You may paint anything you fancy on my land."

Sylvia glanced over her shoulder at him. "I accept your apology, my lord," she said, "but only if I may return to the cliffs."

The earl hesitated, his face suddenly grim.

"Oh, Nicholas, do say yes," Mrs. Hargate exclaimed from where she stood at the foot of the stairs. "Only see this fascinating portrait Lady Sylvia has done of the local legend."

Lord Longueville moved—almost reluctantly, Sylvia noted—to stand beside his aunt. He stared at the picture for a long time; then he swore under his breath and, without a word, turned and strode out of the room, leaving the two women to stare after him.

Sylvia slowly let out her breath. Her gaze returned to the pale scene she had whimsically entitled *Mysterious Lady by Moonlight*. Two violet eyes looked back at her, filled with ambiguous emotions. Was it defiance? Sylvia wondered. Or triumph perhaps? She remembered attempting to capture a mixture of both emotions while she worked on the portrait.

In the dim light of the staircase, Sylvia suddenly had the eerie sensation that the expression in the countess's staring eyes was neither defiance nor triumph. It was fear.

Chapter Seven

~

The First Clue

The following morning, as Lady Sylvia rode into Helston to collect the art supplies she had ordered a month since, she mulled over the earl's strange behavior of the afternoon before.

Mrs. Lydia Hargate had appeared as startled as Sylvia by her nephew's abrupt departure.

"Poor Nicholas," she murmured as they watched the earl's tall figure disappear from sight. "I suspect he is still grieving for Angelica. Even after all these years he cannot seem to put the specter of her death behind him."

"But that tragedy happened ten years ago," Sylvia murmured. "I would expect the pain to have diminished by now."

"Oh, I cannot speak for Nicholas, of course," Mrs. Hargate said as they climbed slowly to the attic studio on the third floor, "but my own experience tells me that certain kinds of pain haunt one forever. I still remember, as vividly as though it happened yesterday, the afternoon they carried my eldest son, Luke, back to the Castle, bruised and broken beyond recognition."

Sylvia heard a catch in her guest's voice and recalled that the death of the countess was not the only tragedy to haunt the cliffs around Longueville Castle. Ten or more years before the earl brought his bride to Cornwall, Lady Marguerite had told her, his favorite cousin had fallen from the cliffs during a game of hide-and-seek. Young Morley had been one of those who carried the battered boy back to the Castle.

Summer festivities had been abruptly cancelled after the service in the ancient Longueville chapel, with all the neighborhood in attendance. Had there been rumors of foul play in that tragedy, too? Sylvia wondered. Familiar with the superstitious nature of the local inhabitants, she would not be surprised, although Aunt Marguerite had never mentioned it.

Sylvia had visited the chapel and committed its austere beauty to canvas several times during her stay at Whitecliffs. She knew it had been built by the first Norman baron who received the land and English fortress as a reward for services to William, Duke of Normandy. She had that first baron's likeness on canvas, too, inspired initially by the blurred features of a harsh-faced man with a full beard discovered in the Long Gallery at Longueville. She had named it *The Invader*.

"What a shocking experience for you," Sylvia murmured, trying to imagine what it was like to lose the son she would never have. "Sudden death in one so young is indeed a tragedy," she added, stating the obvious. "And then the young countess, not yet eighteen, I understand, came to a similar . . ."

"Oh, I was not at Longueville when *that* happened," Mrs. Hargate interrupted, and Sylvia thought she detected a nuance of disapproval in her tone. "I never came back to Cornwall after Luke's death. Until now, of course. The place held too many painful memories for me. It still does, if you want the truth, my dear. But not on account of Angelica. I hardly knew the gel, you see. They were married in London, and Nicholas brought her to Bath on their way down to Cornwall. He has always been quite my favorite nephew."

Sylvia was itching to ask if Mrs. Hargate thought her favorite nephew had done away with his lovely bride, but she could hardly expect a doting aunt to admit such a thing. Instead she changed the subject.

"I am sorry his lordship was upset by my *Mysterious Lady*. I should have explained to him that the romantic combined with the tragic is irresistible for a painter. The death of beauty is inherently tragic, of course, but when it occurs under such mysterious circumstances, the artistic imagination takes certain liberties."

Mrs. Hargate sniffed. "And your imagination was influenced by that silly tale of the ghost rider on the cliffs during the full moon, my dear. An unlikely story, if you will forgive me for saying so."

Sylvia smiled. "I tend to agree with you, ma'am, although many villagers swear to have seen the mystery lady riding along the cliff top on her white horse."

"Poppycock!" Mrs. Hargate exclaimed sharply. "It never ceases to amaze me what ignorant minds are capable of inventing. Pure superstition it is, of course, never doubt it, my dear."

"Perhaps you are right," Sylvia conceded, wondering how she might broach the other tale that still circulated among the earl's tenants concerning his lordship's role in his young bride's death.

Before she could introduce the topic without being offensive, Mrs. Hargate did it for her.

"And if you are thinking there is any more truth in that malicious rumor regarding poor Nicholas having a hand in the accident—and accident it undoubtedly was, regardless of what you may have heard—then you are as addle-pated as that prosy Huntsville fellow," Mrs. Hargate declared heatedly. "I confess I was mortified beyond endurance to hear the rogue give credence to what is nothing but gossip spread by peasants."

"Did you know that Sir Geoffrey composed a narrative poem in the Italian style on the tragedy? Needless to say, that gave shape and substance to the rumors, which have since become a legend around here."

Mrs. Hargate looked alarmed. "I trust that gapeseed has the good sense not to read such nonsense at the memorial service next month," she said uneasily. "I understand Reverend Rawson is determined to continue to celebrate the anniversary of Angelica's demise. Nicholas is quite capable of pounding that pompous nose of his into a pulp," she added with unmistakable relish.

Taking that unflattering remark about noses to refer to Sir Geoffrey's admittedly large appendage, Sylvia smiled. "The vicar has done so every year since the accident," she said diplomatically. "I do not always attend, since I never met the countess myself, but my aunt never misses it if the weather is fine."

Sylvia got the distinct impression from the silence following this remark that Mrs. Hargate was not one of the Countess of Longueville's many admirers.

As she entered the village and made her way towards Connan's Book Shop, Sylvia made a mental note to find out why.

When Sylvia finally stepped across the narrow threshold of the small but well-stocked shop, the clock in the church tower was striking eleven. She had been forced to make an unscheduled visit to Mr. Gordon, the blacksmith, when she detected, from the uneven clatter of her horse's hooves on the cobbled street, that Greyboy had cast a shoe.

Interpreting the smithy's assurances that he would have the horse ready for her in a jiffy to mean at least an hour, Lady Sylvia walked the short distance into the center of the village.

"My dear Lady Sylvia," George Connan gushed effusively as soon as he saw her, rubbing his thin hands together as though he had been stung by an army of ants, "how delightful to welcome you to my humble little shop."

Sylvia smiled at him, but could not help wondering if poor Mr. Connan would ever outgrow his annoying habit of belittling himself and his chosen profession. She knew George Connan to be Oxford educated, with a quite astonishing understanding of art and literature.

"You are too modest, Mr. Connan. Your *little shop,* as you choose to call it, is better stocked than some of London's better establishments," Sylvia responded, intending to bolster the man's confidence.

Her good intentions were wasted, however, for the book merchant's face turned fiery red and his reply was lost in a morass of unintelligible gibberish.

"I trust you have received my supplies," she interrupted, taking pity on his confusion. "I am quite out of canvas, and that naughty Rufus chewed up two of my favorite brushes last week. He is quite in my black book, I can tell you."

Connan cleared his throat. "Oh, yes, indeed, my lady," he said, his aplomb partially restored. "Everything arrived as you instructed, my lady. And Mrs. Radcliffe's latest novel is just in." He paused, and when he continued, his voice had dropped to a plaintive whisper. "Every time a Minerva Press book arrives, I cannot help but remember what pleasure our poor countess derived from those romantical novels she used to order from me."

"I enjoy a good novel myself occasionally," Sylvia cut in bracingly, hoping to avoid the long enumeration of the late countess's many saintly virtues she had heard countless times before.

Mr. Connan appeared not to have heard her. His eyes had taken on that familiar glazed look—very much like those of a dead jellyfish, Sylvia thought—and focused on a fantasy he seemed to be able to conjure up at will. She had always considered it a crying shame that an intelligent gentleman like George Connan should fall into a catatonic trance at the mere mention of a slip of a girl whose sole purpose in life—or so her aunt had declared in no uncertain terms—was to entangle as many unsuspecting gentlemen as possible in her web of seductive games, wring them dry of emotion, then discard them like so many soiled handkerchiefs.

"And now that heartless rogue is back," Connan muttered, as though speaking his thoughts aloud, "and we must defer to him as lord of the manor while we all know that he drove the poor angel to take her own life."

Sylvia was startled at this novel revelation. "We do?" she repeated. "I beg to differ, Mr. Connan. I know no such thing. The countess's death was declared an accident, and I am disappointed to hear an intelligent man like yourself give credence to ignorant gossip. The theory of suicide is plainly ridiculous. No young woman of eighteen with everything to live for would commit such a sinful act. There was no evidence at all to support that theory."

Connan appeared slightly taken aback at the fierceness of Sylvia's rebuttal. "There was the suicide note," he argued. "The poor lady—"

"Did you read that note?" Sylvia snapped.

"No, of course not," the scholar replied stubbornly. "His lordship made quite sure of that."

"Then it is nonsensical to pretend that it was a suicide note," Sylvia insisted, her patience with this romantical faradiddle fast evaporating. She had never seen the timid, self-effacing George Connan express himself quite so forcefully before. His reticence seemed to disappear in the face of an attack on his precious countess.

"You do not know the whole, my lady," Connan countered in less strident tones. "You see, her ladyship confided in me." He glanced uneasily over his shoulder as though he feared being caught divulging a treasonous secret. "Marriage to Longueville was destroying the poor darling. A creature of such exquisite sensibility was understandably outraged at the disgusting appetites his lordship displayed in the intimacy of their life together." Connan's expression contracted into a grimace of distaste.

"Disgusting appetites?" Sylvia repeated, more intrigued than she cared to admit about the earl's secret perversions. "Exactly what disgusting appetites are we talking about here, Mr. Connan?"

Connan turned a bright red and stuttered for several moments without being able to articulate coherently. "I c-cannot sully your t-tender ears, my lady," he finally muttered, his eyes modestly averted.

"Her ladyship evidently sullied yours with her lurid tales,"

Sylvia responded sharply. "None of which I believe for a moment, of course. No gentlewoman would dream of broaching such a subject to a stranger."

Connan's eyes refocused on her face. "Oh, you do not understand," he cried, and Sylvia was horrified to note how close the bookseller was to actual tears. "We were not strangers at all."

Sylvia did not quite know how to take this odd confession, and her expression must have reflected her thoughts, for Connan hastily added, "And it was not what you are thinking, my lady," he stammered, face again flaming a brilliant red. "She called me her soul mate." His voice dropped an octave. "The only man who appreciated the purity of her soul, she used to say."

"Poppycock!" Sylvia snapped back, thoroughly disgusted at this maudlin display of excessive sensibility. "Can you explain to me why the lady happened to wed an earl when you were her soul mate? Or did this so-called confession come *after* she was safely hitched to Longueville?"

Connan's face had turned a pasty white. "We did not meet until after the wedding," he muttered. "But her ladyship assured me that had we done so, her choice would have been quite different. As it was, her father pressured her into what he felt was an advantageous match for the daughter of a penniless French émigré."

And the countess's father was undoubtedly correct, Sylvia mused, but she refrained from pointing out that obvious fact to the distraught gentleman. Already she regretted the harshness of her interrogation. Connan had revealed a new slant to the young bride's character, one that confirmed Lady Marguerite's description of the countess as a shameless flirt who amused herself tormenting a guileless young man in the throes of puppy love.

She sighed and glanced at the table of new arrivals at the front of the shop. Perhaps if she were to read more of those infamous romantical novels, she might learn the countess's secret of stirring such unswerving devotion in the hearts of men.

She might also discover exactly what disgusting appetites the lady had objected to in the privacy of her marriage bed.

Lost in these titillating thoughts, Sylvia was brought up short at the sight of the man standing just inside the door. His granite-dark eyes seemed to bore into her very bones.

How much had the Earl of Longueville overheard, she wondered, conscious of the guilty flush suffusing her cheeks.

*   *   *

Nicholas heard the raised female voice before he opened the door, but he hesitated a mere second before stepping into the shop. If George Connan wished to argue with his customers, that was his concern, but Nicholas had an errand to perform for the dowager, and he intended to discharge it.

The identity of the angry customer stopped the earl in his tracks, and he paused for a long moment to survey the scene. The force of Lady Sylvia's disdain lent a militant glitter to her marvelous gray eyes, and Nicholas was enchanted by the wisps of red curls escaping from beneath her gray straw bonnet with its profusion of pale pink roses.

This pleasant reverie was abruptly cut short as the tail end of Connan's last remarks penetrated the earl's consciousness. He stiffened and the half smile that had played around his mouth vanished. What had Connan said about the daughter of a penniless French émigré? This could only be Angelica. The meddling dolt was gossiping about his wife again, Nicholas thought savagely. And to Lady Sylvia no less.

For some inexplicable reason Nicholas did not want the rumors of Angelica's wanton behavior to reach Sylvia's ears. But of course it was already too late for that, he reminded himself morosely. The entire neighborhood was undoubtedly privy to every flirtatious sally the countess had ever uttered, and to many that she had not. And to all those illicit assignations Matthew had hinted at before he left Longueville ten years ago.

The notion of cuckoldry had always seemed to describe the woes afflicting other men, and Nicholas had simply refused to believe his cousin's mocking accusations. The idea that a newly married husband could possible be crowned with horns was unthinkable.

The ugly question he had refused to answer all those years ago rose again with renewed persistence. Was it possible that his bride's perverse enjoyment of sexual violence had not been limited to the conjugal bed?

Had the trusting, bewitched Earl of Longueville been cuckolded by an enchanting chit of seventeen whose violet eyes had held promises he had believed implicitly?

Connan's voice jerked the earl out of his unpleasant reverie, saving him the pain of facing the truth.

"My lord," the bookseller exclaimed, moving towards the new

arrival with an ingratiating smile on his pale face, "welcome to my humble shop. What may I do for you?"

Nicholas stared at the younger man for several moments, his memory dredging up the past with agonizing detail. Had his mother not protested that Angelica flattered Connan excessively and hung on his every word until the young scholar had become unbearably pedantic? Nicholas had chosen to believe that his wife was merely amusing herself at Connan's expense, encouraging him to make a cake of himself. Now he wondered whether Angelica had not employed less innocent means of tormenting her bedazzled admirer.

"I am here to pick up her ladyship's new books from London," the earl said shortly.

He turned his gaze on Lady Sylvia, who had recovered her composure. On impulse Nicholas stepped closer and raised her gloved fingers to a half inch from his lips. He did not release her hand immediately, but stood gazing down into the cool gray depths of her fine eyes. He was oddly gratified to see pink rise again to her cheeks. At least the lady was not immune to his attentions.

He smiled. Here lay the cure to his restlessness, he thought complaisantly. If the lady was willing, of course. And why should she not be? The Earl of Longueville was a very wealthy man, and he would be generous if she pleased him. He had no doubts on that score. Nicholas allowed his gaze to drift down to the lady's mouth, well shaped and rosy as though she had already been soundly kissed.

Her color deepened, and Nicholas felt his irritation at Connan's impertinence fade. His smile threatened to become a grin as his thoughts anticipated the delights in store for him. Lady Sylvia was indeed a tempting morsel, although she appeared to be unaware of her obvious attractions. She blushed like a veritable innocent.

The incongruity of the notion amused him. Innocence in such a female was all an act, of course. There was no doubt that the lady was as ruined as her aunt and eminently suitable for the kind of liaison Nicholas had in mind.

Chapter Eight

~

The Missing Figure

Sylvia stood as though mesmerized, conscious only of the gleam of approval in the gentleman's dark eyes, and the warmth of his grasp seeping through the thin cotton of her gray gloves. She experienced the insane desire to remain in his hands forever.

A discreet cough from Mr. Connan jerked her back to her senses. Sylvia felt the uncomfortable warmth of yet another blush on her cheeks. She was behaving quite like a besotted schoolroom chit in the presence of a dashing music master. This would not do at all, she told herself firmly. Had she not sworn never to allow another gentleman to beguile her with charm, sweet blandishments, and the magic of unspoken promises in deceitful eyes?

What was the matter with her? she wondered, turning to accept the packet of books and brushes Connan had prepared for her. After ten years of learning the unwritten boundaries of what a woman with her shameful history could and could not do in the eyes of the country gentry, Sylvia had become careless. Most of them stood in awe of her aunt, the flamboyant Lady Marguerite, and her refusal to be treated as a pariah. As a wealthy, titled landowner and direct descendent of the eccentric but well-loved Lady Giselda, her ladyship had been insulated from open snubs, and Sylvia had benefited from her aunt's position in the neighborhood.

It had taken but one disdainful glance from the Dowager Countess's cold eyes, however, to remind Sylvia of her precarious position in local circles. Her aunt's long-standing friendship with the dowager was no assurance that Sylvia herself would be accepted within the august circles over which that cold-eyed dragon held sway.

And now her son was exercising the same prerogatives. She had seen it in his knowing eyes, in the way he smiled at her quite as though . . . as though . . . Sylvia balked at completing that unnerving thought.

"Thank you, Mr. Connan," she murmured, aware that the earl had not moved from her side. "I shall send the trap to pick up the canvas tomorrow. I doubt Greyboy will take kindly to having it tied to the saddle."

"I will send one of the clerks to fetch your horse from the blacksmith's," Connan said solicitously.

"That is very kind of—"

"That will not be necessary."

Startled at the earl's audacity, Sylvia turned to glare at him.

He smiled, and Sylvia was reminded forcibly of her aunt's big gray tabby, whom she had seen only yesterday indulging in his favorite sport. Lounging in the shade of a lilac bush, Jonas had one enormous paw on the belly of a tiny field mouse, which he periodically removed to nudge the victim into action. Sylvia had silently urged the mouse to make a run for it, but the poor creature was obviously so paralyzed with fear that it could only crouch before the green-eyed monster that would eventually destroy it.

She felt a strong bond of sympathy for that doomed mouse as she listened, unprotesting, as the earl spoke.

"I will be happy to take the lady up in my curricle as far as the smithy's." Anticipating her assent, the earl took the packet from Mr. Connan and offered his arm.

To her immense chagrin, Sylvia found herself quite incapable of shaking off years of ingrained civility. Her fingers reached out, seemingly of their own accord, and settled lightly on the earl's arm. In no time at all she was whisked outside and lifted effortlessly into the vehicle standing in the sunlit road. She felt the curricle dip as the earl joined her on the green leather seat, and then they were off, a liveried groom leaving his post at the horses' heads and swinging agilely into place behind them.

Sylvia could have kicked herself. What had become of her fine resolution to send every eligible gentleman to the right about? And more particularly those who were ineligible, like Baron Hazelworth and Sir Geoffrey Huntington, both married with growing families. Of course, the baron was now a widower, but Sylvia was not foolish enough to believe that his intentions were any more honorable than they had been before Lady Hazelworth's death. Lawrence Hazelworth was not looking for a second mother for his brood. At least not at Whitecliffs, Sylvia reminded herself bluntly.

The curricle swayed on the uneven cobbles, and Sylvia grasped the handrail to steady herself. It had been a long time since she had driven in such an elegant rig. Both Huntington and Hazelworth owned these sporting vehicles, but Sylvia had wisely fobbed off all invitations to drive out with either gentleman. Why was it, she mused crossly, that she had been more than able to divert these gentlemen from their designs on her virtue, but she had suddenly lost the use of her tongue when confronted by Longueville's autocratic invitation, which had sounded more like a command?

She glanced over her shoulder and was surprised to see George Connan standing before the door to his shop staring after them. Had Sylvia not known the bookseller to be a self-effacing, kindly, unassuming scholar, she might have described his present expression as lowering, perhaps even malignant. She dismissed this odd impression as a result of her present agitation and cast her gaze down the village street, counting the moments that brought her closer to Mr. Gordon's forge and her means of escape from the predatory man who held her captive.

"Ah, there he is," Sylvia exclaimed, brightening at the prospect of regaining control of her transportation. And indeed, his dappled coat gleaming in the sunlight, Greyboy stood, head nodding sleepily, exactly where she had left him an hour since.

"If I remember anything at all about Gordon, my dear," the earl drawled in an amused tone that set Sylvia's teeth on edge, "it must be his cavalier disregard for the clock. So I would not wager on getting your horse anytime before tea-time."

"Mr. Gordon distinctly said twelve o'clock," Sylvia insisted.

"Did he, now?" There was a world of skepticism in his voice that caused Sylvia to bristle.

"Actually, he said 'in a jiffy,' which I took to mean right away," she clarified, remembering that the blacksmith had not mentioned any precise hour.

"Aha! I take it you have no experience with a Cornish 'jiffy'?"

Sylvia suspected the earl was laughing at her, which did not improve her temper. "Indeed I have," she responded coldly. "I have lived with my aunt for ten years now. I should know something about local dialect."

"So you should," he acknowledged smoothly. "We shall soon discover how attentive a pupil you have been, my dear. Gordon," he called out. "Come out here, man."

The pounding of iron against iron that resounded throughout the yard broke off abruptly, and a giant of a man emerged into the sunlight, blinking like a huge owl. His thickly muscled arms glistened with sweat, and a grimy shirt clung wetly to his broad back.

"Milord," he exclaimed, one hand instinctively tugging on his forelock, his bearded face breaking into a grin. "What ken I do for yer lordship this fine morning?"

"It is long past morning, Mr. Gordon," Sylvia interrupted pointedly. "And I have come for my horse, which you promised to have ready by noon. Remember?"

The mountainous smithy blinked at her. "Did I, now?" he said, glancing curiously at the assortment of animals tethered around the yard. "Ah! Ye be meanin' that gray gelding over yonder." He waved a huge paw in the general direction of Greyboy, who opened one eye at the sound of Sylvia's voice.

"Yes, indeed," she responded sharply, sensing that all was not going as planned. "Have you replaced his shoe?"

"His shoe?" the blacksmith repeated, as though he had never heard of one before. "He lost a shoe, did he, now? Well, let me see." He rubbed his bearded chin with one hairy paw and seemed to ponder the matter.

Sylvia felt her patience evaporating. Worse still, she distinctly heard the earl repress a chuckle. The wretch was laughing at her again.

"Ah, well, now," Gordon exclaimed, his florid face smiling amiably. "I may be the best horse shoer between here and Plymouth, milady, but I ain't that Greek feller Hercales or whatever his blessed name was. Ye brung that gray in less than a half hour ago, milady, and—"

"A full hour ago, sir. And you promised to have him ready for me—"

"In a jiffy," the earl interrupted, with a crack of laughter to which the smithy was not slow to add his bellow.

Realizing she was outnumbered and not wishing to waste her breath arguing with two males obviously intent on thwarting her, Sylvia stared stonily at an outrageously ugly bonnet in puce velvet embellished with yellow pansies in a milliner's shop across the street.

"Tom," the earl commanded finally, turning to his grinning groom, "you had better stay here to make sure Gordon takes no more than his promised jiffy. Then bring the horse to Whitecliffs and deliver it to her ladyship with my compliments."

"There is absolutely no need to inconvenience yourself, my lord," Sylvia protested, knowing she was fighting a losing battle.

"You are not inconveniencing me in the slightest, my dear," he replied truthfully. And before Sylvia could think of a rebuttal, Tom had jumped down and the curricle rattled away at a spanking pace as the earl's team sprang forward smartly.

Stunned by the suddenness of events, Sylvia again found herself wondering why she had not jumped from the vehicle herself, even at the risk of breaking a limb. The answer was not difficult to find. The unpleasant truth was that she had—either consciously or unconsciously, she could not be sure—allowed herself to be bullied by a man whose intentions she knew could not be honorable. Through the sheer weight of his authority, the earl had not only separated her from her horse and the dubious protection of a groom, but was about to subject her to a five-mile drive along deserted country lanes.

Just the two of them alone together.

Sylvia wondered if it was still too late to fling herself from the racing vehicle. At least her battered body, if she survived, would be evidence that she had taken drastic measures to protect her innocence.

What innocence? a little voice inside her whispered insidiously. She could no longer plead innocence to avert unwelcome advances. She had left innocence behind her, back in faraway Dover, in that poky little inn with a man who had broken her heart.

The man beside her, his shoulder brushing hers companionably, must be well aware of this shady chapter in her past. Indeed, he was—if that complaisant little smile that played around his mouth was any indication—counting on her lost innocence to smooth the way for him.

Sylvia clasped her hands tightly in her lap to still their trembling, and bitterness welled up in her throat at the unfairness of life. If the earl thought she would be willing to play that game again, he was in for a nasty surprise, she thought, hoping that her resolution was equal to the challenge.

* * *

After a dashing departure from the village, the earl drew his
team down to a more leisurely pace as soon as they had passed the
last thatched cottage.

Sylvia glanced at him askance, wondering which seductive ploy
he was about to practice on her.

"Have you given further thought to selling *Longueville Castle at
Twilight?*" he said finally, surprising her.

"I thought we had already concluded that subject, my lord," she
replied coolly, her lips flickering into a half smile.

"Not at all, my dear," he drawled. "I have set my heart on it, you
see. And I am accustomed to getting what I want," he added softly.

Was she dreaming, Sylvia wondered, or was that a thinly veiled
threat that referred to much more than a painting?

She laughed shortly, angry that this man could be so sure of her
capitulation. "Then your heart has misled you, my lord, and you
had best prepare yourself for disappointment. That painting is not
for sale." Nor is anything else you may have set your heart on, she
added to herself. "At *any* price," she could not resist emphasizing
to conclude the matter.

"Two thousand pounds," he reminded her, ignoring her last
statement entirely. "My offer still stands. Or perhaps you are fishing for more, my lady."

Sylvia repressed the caustic remark that rose to her lips and
turned to gaze at the farmland that swept away towards the hori-
zon on her left, shutting out the earl's voice. All this was
Longueville land, she knew, as was the village itself, and the desolate moors that lay between the lane and the cliffs, where the
enigmatic stone hut clung tenaciously to the stones above the sea.

Thoughts of that desolate hut and the dangerous secrets it harbored reminded Sylvia of the painting she had been working on
when she first encountered an irate earl. She had thought the
seascape complete, but now it dawned upon her that an important
element was missing. The scene was lifeless, she realized with
sudden insight. A mediocre composition of rocks and sea and gray
sky. In her mind's eye she abruptly saw it, like a glimpse of a scene
perceived through a break in a thick fog, as it should be. As perhaps it had been on that glorious summer evening when the countess had died.

There should be a dark figure standing on the edge of the cliff
gazing down at the hut.

How could she have missed it? True, the figure would be

dwarfed by the arching sky, by the towering rocks, indistinct in the thickening twilight. But Sylvia should have sensed his presence, as she felt it now. She should have *known* the figure would be there. He *had* to have been there, she told herself firmly. Someone had witnessed the last moments of the unhappy bride.

Her artist's imagination would never betray her in such a vital detail. She had failed to visualize the complete scene as it must have happened ten years ago. How had she hoped to capture the mysterious essence of the place if the most important character was missing?

And then, as vividly as the presence of that dark figure had burst upon her consciousness, Sylvia saw the sequel to that scene unfold in her imagination. The dark figure moved towards the edge of the cliff. Unhurriedly, yet with sinister purpose, he descended the stone stairs leading to the open door of the hut.

There was someone waiting inside; she knew instinctively. Was it the countess? Local rumors had linked her to various gentlemen gathered at the Castle that summer. But which one had gone down to the stone hut that evening? What had been his purpose? Amorous dalliance? Dastardly murder? Or had there really been an accident that the dark figure dared not reveal for obvious reasons?

A disturbing thought nagged at her; the figure on the cliffs had seemed oddly familiar. But that was patently ridiculous. Sylvia had known none of these gentlemen ten years ago. Certainly not the earl, who was commonly cast in the role of jealous husband extracting a dreadful revenge on his wanton wife.

"Now I have offended you, my dear," that faintly amused voice remarked from close beside her.

Sylvia jumped and turned to stare at him, eyes blank as she tried to rally her thoughts. Here was the man who must know the truth, she thought. Had he not read the so-called suicide note Mrs. Rawson, the vicar's wife, set such store by? No one seemed to know for certain that it had been a suicide note. Or even that the countess had written it. Although the earl had supposedly identified his wife's writing.

Was it possible, Sylvia thought in sudden panic, that she was riding over the Cornish moors with a murderer who had cleverly covered his tracks? Had the earl been that dark figure on the cliff?

She shook her head to dispel the ugly thought.

"You have been wool-gathering, my lady, have you not?" he chided her. "Have you heard a single word of my latest proposition? I am crushed," he added, sounding amused rather than annoyed.

Sylvia assayed a faint smile. She wished she could ask this arrogant man if he had been on the cliffs the night the countess died, but something told her the dark figure had not been the earl. Or was she unconsciously rejecting the possibility of his guilt?

Uncomfortable with this question, Sylvia opted to stick to the truth, at least as far as possible.

"Actually, I was thinking of a recent painting of mine," she admitted. "I had considered it complete, but now I realize that there is an important piece of the story missing. I cannot wait to get back to my studio and rectify that omission."

"Can you tell me what that missing piece is?" he demanded in a voice suddenly devoid of all humor.

She laughed uneasily. "I cannot do that, my lord," she prevaricated. "I am not sure myself if the addition I have in mind fits into the picture or not. You see, I do not know the whole story; I merely follow my imagination. You are welcome to see for yourself when I finish the painting."

He glanced at her briefly, and Sylvia had a premonition that the earl had guessed the story she had referred to. "I shall hold you to that invitation," he said dryly. "In the meantime, what do you say to my other proposition?"

For a sickening moment Sylvia's heart pounded uncomfortably. Had the rogue offered her a *carte blanche* while she had been thinking of his late countess? she wondered. The incongruity of it amused her, and she was able to reply with some composure. "And what proposition is that, my lord?"

He grinned at her, a devilish, cat-like grin that reminded again of Jonas playing his macabre games with the defenseless mouse. Had he read her thoughts?

"I offered you the chance to contribute to the art collection in the Long Gallery at Longueville, my dear. A singular honor, I might add. My mother is anxious to add my likeness to the family heirlooms."

"And the dowager suggested that I be chosen for this singular honor, my lord?" She could not keep the skepticism from her voice, and her question brought an answering smile from her companion.

"Actually, you are *my* choice, Lady Sylvia." The softly spoken words seemed innocent enough, but as Sylvia stared into the warm glow of his dark eyes, they took on quite another meaning.

She blushed and glanced towards the cliffs. The prospect of hours of intimacy with this man, alone in her studio, unnerved her. He was right, of course—this was indeed an honor. Her reputation in the art world would benefit immeasurably; she knew several major portrait artists who would kill to receive such a commission from the Earl of Longueville. But . . . her thoughts trailed off as she came face to face with the disturbing truth.

But what of her heart?

Chapter Nine

~

Jason

The remainder of the drive back to Whitecliffs passed so quickly that Nicholas found no opportunity to broach the subject that was uppermost in his mind. He suspected that Lady Sylvia had divined his intentions and deliberately kept her flood of amusing anecdotes about the art world flowing to thwart him.

But she would not escape him so easily, he told himself cynically as the curricle swept through the stone gates of the Sutherland estates. If not today, then tomorrow or the next he would make her an offer she could not refuse. He already owned a house in Falmouth where he could install her, but he would willingly purchase another in Penzance or anywhere else she chose to name. Within easy riding distance, of course. What was the use of keeping a mistress in London or Bath when he spent most of his time in Cornwall?

Nicholas glanced at his companion and was charmed afresh by the elegant profile under the floppy brim of the gray straw bonnet. He found the delicate shape of her mouth enchanting as she suddenly turned to smile at him. Her gray eyes sparkled with intelligence and a hint of mischief that delighted him. Nicholas enjoyed educated females who used their brains instead of their petticoats to attract a man.

He found himself grinning at her, something he had not done with a female for a very long time. Suddenly the summer stretched ahead of him, offering a delightful alternative to the tedious revision of estate accounts and the necessary shipping business he must attend to in Falmouth.

The anticipation made his blood sing.

But first there was the small matter of convincing the lady. It would not happen today, as he had hoped, but Nicholas could wait. The sweetness of the chase was half the fun, he thought, lifting Lady Sylvia down from the curricle, relishing the feel of her trim waist beneath his fingers. He had little hopes of receiving an invitation to linger at Whitecliffs that afternoon, but tomorrow he would invent some excuse to call.

"Thank you, my lord," Lady Sylvia said, a trifle breathlessly, he thought. "You are very kind."

"Nothing of the sort," he answered lightly. "It was all a bribe to seduce you, my dear," he added daringly.

"Seduce me?" she echoed, the flush he had deliberately provoked flooding her cheeks.

"Yes," he said, his voice smooth as silk. "Seduce you into painting my portrait." He paused and gazed down at her from beneath hooded lids. "Tell me I have succeeded, Sylvia."

Lady Sylvia gasped at his daring use of her name and opened her mouth, doubtless to protest the impertinence. A voice from the front door interrupted them, and they turned to see Lady Marguerite hurrying down the stone steps, her face wreathed in smiles.

"My dear Nicholas," she cried, grasping his arm and urging him towards the house. "You will never guess who is here, my dear boy. Oh, what a lovely surprise. I am so glad you stopped in at Whitecliffs." She paused, glancing at her niece, whom she appeared to notice for the first time. "Sylvia? What happened, dear? Where is Greyboy? I do hope you did not have an accident." She glanced apprehensively from the earl to her niece.

"Calm yourself, my dear lady," Nicholas said soothingly, patting the hand that clutched his sleeve. "Lady Sylvia's horse cast a shoe, and you know how lackadaisical Gordon is about his work. I happened to be in Helston on a errand for my mother, and we ran into each other at Connan's."

"Oh, how kind you are, Nicholas," her ladyship said distractedly. "But do come inside, both of you. There is someone I want you to meet, Sylvia. And as for you, my lord"—she slanted her eyes at him provocatively, then paused again—"I shall say no more. Come in and see for yourself."

As they approached the Italian Saloon, Nicholas heard a crack of male laughter that he recognized instantly. "Jason!" he exclaimed delightedly. "I was not expecting that scurvy rogue for another month." He strode unceremoniously into the drawing room, leaving the ladies to trail behind him.

"Jason," he drawled, "you never cease to amaze me, old man. I imagined you still out on the high seas somewhere between Corunna and St.-Pol-de-Léon. Not lost another of my ships, have you, lad?"

A tall, rangy gentleman, dressed informally in buff breeches and a coat of no particular style, unfolded himself from a deep chair and strode across the room to clasp Nicholas in a bear hug.

"If memory serves me, Nick, it was not I who lost the *Intrepid* last year, but Rogers, who could no more tell the poop from the prow if his life depended upon it. And to think I warned you how it would be, lad, but did you listen, you pig-headed—"

"Hush, lad," Nicholas cut in, interrupting an argument they had had before. "You are right, of course. 'Tis true I misjudged Rogers, but how was I to know he would take to the bottle when things got rough?"

"Had you listened to me . . ."

"I promise to do so next time, old man, never fear. And it so happens you may get your chance sooner than you think. Old Barker tells me that the Horton brothers are selling off their fleet. The *Voyageur* will be the first to go, Ned assures me, and if we can pay cash, he guarantees—"

"The *Voyageur?*" Ransome repeated excitedly. "One of the finest ships in the trade, Nick. Worth every penny you pay for it, too. Are you going to purchase her?"

"I want you to see her first, Jason. Perhaps we can ride over to Falmouth tomorrow."

Nicholas suddenly became aware that his friend's attention had strayed. Jason was staring over the earl's shoulder, an admiring look in his startling blue eyes. He turned slowly, a rueful grin on his face.

"My apologies, ladies," he began, cursing himself for his appalling breach of etiquette. "I am behaving quite abominably."

"Think nothing of it, my boy." Lady Marguerite chuckled and moved forward, her niece in tow.

"This is Lord Jason Ransome, Sylvia," she said, indicating the captain with one slender hand. "Quite one of my favorite gentlemen, I should add. A confirmed rogue and philanderer, of course, but quite charming."

Nicholas grimaced. Her ladyship's assessment of his friend was undoubtedly true. Jason Ransome, youngest son of the Marquess of Milford, came from an impeccable lineage and possessed everything but rank and fortune to make him the catch of every Season he had graced London's saloons over the years. While his dry stick of a brother stood to inherit their father's title and fortune, Jason had more than enough charm to delight every hostess in Town. He might have wed any number of heiresses who had thrown their handkerchiefs at him, and settled into the easy life of a wealthy landowner. But Jason's love of adventure precluded anything so mundane. Fascination for the sea had brought them together at Oxford, and that bond had only strengthened throughout the years.

In his heart of hearts, Nicholas envied his friend for being a younger son, free to venture forth on madcap adventures at the drop of a hat. Jason had gained his sea legs with an old captain in Portsmouth, long since passed on. But the old man's love of the sea lived on in Jason, and when Nicholas had bought his first trading vessel, it was a foregone conclusion that Jason would captain her.

Their partnership had been profitable for both of them. Before the loss of the *Intrepid,* Nicholas had owned six vessels and now, if the purchase of the *Voyageur* materialized, he would again own six prime trading ships, which brought in more money than he knew what to do with.

"Your most humble servant, my lady."

Nicholas watched with mild amusement as Jason raised Lady Sylvia's fingers to his lips with an extravagant flourish. The rogue certainly had a way with the ladies, he thought, noting the warmth in this particular lady's eyes as she smiled up at Captain Ransome.

Had he not known that his friend was more interested in ships than females, Nicholas might have had a moment of uneasiness as the party moved onto the back terrace, where Hobson had laid out the tea things. As it was, he only smiled as the captain settled himself between Lady Sylvia and her aunt and regaled them with humorous tales of his latest adventures on the high seas.

"I do envy you, Captain Ransome," Lady Sylvia remarked after she made sure Jason had a generous helping of gooseberry tarts. "Our lives here in Cornwall seem so tame after hearing of such fascinating places and exotic people. You must find us terribly dull and stodgy."

"*Au contraire,* my dear lady," the captain responded gallantly, "nowhere in the world have I seen anything that comes close to the perfection of our own English rose. One tires of the exotic, my lady, and grows nostalgic for the radiant beauty of an innocent English lass. Would you not agree, Nicholas?"

The earl stared at his friend in astonishment at this piece of arrant nonsense, then let out a crack of laughter. "Your brains have been addled by the Indian sun, my lad. That is what ails you. And if you do not have a care, Jason, you will find yourself banished from Whitecliffs until you learn to comport yourself like a proper English gentleman."

"You are too harsh, my lord," Lady Marguerite burst out impetuously. "Captain Ransome is utterly charming, as usual, and he is welcome to take his meals with us anytime he pleases. Besides," she added with a mischievous twinkle in her eyes, "neither Sylvia nor I are particularly impressed by what passes for proper English gentlemen these days. Are we, dearest?"

Nicholas glanced at Lady Sylvia and noted that her cheeks were rosy. She was smiling at Jason, and at his prompting, she admitted that English gentlemen tended to be stuffy, pompous, and too concerned with their own consequence.

At this frank admission, Jason echoed the earl's mocking laughter. "Touché, old man," he drawled wryly. "It would seem that you are the one in need of lessons in proper comportment, Nick. I shall be happy to give you some pointers, if you wish."

None too pleased with the direction the conversation had taken, Nicholas turned to Lady Marguerite and changed the subject.

Sylvia let her fingers stray idly over the keys of the rosewood pianoforte in the drawing room. She was in a pensive mood. The events of the afternoon had left her mind in an unaccustomed turmoil. First the disturbing suspicion—derived from Mr. Connan's revealing comments that morning—that the bookseller had not told the magistrate all he knew about the sudden death of the Countess of Longueville.

Had Connan been on the cliffs that fatal summer evening? she wondered. Had he seen someone else there? What secrets had the young woman confided to this unprepossessing scholar she had called her soul mate? Was it even true that the pair had not met until after the wedding?

Sylvia shook her head impatiently. She was becoming suspicious of everyone even remotely connected with the countess. Even poor George Connan, who was the least likely gentleman of her acquaintance to be embroiled with another man's wife.

Or was he?

The thought startled her, and her fingers fumbled on the keyboard. Sylvia curled her hands nervously in her lap as fragments of that morning's conversation drifted back to her.

When he had spoken of the countess, Connan's voice had taken on the strident tones of a fanatic. He had given the impression that their relationship had been more than a casual acquaintance.

We were not strangers at all.

Those were his very words, but what did they mean? Could they have been . . . lovers? Sylvia had difficulty imagining the bespectacled scholar in that role. Knowing as she did from firsthand experience the sometimes embarrassing intimacies associated with such amorous activities, Sylvia had a hard time placing George Connan in any lady's bedchamber, much less that of the flamboyant, obviously uninhibited young countess.

Had she lived, the Countess of Longueville would have been about Sylvia's own age, she mused, nearing thirty, but what a difference in their situations. From relative obscurity and modest circumstances, Angelica DeJardin had been elevated to the rank of countess through the love of a man. Sylvia had not been so blessed. The love of a man—in whom she had placed her trust and innocence—had plunged her into disgrace and banishment.

"Daydreaming about your latest admirer, *cara mia?*" Giovanni's laughing voice cut short her musings, and Sylvia guessed she must have been sitting at the silent instrument for some time, lost in thought.

"Come and pour tea for us, darling," her aunt said, and Sylvia saw that Hobson had brought in the tea-tray without her noticing. "I want to hear what transpired between you and Longueville this morning, Sylvia, although I suspect I already know. I trust you will not be foolish enough to harbor impossible dreams in that quarter, my dear. I would hate to see you hurt all over again."

Sylvia saw the genuine concern on her aunt's face and forgave her for touching on a sore subject. "Oh, never fear, Aunt," she responded lightly. "My heart is quite safe from his lordship's blandishments. I promise not to tread that primrose path again, no matter what prestigious commission he flings my way."

"I still believe you would do well to paint his portrait, child," Lady Marguerite said, branching off on another topic. "You owe it to your career, Sylvia."

"I was not referring to his lordship," Giovanni interrupted, waving an elegant hand as if to dismiss the earl and his commission. "I think the dashing Captain Ransome was definitely *épris* by our lovely Sylvia. He could not take his eyes off you, my dear."

"A charming rogue, I will agree," Lady Marguerite remarked, accepting her cup and setting it down beside her. "But he is a rover, my love, as all sailors are. Only think what poor Penelope had to endure with her Odysseus. And even your own Cristobal Colombo, my love," she added, turning to her lover as though Giovanni were personally responsible for the Italian explorer's wandering ways, "must have had a wife somewhere, yet we hear nothing of the unfortunate creature."

"I know nothing of Colombo's home life," Giovanni responded with a laugh, "but I did see the captain's face when he looked upon our Sylvia. He is smitten, for certain."

"I have no romantic interest in the good captain," Sylvia assured them. "My interest is purely artistic. I would dearly love to paint his portrait. With that red hair and blue eyes, he reminds me of my brother John. Do you not agree, Aunt?"

"I was startled by his resemblance to the Sutherland men ever since I met dear Jason ten years ago," Lady Marguerite replied. "But his mother was a Corrington, and half of them have red hair." Her ladyship took up a delicate watercress sandwich and examined it as though she expected a tadpole to wriggle out onto her plate. "But tell me, Sylvia, do you intend to paint the captain before you start Longueville's commission? Knowing the earl, I can guarantee that he will not be pleased."

Sylvia laughed. "Am I supposed to spend my life trying to please his lordship?" she inquired facetiously. "You taught me long ago, Aunt, that a true artist paints to please himself. I doubt that I will derive much pleasure in painting the Earl of Longueville."

"But you will paint him, dear? Promise me you will," her aunt insisted.

"If you wish it, Aunt, then be assured that I shall," Sylvia replied with a smile. "But first allow me to capture some of the good captain's charm on my canvas."

"I daresay poor Nicholas will be furious with you, darling."

Tired of hearing about the earl's disapproval, for which she cared not a jot, Sylvia returned to the pianoforte and selected a lively country dance to banish her blue devils.

Chapter Ten

~

Past Deceptions

Longueville Castle
July 1804

"I thought I had expressly asked you not to go down to the cliffs, Angelica," Nicholas said, deliberately keeping his tone from betraying his anger.

His lovely bride invariably took exception to his rare insistence on wifely obedience, chiding him for his antiquated notions. But deliberate thwarting of his wishes was something even Nicholas, enchanted as he admittedly was by his young countess, would not tolerate.

"Did you, darling?" Angelica's voice was as soft and languid as her person, presently reclining on an opulent chaise-longue beside the open window in her bedchamber. "I do not recall you saying such a silly thing."

She smiled seductively at him, and Nicholas felt himself weaken. Should he let it go? he wondered. If he provoked a quarrel, his wife would react violently, as she always did when confronted with her peccadilloes or denied her more outrageous whims. Doubtless she would deny him her bed if he pursued his grievance. Unlike some of his friends, Nicholas had never been a particularly innovative lover, preferring the traditional to the exotic in his dealing with females.

Angelica had changed all that.

Now he found himself—more often than not in his own Green Saloon, with one of his mother's delicate Wedgwood tea-cups balanced in his hand, wishing for the day to be over so he could discover what new delights his wife had in store for him. Avoiding the dowager's accusatory stare as she sat, stiff and rigid like some watchdog of propriety, his gaze would follow Angelica's elegantly clad figure about the room. She was invariably the center of attention, a tantalizing butterfly among the usual throng of dark-suited gentlemen who flocked to listen to her tinkling laughter and bask in the flirtatious warmth of her pansy blue eyes.

He resolutely put this thought aside.

"Well, I certainly did say so, my dear," he responded doggedly. "And now I find that you were seen down there yesterday afternoon. In defiance of my express wishes to the contrary."

Bracing himself for a bitter argument, Nicholas watched the lovely face turn petulant, the full lips pout enticingly. God, he thought, she was beautiful even in her worst moods.

"I am concerned for your safety, my love," he added, feeling the need to avert the storm before it broke. "There have been numerous accidents on those cliffs, Angelica, one of which happened to my own cousin, Luke, who fell and died there one summer."

"Oh, you mean Matt's brother?" she interrupted nonchalantly. "I know all about that. Matt told me. He claims it was a rather fortunate accident for him, since he is now the heir." She paused to stare at him, as if gauging the effect of her outrageous statement.

Nicholas could not quite believe his wife had said that. Yet he knew from experience that she delighted in shocking him. All too often the indiscreet, often offensive language that sallied from those shapely lips jarred his sensibilities. He understood why the dowager disliked his wife. His mother's keen sense of decorum would have instantly detected this streak of vulgarity in the new countess.

"If indeed it really was an accident at all," Angelica added softly, a malicious little smile pulling at the corners of her sensuous mouth.

The earl felt his breath catch in his throat. "What did you say?" he demanded brusquely. "Where did you hear such foolishness, Angelica? I know it could not have been from my cousin."

This appeared to amuse the countess, for she laughed, a knowing little sound that sent a chill down his spine. "Oh, my dear, innocent Nicky," she crooned, evidently highly pleased with herself, "still trusting everyone, I see. Let me tell you, my love, that you do not know your precious friends as well as you think you do."

Nicholas knew this accusation to be false, but he had to make sure. "I assume you are including my cousin in this calumny."

"Among others," she replied enigmatically. "People are not always what you imagine them to be, Nicky. There is more evil in the world than you suspect. It has already touched you, my love, but you refuse to see it."

She extended one shapely limb, which Nicholas could clearly see beneath the diaphanous night rail, and wriggled her toes provocatively. But Nicholas refused to be distracted.

"Does that include you, too, Angelica?" he blurted out before considering the wisdom of his words. "Are you everything I imagine you to be?"

The countess opened her eyes wide, dazzling him with their brilliance. "Of course not, silly," she murmured, "no woman is that perfect, Nicky. And certainly no gentleman I have ever met." A shadow passed across her face. "They are villains and deceivers all," she added with a suppressed fury that startled him.

"Surely you exaggerate, my love," he said mildly. "And I know you are mistaken about my cousin. We have been friends since childhood—"

"Fiddle!" the countess exclaimed impatiently. "You deceive yourself if you think you can trust relatives, Nicholas. They are the worst kind of predators."

She looked so distressed that Nicholas was about to forget his wife's disobedience when an ugly thought crossed his mind.

"Are you trying to suggest that it was my Cousin Matt who was on the cliffs with you yesterday?" His source of information had been unable to identify the gentleman who had been seen with the countess, but Nicholas had an uneasy suspicion it might have been his cousin.

The earl watched his wife's face carefully. She appeared to be searching for an appropriate reply to his question. He hoped she would not lie to him.

His hopes died abruptly when the countess dropped her gaze and fiddled briefly with the folds of her pink satin dressing gown. When she raised her eyes, they were cold and stormy.

"Why must you pick on poor Matt?" she cried in a voice verging on hysteria. "He is not the only gentleman deserving of your scorn, my lord. Your precious friend Lord Jason is hardly as lily white as you seem to think. Have you not seen him stare at me with those sheep's eyes of his?"

Nicholas felt his heart sink. His incorrigibly self-centered cousin he could understand, even forgive; had he not overlooked many such selfish, thoughtless acts over the years? But Jason? Not Jason, please Lord. Betrayal from such a quarter would be unbearable. They had been as brothers since their days together at Eton. And ever since that shattering summer of 1790 when his Cousin Luke had fallen to his death from those same cliffs, Jason had become an indispensable part of his life. Much more so than Matt had ever been. Or ever would be, Nicholas admitted.

"Are you saying that Jason was there with you, Angelica?" He knew it could not be true, but some perversity in his soul forced him to ask.

His wife's reaction was instantaneous and violent. Swinging herself up from the chaise-longue, she stood facing him, fists clenched, eyes blazing blue fire.

"Why is it that you are so ready to believe your spies before you can trust me?" she hissed furiously, her face suffused with angry color.

"I set no one to spy on you, Angelica," he said slowly. And he had not done so; the idea would not have crossed his mind before today. He had trusted her. But it appeared Angelica had spoken the truth: one could not trust relatives, even one's own wife. Particularly not one's own wife, it appeared.

But then perhaps he had been too quick to believe his steward's report of seeing the countess and a gentleman on the cliffs yesterday afternoon. Tom Gates had not been instructed to report on his mistress's activities, and his comment this morning had seemed casual enough. And what possible reason could Gates have for making up such a story?

"Then some busybody obviously took it upon himself to do so," Angelica raged. "And went running to you with the story, hoping for a pat on the head, no doubt."

"Then you admit the story is true?" Nicholas said heavily, as the implications of her words sank in. "You were on the cliffs?"

Angelica's face turned livid with rage. "I was nowhere near your silly cliffs," she cried, stamping her foot in frustration, "and I resent being forced to account for my actions like some irresponsible schoolroom chit. I thought I left all that behind me in my father's house. Believe me, Nicholas, I may not be the perfect wife, but I am innocent of this particular sin."

Nicholas recognized an olive branch when one was offered, but there was something in his wife's story that did not ring true. How could Gates, who knew her ladyship well, mistake the matter? Faced with accepting an uneasy truce or discovering an unpalatable truth, Nicholas opted for the latter, fully aware that he was burning his bridges for the night.

"If you are innocent, my love," he said as gently as he could, "perhaps you will tell me exactly where you were yesterday afternoon?"

The countess stared at him for a long while before responding. Nicholas tried hard not to imagine that she was again searching for an appropriate answer to appease him. When she finally spoke, the earl could tell from her supercilious tone that he would sleep in his own bed that night.

"Since apparently I am expected to account for every single action I take," she said disdainfully, "then I must confess I spent most of the afternoon with that insipid Martha Grenville. As you know, I am painting her portrait. It is not going at all well, of course, but what can you expect? The silly little fool looks as though she is sucking on a lemon half the time. I did not enjoy the visit in the slightest, but I had promised her mother I would try to produce a reasonable likeness."

Nicholas let her talk, knowing that he was listening to a pack of lies. "Did you not enjoy Lady Grenville's famous currant tarts?" he inquired innocently. "I imagine you stayed for tea."

"Of course," Angelica answered instantly, confirming the earl's suspicion that his wife had not been anywhere near Grenville Hall yesterday, either to paint or to eat currant tarts.

"And now you must leave me, Nicky," she said petulantly, confirming another of the earl's predictions. "I can feel one of my megrims coming on."

Nicholas bowed without a word and turned on his heel. As the connecting door closed behind him, he knew that he could never again trust in his wife's innocence. She had lied to him deliberately about spending the afternoon at Grenville Hall. And Nicholas did not need Tom Gates's report to confirm this lie. He could confirm it himself.

The earl and his mother, who believed in spreading her patronage evenly amongst the gentry, had been at Grenville Hall that afternoon, and had sat for nearly an hour drinking tea and eating currant tarts with the family.

The Countess of Longueville had not been there at all.

Chapter Eleven

~

Portrait of a Pirate

"Oh, do hold still, Captain," Sylvia said for the fourth time that afternoon, stepping back from her easel and squinting through half-closed eyes at the canvas. "Unless you really wish to have a crooked nose, sir. That would be no trouble at all, but I rather think it would spoil the overall effect of piratical elegance."

"I had no idea pirates were elegant creatures," the captain replied with a laugh. "The only ones I ever met were a ragtag, motley crew, sadly in need of a bath. Bad teeth, too, most of them. Something to do with their diet, I have heard. And too much Blue Ruin, of course."

"You have actually met real pirates?" Sylvia gasped, her attention momentarily diverted from the captain's nose. "How thrilling! Although I suspect they are not quite as romantical as Mrs. Radcliffe paints them in her novels."

"Quite the opposite, my dear. Scurvy rogues, every last one of them. Just as soon cut your liver out and fry it for breakfast as give you a civil good-day."

"Surely you exaggerate, Captain," Sylvia protested with a laugh. "And I trust you are, because the Sutherlands have a real live pirate in their closet, and we like to think him respectable. Although Papa had some difficulty in maintaining that fiction when my brother John discovered the record of his hanging at Tyburn in the 1680s."

The captain's eyebrows rose, and another smile lit up his face. "It is good to know that I am not the only black sheep of your acquaintance, my dear," he remarked lightly. "My father disowned me when I took to the sea. He tried to convince me I had sullied the honor of the family by dabbling in Trade. Family tradition had me condemned to the clergy; can you imagine anything more ludicrous?"

Sylvia shook her head and smiled. "What a waste that would have been," she agreed, her vivid imagination picturing the handsome, red-headed captain in a more dashing role. "I think you might have made a wonderful pirate, though. Dressed in a red silk shirt, studded belt, and swinging a scimitar as you boarded a fat Spanish galleon bloated with chests of gold." She paused and eyed him speculatively. "Have you ever considered—"

"No, I have not," the captain broke in emphatically. "A life of crime rarely leads to anything except the gallows or a knife in the back, lass." He grinned at her, quite charmingly, Sylvia thought. "You must rid yourself of these romantical notions, my dear. Just consider your own family. Did your ancestor not end his career at the end of a rope?"

"Yes. At least that is what the records show. But he was only a relative by marriage, I will have you know, sir," Sylvia clarified. "Actually, he was a brother to our famous Lady Giselda, that intrepid lady who came over from France to wed the fourth earl. Jacques Dubois his name was, and he acquired Whitecliffs as a dowry for his only sister. Doubtless with pilfered Spanish gold," she added with a twinkle.

"Doubtless," the captain echoed wryly, settling back into his pose again. "But I have no fancy for hanging just yet. Besides, pirates do not wear red silk, nor do they swing scimitars around except in novels from the Minerva Press. Is it not time for tea?" he demanded a short while later.

"I am not quite finished for today, Captain, so you will have to wait for your tea."

An hour later, Sylvia sighed and stepped back to view the results of her afternoon's work. She glanced at the captain and noticed he was watching her, a faint smile curving his sensuous mouth. Sylvia returned his smile. For some reason she felt entirely at ease with Jason Ransome. Although he obviously admired her, she felt she could trust him, something she had not done for a long time with any gentleman but Giovanni.

As she gazed at the half-finished portrait of the captain, Sylvia suddenly realized that with a few changes to the angle of the cheekbones, the length of the red hair, the color of the eyes—from

Jason's deep blue to John's hazel—she might easily turn the captain into her brother. The resemblance was uncanny, and Sylvia realized why she felt so comfortable with Jason; he was an older, more experienced version of John.

Quite unexpectedly, Sylvia felt her throat tighten. She blinked back tears, angry at her lapse into maudlin sentimentality.

"This brother John you mention, I take it you miss him," Jason remarked softly, as if reading her thoughts.

"Oh, yes," she murmured raggedly. "John and I were as close as siblings can be. My mother had four girls, and then when she thought there would be no more, John and I came along. We are twins, you know, and did everything together. He was the one who insisted I take lessons with his tutor. Father was furious, naturally. He has no use for educated females." She laughed shortly.

"Some men never learn," Jason said gently, his eyes reflecting his compassion.

"You sound just like John," Sylvia confided incautiously. "That is exactly the sort of thing my brother would say. Oh, how I wish . . ." she began impetuously, then broke off, mortified at the foolishness of her inchoate thought. "But that is impossible." She laughed shakily. "And I have only myself to blame. Had I not been so young and naive as to think . . . as to believe . . . to b-believe that gentlemen m-mean what they say—"

She stopped abruptly, quite unable to continue, and distressed that she had revealed more than she intended to a complete stranger.

"If it is any consolation, my dear, I sincerely doubt you were to blame for anything," the captain said in a low voice. "And you can take it from me that age is no guarantee against naiveté, Sylvia. Only consider poor old Nicholas. Was ever a man so taken in by a beautiful face?"

Startled at the bitterness in the captain's voice, Sylvia stared at him, her own despair momentarily forgotten. "You knew the countess well, then?"

Jason's expression turned harsh. "Oh, yes. I knew her, all right. Nicholas and I went up to London together for the wedding. His brother, Stephen, was still alive then, and he and I stood up with Nicholas." The captain paused, and Sylvia could see that his thoughts still lingered in the past.

"I understand it was the event of the Season."

"Ah, yes, it certainly was that. Nothing was too good for his Angelica. Even Prinny was there." He grinned mirthlessly. "The Longuevilles have a long history of service to the Crown, starting with that Norman barbarian Henri Morlaix, the first baron, who came over with the Conqueror and received the Castle as a reward for his loyalty. The new countess never tired of hearing tales of the Normans; she was forever twitting Nicholas about his French ancestor, the first baron. The English had the last word, of course, for Morlaix soon became Morley. Angelica was French herself, you know, and it amused her to remember that her countrymen had conquered the English and become kings here."

"No mean accomplishment if what the history books say is true," Sylvia remarked, more interested than she cared to admit in the events that had shaped the more recent history of the Castle. "I wonder if the new countess saw herself as continuing that first Norman's invasion?"

Sylvia had meant the remark as a jest, but the captain's reaction warned her that she had trodden on sensitive ground.

"I do not doubt it for a moment," he said shortly. "No Englishman was safe from Medusa's reach. Even poor old Stephen loped off after a month to join the Army. He considered retreat his safest option. After all, she was his brother's wife."

"Medusa?" she repeated. "I understood that the young countess was stunningly lovely."

"Oh, she was that, all right," the captain admitted. "But so was Medusa before she allowed her beauty to go to her head. She dared to compare herself to one of the goddesses—Athene, I believe it was. Unwise of her, of course, but there you have it. The irate goddess turned Medusa's hair into snakes, and any man who ventured to gaze upon her lovely face was turned to stone."

"Petrified by beauty," Sylvia murmured, an idea for a painting already forming in her mind. "I shall have to put that on canvas."

"Precisely, my dear," the captain confirmed with a cynical smile. "And for the stone faces, just copy every male phiz up and down the Cornish coast and you will have a pretty fair notion of what happened when Angelica DeJardin set foot in Longueville."

The Earl of Longueville lounged very much at his ease on the brick terrace at Whitecliffs. He had arrived more than hour since, his excuse a hand-delivered invitation from the dowager to a small dinner party she had planned for three days hence. Instead of riding on to Helston, where he had told his mother he had business with a tenant, Nicholas had allowed himself to be talked into staying for tea.

This had not been entirely untrue, he told himself as he settled into a comfortable garden chair; he had merely omitted to clarify that the business was not urgent. Old Joel Dudley over on Laurel Farm was getting along in years and had asked permission to bring his youngest boy back from the shipyards in Falmouth to help him with the heavy work. He might have told Tom Gates to take care of the matter, but the lane to Laurel Farm ran past the Sutherland estate, and he was curious to see how Lady Sylvia's new painting was progressing.

If he was honest with himself, Nicholas thought wryly, he would have confessed that he actually wished to see the red-haired lady herself. But he was not ready for such honesty, which seemed like a highly dangerous admission to make. Far too revealing, furthermore. Nicholas had no wish to expose himself to any misunderstanding on the part of the lady. It was not his heart he was offering—had that organ not been wrenched from him by a perfidious wife?—but his protection. That should more than satisfy any female in Lady Sylvia's tarnished circumstances.

Nicholas smiled at his hostess. He suspected that Lady Marguerite's fine hazel eyes had seen through his little ploy, but what did he care? What objection might she conceivably raise to an arrangement that she herself had enjoyed for years with the Italian sculptor?

"I had forgotten what a mass of rose-bushes you have here at Whitecliffs," he said, amused to find himself talking of gardening. "They seem to do so much better here than at Longueville. Yet the soil must be identical."

Lady Marguerite laughed, and Nicholas was reminded of her niece in one of her milder moods. "It is not only the soil, my lord," she explained. "Roses are like women; they flourish almost anywhere with the right care."

The earl glanced sharply at his hostess. What had she meant by that odd remark? Females as roses was a common conceit among poets, of course, but Nicholas had little use for such hyperbole himself. At least, not any longer. There had been a time, ten years ago, when he had indulged in such foolishness with his wife, comparing her to flowers far more exotic than a simple English rose. Angelica had seemed so perfect, almost untouchable, he had imagined in his infatuated state. All too soon he had discovered the flaw in his private paradise. Angelica had not been untouchable, and his paradise had been private no longer.

For the longest time, he had refused to admit what his eyes were telling him, Nicholas recalled. But gradually Jason's veiled warnings and Stephen's precipitate departure from Longueville had taken on sinister significance. Isolated incidents began to add up to more than idle rumors.

Then one afternoon he had visited the ancient chapel to inspect a window one of the gardeners had reported broken. As he approached, the unmistakable sounds of female giggles issued from the Norman relic. Incensed that some serving wench and her swain had dared use his family's holy place for their tryst, the earl had dismounted and strode inside.

The dimness of the interior had prevented him from seeing more than two figures, apparently embracing before the altar. But to his surprise and dismay, the woman who emerged after a prolonged pause had been his wife.

"Who was in there with you, Angelica?" he had demanded, prepared to tear the scoundrel limb from limb.

An insouciant masculine laugh had fanned his fury into white hot intensity. Then, like a bucket of cold water, a languid voice had identified the gentleman.

"None but her own brother, my dear Nicholas," Jean-Claude DeJardin drawled as he sauntered out into the sunlight, his handsome features set in their habitual sneer. "Have we offended your so English sense of propriety, *mon frère?*" The Frenchman snickered under his breath, his cold eyes raking the earl insolently from head to toe.

Angelica rewarded this impertinence with a rich chuckle. "Do not be such a tease, *cheri*," she remarked with deplorable levity, the earl thought. "*Cher* Nicholas only concerns himself with protecting my virtue, Claude, and you would not wish a husband to do anything less, now, would you, *cheri?*"

DeJardin had shrugged his immaculately tailored shoulders, encased in one of Scott's finest creations—one of the many the young Frenchman had casually ordered from the earl's own tailor. "*Enfin, cherie*, if it pleases you to be forever censured by an English watchdog," he murmured half under his breath so that Nicholas could not be sure he had actually heard this additional rudeness.

The earl had stared closely at his wife, but Angelica had returned his gaze steadily, as if daring him to find fault with her. Nicholas had been quite unable to do so, although his first impression that the couple in the chapel had been engaged in anything but pious entertainment stayed with him for an uncomfortably long time. He was able to shake it off only by reminding himself repeatedly that Angelica and Jean-Claude were, after all, brother and sister. What harm could there be?

The earl's uneasy memories were dispelled by the welcome appearance of Hobson with the tea-tray. In any case, Nicholas mused, watching the deft way the butler transferred the tea-cups from tray to table, Angelica no longer had the power to torment him. She was safely laid to rest in the Longueville cemetery, a short distance from that Norman invader with whom she had so often identified herself. As for Jean-Claude, after being informed that he was no longer welcome at Longueville, he had attempted a vicious but futile campaign of blackmail against his brother-in-law. Then DeJardin had disappeared, and the earl hoped never to set eyes on him again.

A very different kind of laugh from the one that had invaded the earl's thoughts from the past echoed in the doorway. His eyes were drawn to the sound, and he was greeted by a sight that drove all unpleasant thoughts from his mind. The young woman who stepped onto the terrace was as unlike the sultry Beauty he had loved and lost that nightmarish summer as any woman could be.

What had Jason called her? An English rose? And no female he knew fit the description as well as Lady Sylvia Sutherland as she trod lightly across the terrace beside the captain to join the group at the tea-table. Her translucent skin was tinged with color—not the heightened red of nervousness, but the muted pink of good health, enjoyment of life, and inner joy. She fairly exuded happiness, and in a sudden flash of insight Nicholas realized that at no time in his brief marriage had he experienced the happiness he had expected to find with a wife. Passion, yes, there had been a surfeit of that, but not the kind of happiness he saw reflected on Lady Sylvia's face as she laughed gaily at something his friend was saying.

Nicholas felt a dull ache for all the lost years of his life. All those years spent in India, far from his Cornish homeland, from his beloved Longueville. Far from females like this one, whose English beauty was unblemished, unenhanced by pots of rouge and lotions. Whose laughter was filled with joy, not seductive overtones, whose smiles were devoid of calculation and cynicism. Whose respect for the marriage vows would be as steadfast as his own had once been.

Suddenly realizing where his maudlin ruminations were leading him, Nicholas jerked his thoughts back to the present. He must be mad indeed to allow himself, even for a moment, to think of Lady Sylvia in those terms. A discreet liaison with her would be a pleasant distraction from his present celibacy. A summer of delightful dalliance before he removed to London for the Season to begin his inevitable search for a second wife. Nothing more than that.

He rose to his feet as the laughing couple came to a halt beside the tea-table.

"My lord," Lady Sylvia said, greeting him with a smile of such sweetness Nicholas was momentarily at a loss for words. "I must inform you that your pirate friend has turned out to be a most difficult subject. Not only does he jump up without warning to stride about the room like a caged tiger, but when he is sitting down, he will not keep his head still. I swear he will have a crooked nose if he does not have more care."

"Pirate?" Nicholas echoed, noting with some alarm the teasing glance the lady threw at the subject of her criticism. "So her ladyship has discovered your secret ambition to fly the Jolly Roger and plunder Spanish galleons, has she?"

The captain laughed good-naturedly. "I seem to remember I was all of seven years old when I expressed such rash ambitions, Nick. I believe you favored the High Toby over life on the high seas."

To the earl's surprise, Lady Sylvia accepted a chair next to his and gazed at him speculatively. "Did you indeed?" she murmured. "How very interesting, my lord. I never would have thought you so bloodthirsty. What do highwaymen wear these days? I have never met one, you see. Not that I have ever met a pirate either," she added with a guileless chuckle that caused Nicholas to smile. "Except for Captain Ransome, of course, and he does not qualify as a real pirate."

She accompanied this remark with a dazzling smile across the table for the captain, whom Nicholas had a sudden urge to strangle.

"Perhaps you might portray old Nicholas as a highwayman on a flea-bitten old nag and a black patch on one eye," Jason suggested, casting a devilish grin at his friend.

"I doubt future generations of Morleys would appreciate having such a flamboyant character hanging in the family gallery," Lady Marguerite put in gently. "Are we to understand, then, that you have decided to accept his lordship's commission to paint his portrait, dear?"

Nicholas saw something akin to annoyance flicker in the lady's gray eyes and wondered if she would deny him again. As quickly as it came, the annoyance disappeared, replaced by a look of pure mischief that made him suddenly wary.

"Perhaps if his lordship would consent to pose as his unfulfilled dream of haunting the hedgerows, Aunt," she replied with a saucy toss of her bright curls, "I might well do so."

As Nicholas had anticipated, Jason let out a delighted crack of laughter. "Now, that is something I have to see, old man," he chortled. "What a splendid pair of ruffians we shall be, forsooth. I dare you to do it, Nicholas."

Everyone at the table chimed in with words of encouragement until Nicholas felt he could no longer refuse.

"Very well," he said finally, "when shall we start?"

The conversation became general at that point, with everyone contributing ideas on where a spavined nag might be had, whether a gentleman criminal might conceivably be expected to sport one of Scott's coats, and whether a suitable tricorne might be found in the trunks in the Longueville attic.

The earl said nothing, contenting himself with watching the animated expressions on Lady Sylvia's lovely face. Strange, he had not thought of her as beautiful before, but he now saw there was a quiet loveliness to her features that he was beginning to find both soothing and attractive.

Perhaps, he thought, accepting his cup from the lady he was admiring and basking in another dazzling smile, he might entice this English rose to accept his offer by the time his portrait was finished.

The vision of Lady Sylvia in the intimacy of her bedroom made his blood sing in anticipation.

Chapter Twelve

~

The Dinner Party

"So, tell me, Sylvia, are you happy with the captain's portrait?"

Sylvia glanced at her aunt, who sat across from her in the chaise that bore them to Longueville Castle. Lady Marguerite was looking radiant in a gown of deep blue edged with Brussels lace at neckline and hem. No pale colors for her aunt, whose gowns were invariably as vivid as her personality.

Beside her aunt, Giovanni held her gloved hand in both of his, and gazed at his beloved with a tenderness that Sylvia still had difficulty associating with a couple whose liaison had lasted twenty years. She often wondered whether the love they shared would have remained as strong had they married. The Italian had recently become more insistent that they formalize their relationship, but Lady Marguerite appeared to be content with the way things were.

She smiled at them. "I believe Captain Ransome makes a very dashing pirate. He was a little dubious when I suggested it, but he seems pleased with the results. So, yes, Aunt, I am certainly happy with the portrait."

"Did the captain not offer to purchase it, dear?"

"Oh, yes," Sylvia said with a chuckle. "When he saw how dashing he looked in his pirate costume, he immediately made me an offer. I told him, of course, that without a scimitar he was only a make-believe pirate. He absolutely refused to wear one, even had I been able to locate such an exotic weapon in the heart of Cornwall."

"So you would not sell?" her aunt insisted.

"No. I rather took a fancy to it myself, you see. The captain reminds me of my brother, John. Did you know that, like John, the captain dreamed of being a pirate when he was a boy? He tells me that the earl wanted to be a highwayman, but only if he could wear his velvet breeches and tailored coats, and ride a blooded horse. No broken-down nags for the heir to Longueville."

"I should hope not," her aunt responded with a laugh. "Unlike your happy-go-lucky pirate, who enjoys all the freedom of a younger son, the responsibilities of rank and position have always weighed heavily upon Longueville's shoulders."

"No doubt he also enjoys the wealth and power that goes with the rank, Aunt," Sylvia countered belligerently. "He certainly threw enough of it in my direction when I declined to paint his portrait."

"And why should he not enjoy these small privileges?" Giovanni broke in gently. "You are too harsh, *cara mia*. The man has not had much happiness in his life. That precious wife of his brought him nothing but trouble."

Sylvia thought the sculptor would have said more, but she intercepted a quelling glance from her aunt, and he relapsed into silence.

"Yes, indeed, my dear," her aunt added, deftly diverting the subject, "what Giovanni says is quite true. Nicholas lost his father when he was very young, and since then a series of calamities have dogged the family. First his Cousin Luke fell to his death here at Longueville; then he lost his brother, Stephen, at Talavera after the dreadful business with the countess . . ." Her words faded into a sigh.

The Italian raised her ladyship's fingers and held them tenderly against his cheek. "Do not fret your pretty head with Lord Longueville's troubles, my love. He is quite capable of handling his own affairs."

Lady Marguerite seemed unconvinced. "I trust you are right, dearest, and that his lordship has learned that—as our redoubtable Mrs. Violet Rawson would say—all that glitters is not necessarily gold."

The same thought crossed Sylvia's mind as they were ushered, twenty minutes later, into the impressive drawing room at Longueville Castle, where the earl and his friend rose to greet the guests.

After they moved into the room, it was Captain Ransome who

escorted Lady Sylvia to make her curtsy to the Dowager Countess, who surprised her with a stiff though gracious smile.

"You are in looks tonight, my dear," the captain murmured under his breath, observing her with open admiration.

Sylvia felt herself blush with pleasure. It had been a long time since she had enjoyed an honest compliment from a gentleman like Captain Ransome. More often than not, she would detect a speculative undertone to any such pleasantry that alerted her to the direction of the gentleman's thoughts. There was no hint of ulterior motives in the captain's voice, and Sylvia prepared to relax and enjoy the evening as he settled her on a green brocade settee between Mrs. Hargate and the vicar's wife.

Mrs. Rawson lost no time in launching into a detailed account of Lila Jones's salvation from sin and imminent wedding to the father of her unborn child. Since Sylvia had heard all about Tom Daly's perfidy before, she let her eyes wander about the room, but desisted as soon as she caught the earl's intense gaze resting upon her for the third time.

Once the party removed to the formal dining room, the remainder of Sylvia's enthusiasm for the evening quickly dissipated. She found herself seated—quite unexpectedly—beside Lord Longueville. Her aunt, who sat across the table on the earl's right, flashed her a glittering, decidedly smug smile.

"How convenient, darling," Lady Marguerite cooed, "you will be able to discuss the details of his lordship's portrait without annoying interruptions."

Sylvia could see where her aunt's mind was leading her, and blushed to think that the earl might conclude that Sylvia wished for a private tête-à-tête with him.

"I was under the impression that the details had already been agreed upon," she responded coolly. "His lordship is willing to be portrayed as a highwayman, and I am quite looking forward to the challenge of presenting him as a shady character."

The earl threw her a quizzical glance. "I was hoping you would reconsider, my lady," he said. "I must have been in my cups to consider such an unflattering suggestion. Perhaps we might dispense with the spavined nag you spoke of. I cannot see myself riding such a beast. Besides, I doubt you could find one in this part of Cornwall."

Sylvia laughed, enjoying his discomfiture. "There you are mistaken, my lord," she pointed out. "I approached Mr. Gordon only yesterday, and he assures me that he knows just the horse I have in mind. It belongs to a Mr. Dudley of Laurel Farm, one of your own tenants, I believe, my lord. Both horse and master are quite past their prime, Gordon tells me, so the nag seems to be exactly right for the part. I intend to ride over there tomorrow to obtain permission to borrow the horse."

"I do wish you would choose one from the Longueville stables," the earl said, his dark eyes fixed on Sylvia's face, as if willing her to relent. "I am convinced it is mere capriciousness on your part, madam, to punish me for my uncouth behavior during our first unfortunate encounter."

Sylvia felt herself relax slightly. If the earl wished to cross swords with her, she was more than willing to oblige him, but since she was under no obligation to make a favorable impression, there was no need to give him any quarter. She might even enjoy the challenge of bringing the gentleman down a peg or two.

There were certain advantages, she reminded herself philosophically, to being a female beyond the pale. The lines were more clearly drawn. This was not the London Marriage Mart. Lady Sylvia Sutherland was no innocent young miss whose sole purpose in life was to throw out lures to eligible gentlemen—preferably titled and wealthy. Snaring a husband was no longer one of her options, far less the main reason for her existence.

Regardless of the smug expression her aunt wore at that moment. Regardless of her own secret desires.

To prove that she was comfortable with her husbandless destiny, Sylvia smiled one of her sweet smiles, and was dismayed at the instant flicker of response in the earl's dark eyes. When his gaze dropped to her lips, Sylvia realized she had made a grave tactical error. The conceited fool imagined she was flirting with him.

"Oh, no, my lord," Lady Marguerite broke in before Sylvia could gather her wits together. "My niece is rarely capricious, and never vindictive. So you may rest assured that she does not hold that incident against you."

Sylvia frowned at her aunt. Had that devious lady noticed the admiring look in their host's eyes and concluded that a match was in the making? She felt the need to squash such ridiculous notions irrevocably.

"I fear you are mistaken, Aunt," she said coolly. "Like many females who find themselves on the shelf, I am often capricious, and quite possibly vindictive, besides any number of other disagree-

able qualities." Ignoring the mortified expression on her aunt's
face, Sylvia turned to the earl and favored him with another charming smile. "My aunt is a prejudiced witness, my lord. She tends to
overlook my faults, and I love her for it, of course. But I would not
wish her partiality to distort the truth."

"Rubbish!" Lady Marguerite exclaimed with such vehemence
that Mrs. Rawson interrupted her detailed account of the latest
scandal in Cury Cross to glare avidly in her direction.

After an awkward pause, the dowager drew the vicar's wife
back to her subject, and the earl returned Sylvia's smile. She did
not trust the mocking twitch on his lips, but for some reason could
not tear her gaze away. His next words jerked her mind back from
the delicious but indecorous images of the havoc that sensuous
mouth might create should it come into contact with her person.

"Perhaps you will enlighten us, my dear," he said with deceptive smoothness. "Since her ladyship is obviously unaware of
these disagreeable qualities you mention, and I confess not to have
noticed any. Beyond a tendency to willfulness, of course," and
here his smile broadened. "But in my experience, willfulness is
never held as a fault but a privilege in beautiful women. Would
you not agree, Lady Marguerite?"

Although he addressed her aunt, the earl's eyes never left
Sylvia's face, and she felt suddenly quite out of breath, as though
she had run across the Lower Meadow, chased by one of Giovanni's prize Jersey bulls.

The wretch had just called her beautiful! Sylvia could not believe her ears—did not wish to believe such blatant farradiddle.
She knew herself to be passably attractive, but never, by any
stretch of the imagination, *beautiful.* As the earl's former countess
must have been beautiful, she thought with a stab of something
like envy. Beautiful enough to drive men to distraction. To drive
her own husband to reveal his baser instincts. What had Connan
called them? Disgusting appetites? Yes, that was it, and Sylvia was
again beset by an irrational desire to know the precise nature of
such depravity. In a reckless moment she contemplated his reaction should she demand to know the nature of those disgusting appetites.

The notion of bringing up such a topic at the dowager's dinner
table appealed to her sense of humor, and she stifled a giggle.

"Well?" the earl insisted, his mouth curling at the corners in a
singularly seductive smile. "We are all agog to hear you confess

your secret peccadilloes, my lady. Surely you are not so heartless as to disappoint us?"

Her aunt was regarding her quizzically from across the table, evidently uneasy with the implications of the earl's request.

Sylvia was uneasy, too, but refused to let it show. She smiled back and then dipped her spoon in the steaming turtle soup the servant had placed before her.

"Disappointing you, my lord, may be considered one of my lesser crimes. As for my other sins, as you presume to call them, I prefer to keep them well hidden for fear of offending Mrs. Rawson. But of one thing you may be sure, sir," she added pointedly, "I am indeed heartless, make no mistake about that."

Hoping that his lordship would take the hint and cease his foolish banter, and wipe that tantalizing smile from his face, Sylvia transferred her attention to the soup.

Chapter Thirteen

~

Portrait of a Highwayman

Nicholas heard her laughter before he reached the door to the sprawling thatched barn that housed the horses at Whitecliffs. Like everything else about the estate, he had noticed, an air of careless charm hung over the building, belying the unobtrusive efficiency that prevailed beneath the casual surface.

Informality was not something that came easily to the earl. Except with his closest friends, Nicholas much preferred life to follow regular patterns. The comfortable chaos of existence at Whitecliffs had initially offended his sense of order, but as he paused on the threshold of the stables, he was struck by the cheerful atmosphere that greeted him.

His gaze was drawn to the tableau in the center aisle, where Lady Sylvia stood talking to a gray-haired individual with the unmistakable stamp of head groom about him. They seemed to be absorbed in the inspection of a dejected-looking specimen of horseflesh, standing hip-shot between them, his ears hanging limply beside his ugly, box-shaped head. His eyes were closed, and he rocked gently to and fro on knobbly legs, ending in ragged hooves that were badly in need of a trim.

Nicholas groaned aloud as he realized that this equine apparition must be Dudley's nag, destined to be immortalized on canvas with him.

Lady Sylvia turned her head at his approach and flashed him a cautious smile. It seemed the lady might be having second thoughts about including the nag, who looked quite dead on its feet, in her portrait. Nicholas hoped so, for he did not relish the prospect of acknowledging any connection, however remote, with this pathetic bag of bones.

"My lord, good morning," the lady greeted him, her smile warming. "Evans and I are debating what can be done to spruce up your trusty steed a little. The truth is, he turns out to be more decrepit than I had imagined any horse could be. What do you suggest, my lord?"

Nicholas was blunt. "I suggest you take him out and shoot the poor beast," he replied emphatically. A glance at the groom suggested that Evans agreed with him, but would be unlikely to admit as much in front of his mistress.

"That I shall never allow," Lady Sylvia responded sharply. "This poor beast you refer to was once the pride and joy of half of Cornwall. Evans tells me that Hercules—that is his name, improbable as it sounds—won every race at fairs all up and down the coast. Made Mr. Dudley a respectable amount of money, or so I hear. Is that not correct, Evans?"

"Indeed it is, milady. Old Hercules made history hereabouts in his time. I would hate to see the old horse put down just because he is getting a little long in the tooth."

Nicholas felt this latter reproach was directed at him. Perhaps he had misread the groom's enthusiasm about the nag, in which case the old cadger must be as addle-brained as his mistress.

"I am surprised to hear he has any teeth at all," he remarked, glowering at the offending nag from beneath lowered brows. "The animal is a walking skeleton."

"If we honor old soldiers for their past glories, surely we should treat a fine old horse with a little respect," Lady Sylvia said, running a white hand down Hercules's scrawny neck without eliciting any noticeable response from the dozing animal. "I have instructed Evans to put him on a special diet to bring back a little shine to his coat, at least. Much more we cannot expect."

Privately the earl thought it was a little late for that, but all he said was: "I would rather you abandon the whole idea of including a horse in the painting at all, my dear. Surely you cannot wish to waste your talent on such a pathetic creature?"

"Oh, quite the contrary," she responded with spirit. "I believe it is high time poor old Hercules received some recognition for his lifetime of putting guineas into Mr. Dudley's pocket. I shall deem it an honor to do so."

Nicholas considered this startling statement a prime example of feminine gibberish, but—having experienced similar aberrations with his mother—he did not betray his alarm by so much as a flicker. Instead, he cleared his throat and remarked mildly, "From what I know about horses, my lady, every last shilling he may have earned went into oats, and not many found their way into Dudley's pocket."

Lady Sylvia surprised him with an unladylike but delightful giggle. "I do believe you are jealous of old Hercules," she remarked, with a teasing smile that did odd things to the earl's pulse. "Do not fear, my lord. You will not be outshone by a horse, although . . ." Her voice trailed off, and Nicholas held his breath. What would this incredible female come up with next? he wondered apprehensively.

"Although what?" he prodded.

Her gaze, which had been fixed speculatively on the nag, as if she were wrestling with important artistic decisions, swung up to meet his, and Nicholas felt his heart lurch uncomfortably.

He had looked into Lady Sylvia's gray eyes many times before, and admired their luminosity and the lively intelligence reflected there. She normally lowered her gaze, as any well-bred female would, when she caught him staring. Nicholas enjoyed this mildly flirtatious game, enjoyed the vicarious feeling of momentary dominance over a beautiful, independent female. He could look at her and subdue her. The thought pleased him, satisfied a primitive, predatory instinct that he barely acknowledged. Or if he did, took as his male prerogative, like so many others he enjoyed.

But today Lady Sylvia did not lower her gaze.

As he returned her stare, Nicholas waited for the normal pattern of events to take their course. As it would, he reminded himself confidently as the moments dragged by. The silence of the stable, broken only by indistinct rustlings of invisible horses in their stalls, closed in around them, isolating them from the world outside. He waited for his implacable male power to assert itself.

After what seemed like an eternity, Nicholas began to wonder if he had not overshot his mark. Ridiculous, he thought. But even as he tried to convince himself, he felt the pull of those liquid gray pools reaching out to lure him into their tantalizing depths. His power to subdue this woman was slipping away. In an inexplicable shift in the nature of the game he had so often and carelessly played, Nicholas felt his will to resist draining away. He was losing his power, he realized in sudden panic. Instead of subduing the female as he had anticipated, he was being subdued.

Their roles were reversed. He knew it instinctively by the quickening of his pulse, the shallow breathing, the dampness of his palms, the odd sensation of dizziness in his head. But most of all he recognized the symptoms of surrender in the unfamiliar urge to lower his gaze.

A long-forgotten scene from his past flashed through his mind. One of his favorite summer haunts as a boy had been a deep, secret pool in the middle of the Home Wood. His father had forbidden Nicholas and his brother to go near the place, but the threat of a beating had not deterred them. His cousins, Luke and Matt, had been equally fascinated by the mystery of the hidden pool, and the four boys had invented many a fantastic story to explain its presence in the wood.

One afternoon, after a particularly violent storm, they had found a huge beech tree toppled across the small pond. As the eldest, Nicholas had claimed the right to be the first to crawl out on the fallen tree to gaze down into the murky depths of the dark water. He still remembered the thrill of fear he had felt seeing his pale face reflected on the surface of the pool. Then he had seen—or imagined he had seen—strange shapes writhing deep down in the brackish water.

Nicholas had been petrified with terror, but oddly exhilarated at the same time, attracted by some force he could not name. He had not thought of that pool in many years, but the feeling he was experiencing now as he gazed into Lady Sylvia's eyes brought it all back in frightening detail.

Perhaps the most disturbing part of this recollection from his childhood was the fact that he had fallen into that mysterious pool. Had he lost his balance, as his cousin had insisted, or had Matt pushed him? All he remembered was thrashing about in the ice-cold water and seeing Matt's face peering down at him, and hearing his cousin's familiar crow of mocking laughter. Given his cousin's long history of small, vindictive acts, Nicholas was convinced he had been pushed.

With something of a shock, Nicholas discovered that he was no longer gazing into Lady Sylvia's eyes, but at the sorry excuse for a horse that still stood—head hanging even lower at an awkward angle, wrinkled gray muzzle inches from the dusty floor—between them.

"Although I am seriously considering the possibility of making Hercules the central focus of the painting," she continued, quite as though she were unaware of the shattering emotional upheaval she had caused. "After all, is he not the quintessential relic of a life of crime?"

"I thought this was supposed to be my portrait, madam," Nicholas said stiffly, annoyed to find himself relegated to second place by a broken-down nag. He refused to believe that the lady was ignorant of the power she had wielded over him. But since he was paying for the portrait, he reminded himself, he had every right to dictate what would or would not be featured in the picture. He would insist upon it. "And furthermore," he added dryly, "I have not led a life of crime, so have no need for a moribund horse to suggest that I have."

She made no reply to this outburst, merely giving him another melting smile that threw his pulse into further disorder.

"I quite agree," she murmured soothingly, rather like a doting mother to a recalcitrant child. "And there is little point in arguing over poor Hercules until we see what improvement Evans can achieve to his appearance. I have no wish to embarrass you, my lord," she added as they strolled back to the house together, "but I have conceived a fondness for the animal, and must insist that he be included in the portrait as agreed."

Nicholas cursed himself for allowing a mere female to talk him into a course his every instinct warned him would end in disaster. He had half a mind to cancel the commission entirely and contact a portrait artist in London, which he should have done in the first place.

Curiosity, and something else he could not put a finger on, impelled him to see this farce to its conclusion. No mere female would be permitted to deny the Earl of Longueville the right to do as he pleased. Hercules would have to go.

And Lady Sylvia—no mere female by anyone's standards, but a female nevertheless—would not be permitted to deny him anything he wanted.

Nicholas smiled at the thought of her ultimate submission, his spirits miraculously revived.

When they entered her studio twenty minutes later, Sylvia knew that this sitting with the earl would be nothing like the comfortable arrangement she had enjoyed with Captain Ransome.

It soon became apparent that, unlike the captain, Lord Longueville was not going to be easy to work with. Ignoring Sylvia's instructions to exchange his elegant blue superfine coat for the nondescript brown homespun she had gone to considerable trouble to obtain for him, his lordship sauntered about the spacious room, browsing through the collection of finished canvases stacked against the walls and hung on every inch of space available.

Sylvia regarded him impatiently for a few minutes, but when he reached up to remove the cloth she had placed over the painting of the cliff hut, with its newly added male figure, she stopped him with a sharp rebuke.

"My lord, I must request that you not presume to look at those of my works not intended for public view."

The earl glanced at her over his shoulder, his expression perplexed. How many times had his lordship been denied his will? Sylvia wondered. Not very many, she estimated, given the faint frown of annoyance that marred his rugged features.

"What is so special about these works that I may not see them?" he demanded, in a tone Sylvia speculated he used to rebuke incompetent servants.

Amused rather than offended that the earl imagined he might use that same dictatorial tone with her, Sylvia gave him one of her sweetest smiles. She had noticed that such smiles appeared to disconcert his lordship. This very morning in the stables he had turned quite pale when she had returned his impertinent stare with one of her own.

The earl was undoubtedly a strange, moody man, but not so different from the vast majority of gentlemen of his class in his assumption that he could dominate a female with a mere glance. It was high time he learned that Lady Sylvia Sutherland was not to be intimidated so easily.

"They are special because I choose not to share them," she replied calmly. "So again I beg your lordship not to peek."

Unexpectedly he grinned, a quite devastating, devilish grin, and Sylvia felt a flutter of apprehension. It reminded her that they were quite alone in the studio, a circumstance that had never bothered her while she was alone with Captain Ransome. Of course, the captain had reminded her of John, perhaps given her a false sense of security.

The earl was nothing like her brother.

Sylvia felt a prickle of fear course up her spine as she watched him saunter back towards her, that wanton smile still on his lips. Flustered she took refuge in practicality.

"If you will remove your coat, my lord," she said stiffly, picking up the well-worn homespun, "and try on this more modest garment, I think we shall be well on the way to turning you into the ferocious Hedgerow Harry himself. And if we add this elegant hat"—she reached for a tattered tricorne with a once lavish feather curling jauntily from the high crown—"none of your friends will know you."

"That I can well believe, my dear." He had come to a halt close beside her—inappropriately close, Sylvia thought, focusing her attention on a small rent in the worn collar of the coat. She picked at a loose thread, intensely aware of the smell of maleness emanating from the man beside her.

Wordlessly, she handed him the well-worn coat, which he accepted gingerly, holding it up for inspection.

"I trust this monstrosity has no resident fleas or lice," he drawled, eyeing the garment as one would an unwashed, mangy dog.

"It is perfectly clean, my lord," she assured him. "And if you will condescend to put it on, we can throw this cloak over one shoulder and get you set up in the proper pose." She indicated a nondescript woollen cloak that had possibly once been green, but now appeared a dull greenish gray with darker, rust-colored stains that Sylvia shied away from identifying.

The earl glared at the cloak in disgust. "It is too hot to wear a cloak," he protested. "And furthermore, the meanest under-gardener on the estate would balk at being seen in such a thing. Besides, highwaymen do not wear cloaks in summer."

"Oh, yes, they do," Sylvia countered firmly, although to tell the truth she knew next to nothing about life on the High Toby except what she had gleaned from romantical novels.

"How do you know they do?"

"How do you know they do not?"

She stared at him for several moments, wondering which of them would have to back down, determined it would not be her.

When she saw the flicker of uncertainty in his dark eyes, Sylvia knew she had won. As it had earlier in the stables, the earl's gaze faltered, then slid back to the disputed garment. She felt an unfamiliar thrill of triumph at having out-stared the gentleman again.

"To avoid an argument, I will agree to wear the cloak if you will dispense with Hercules," he proposed at length, sounding so reasonable that Sylvia momentarily considered accepting his terms. A telltale smirk on his bronzed face instantly changed her mind.

"Both horse and highwayman as agreed, my lord," she said shortly. "But naturally," she added after an awkward pause, "you may always choose to cancel the commission and select another artist. I am sure there are any number of painters in London who would be happy to portray you just as you are, without the romantical touches that seem to offend you so much."

Her eyes strayed to the portrait of the captain, occupying a prominent position above the mantel. She indicated the painting with a graceful gesture. "Now, there you see what a romantic touch can do to an otherwise commonplace portrait, my lord. Does the captain not look grand as a pirate? It suits his personality and brings out the inner essence of his character."

"What has that damned nag got to do with the inner essence of my character?" the earl demanded explosively, evidently losing his patience. "And I am not so sure I wish my inner essence—whatever that may be—to be exposed for all the world to gawk at."

Sylvia could not help smiling at this outburst. Perhaps she should not have mentioned something as personal as inner essence to a man as jealous of his privacy as the Earl of Longueville. She had discussed it openly with the captain, who had instantly understood what she meant. But the earl was a different man entirely. How would he react, for instance, if she told him that he was more like the legendary Hedgerow Harry than he guessed? Was he not dark, secretive, predatory, with a mysterious, perhaps violent past? The handsome captain was none of these things.

Sylvia infinitely preferred the sunny disposition and comfortable camaraderie she had shared with the captain. However, the artist in her—and the woman, too, she had to confess—longed to explore the secret depths of Nicholas Morley, a man still held responsible—in one way or another—for his wife's death.

Would her artist's eye and intuition discover the truth of that tragedy from long ago? she wondered, watching the muscles of the earl's jaw contract as he tried to regain control of his temper. Would she be happy with that truth if she found it? Or would she wish she had never meddled in the past of a man as shadowy as this one?

Chapter Fourteen

~

The Flowers

A week later they had worked out an uneasy truce. The earl would ride over to Whitecliffs every afternoon for his sitting, submit to being disguised as a ruffian of the first stare—as he liked to call Sylvia's efforts to turn him into a romantical figure—and then accept Lady Marguerite's invitation to take tea with the family. Sylvia would prudently refrain from any mention of Hercules, since that pathetic creature seemed to exacerbate the earl's natural predisposition to stubbornness.

Lord Longueville never declined her aunt's invitation, and Sylvia suspected that he was beginning to enjoy the informality of tea-time at Whitecliffs. Having taken tea one sultry afternoon in the impressive Green Saloon at the Castle, under the disapproving eye of the Dowager Countess, and amidst the muted sounds of polite conversation, Sylvia knew exactly what his lordship was accustomed to. She could well understand that the rustic simplicity of sitting down among the rose-bushes, or under the willows by the pond, or on the terrace with its tubs of vivid scarlet geraniums, with a dog's head resting comfortably on his lap might offend his sense of propriety.

She was pleasantly surprised when the earl accepted Rufus's presence at the tea-table without noticeable alarm. She did experience a moment of alarm herself when the collie abandoned his usual place by her chair to fawn over the visitor.

"It appears that I am forgiven," the earl remarked, stroking the dog's silky ears with his long fingers.

Mesmerized by the gentleness of that unexpected caress, Sylvia instinctively fought the tremor that ran through her. She knew immediately what the earl referred to, and this reminder of their first, unpleasant encounter helped to steady her nerves. What had the odious wretch called her? *A redheaded ape-leader of dubious breeding*? The insult still rankled, and unlike Rufus, she had not entirely forgiven him for his unspeakable rudeness.

"Forgiven?" her aunt repeated. "Now, why would Rufus need to forgive you, my lord?"

The earl laughed, somewhat ruefully, Sylvia thought. "Our first encounter was not at all propitious," he replied. "You might even call it bellicose. I was in serious danger of losing a piece of my hide. Entirely my fault, I have to admit. An unfortunate misunderstanding," he continued, and Sylvia suddenly realized that he was not talking about the dog at all, "for which I am heartily sorry."

So the wretch was sorry, was he? she thought, keeping her eyes resolutely on her spoon as she stirred her tea with more vigor than was strictly necessary. This was probably the closest his lordship would ever come to an apology for his abominable rudeness, she told herself philosophically. But was she ready to accept it? Her head wanted to resist—why should she let him off so easily?—but her heart still fluttered at the sight of those long fingers on the dog's head. How would it feel if those same warm fingers were to—

Abruptly she tore her thoughts away from those forbidden longings and looked across the table. He was indeed staring at her, his dark eyes enigmatic, but his half smile telling her that he had read her thoughts.

Sylvia willed herself not to blush. She glanced at her aunt, who must have sensed her distress, for she jumped into the awkward moment like the consummate hostess she was.

"How is the portrait going, dear?" she asked, reaching for the earl's empty cup. "I do think it was an inspired choice to depict his lordship as a highwayman. There is something so dashing about social outcasts like pirates and criminals and smugglers. No wonder they are to be found in all the romantical novels in the circulating library. They make excellent heroes."

Sylvia could not help laughing. "You are sadly mistaken, Aunt," she said. "According to Captain Ransome, pirates do not bathe regularly and have bad teeth. I imagine highwaymen have similar faults, considering the irregular lives they lead."

Lady Marguerite wrinkled her nose in distaste. "I do wish you had not told me that, Sylvia. You have quite destroyed all my romantical notions of the adventuresome life."

"Well, Captain Ransome destroyed mine with his gruesome details of life under the Jolly Roger, which is not at all as I had imagined it. But to answer your question, Aunt, the portrait is progressing very well. Another week should see it finished."

This was not strictly true, Sylvia knew, since there still remained the addition of Hercules in the background. She dared not mention the old horse for fear of disrupting the pleasant atmosphere of the tea-table, but she was determined to include the horse as originally planned.

To this end, she sent a note over to the Castle the following morning, cancelling the afternoon sitting. "I believe there will be less friction if his lordship discovers the presence of Hercules as a fait accompli," she told her aunt at breakfast.

"I fear you may be a little premature, my dear," Giovanni remarked as Hobson sliced a second helping of ham and served it to the sculptor. "I was down in the stables yesterday, and that Hercules of yours is still more dead than alive. Evans tells me the beast eats enough for three ordinary horses, but has not gained more than an ounce or two. I hardly blame Longueville for refusing to go down in history in the company of such a bone-setter."

"He has not refused," Sylvia corrected him. "That was part of our initial agreement."

"You are too harsh, dear," her aunt remarked. "If the horse is as ugly as Giovanni says, perhaps you should reconsider your agreement, Sylvia."

Later that morning, as she stood beside Hercules's stall, watching the old horse ravenously devour a double ration of oats, Sylvia wondered if perhaps she should listen to her aunt's counsel. The nag was truly decrepit, and she suddenly felt a pang of pity for the earl, which she ruthlessly repressed as soon as she recalled his unflattering comments about her age and breeding.

His arrogant lordship would learn what it was like to be insulted, she told herself, surprised at her desire to get even. Hercules would be her instrument, but she would wait until he was slightly more presentable.

Faced with a free afternoon, Sylvia decided on impulse to take her sketching pad and paints out to the cliffs again. Something drew her to that tragic spot where so much mystery still lingered. Did anyone but the unfortunate countess really know what had happened that moonlit summer evening in that isolated stone hut? Had she really written that so-called suicide note discovered there? And if not, who had?

Her head filled with these and other enigmas, Sylvia was startled when Puffin came to a stop some distance from the edge of the cliff. She had discovered during her first expeditions to the stone hut that the pony could not be persuaded to go a step farther. It was as though he came up against an invisible wall, and no amount of scolding could make him budge.

Sylvia could not blame him. She herself had ventured down to the stone hut only twice in all the years she had lived at Whitecliffs, but never inside, and the heavy pall of tragedy that hung in the air around that small, dark hut had made her skin crawl. She had imagined that evil haunted the place, but her common sense told her that any evil that had existed there ten years ago was long gone. If some terrible, violent act had been committed against the young countess in that hut, as the local villagers still believed, Sylvia refused to credit the rumors of the earl's guilt.

Turning Puffin off the main track, Sylvia drove the little trap up a shallow incline and stopped in the shade of a copse of storm-bent hawthorns and a scattering of old oaks. Leaving the pony to doze in peace, she set up her easel under a cluster of scraggly pines that afforded some protection from the sun. From this vantage point, she could clearly see the door to the hut, facing towards the rough-hewn steps leading up to the cliff road.

As was her custom when beginning a new work, Sylvia set up her canvas and sat motionless for a long period, scanning the scene in front of her, her eyes noting every detail that might be relevant to her interpretation of the subject, and those that were not.

After about ten minutes an uneasy sensation assailed her. From where she sat, she could see without being seen. Assuming that the sprawling gorse bushes and stunted trees were there ten years ago, it was entirely possible that prying eyes might have witnessed the comings and going at the stone hut on the cliff. And if they had, such a witness might just as easily have been driven by prurient curiosity or violent intent, she realized, her heart beating wildly as the possibilities unfolded in her vivid imagination.

Might not the murderer—if indeed there had been a murder committed in the hut that summer night—have crouched here in this very spot where she now sat, his heart beating even as hers did, his eyes watching for the right time to descend on his victim?

Sylvia suddenly felt very exposed, vulnerable, and alone. The sun shone warmly above her, but she sensed a chill where no wind blew. Where was Rufus? she wondered. That dog was never about when she needed him. She cast a glance down the slope, searching for the black and white shape of the collie rooting about in rabbit holes. Nothing moved in the still afternoon.

And then she heard a twig snap, and her blood froze.

The hairs on her neck rose as she thought of the phantom lady in white who rode across these moors in the moonlight.

Nonsense, she told herself firmly. Phantoms do not tread on twigs. Much less in full daylight.

No, there was somebody standing behind her in the grove of hawthorns. Watching her.

Sylvia clearly felt that gaze on her back.

The absolute stillness of the afternoon wrapped itself about her like an invisible embrace. Feeling suffocated, Sylvia gasped for breath, her eyes fixed unseeing on the empty canvas before her. Her mind reverberated with echoes of her recent thoughts. Who had used this very spot to spy on the countess? Had he been a peeping Tom? Or something much more dangerous? Had he returned for some inexplicable reason? Was she herself in danger?

The possibility of danger jerked Sylvia out of her trance. She was behaving like a veritable ninny, scared of her own shadow. Suddenly she remembered what her old Nanny would tell her when she woke up screaming, convinced there was a monster under her bed. "Get up and look, child," she would say, standing beside Sylvia's bed in her voluminous flannel night rail, her night cap perched rakishly on her gray head. "You will find that monsters only exist in the imagination, dear."

Her courage bolstered by this comforting memory of her childhood, Sylvia stood up and turned around to face down this particular monster.

Nanny would have been proud of her, she thought, staring at the man standing at the edge of the copse. Anyone less monster-like than mild-mannered George Connan Sylvia could scarcely imagine.

"I d-did not m-mean to s-startle you, my lady," he stammered, obviously more than a little startled himself. "I d-did not expect . . . that is to say, I was unaware that anyone w-would be here."

"Well, you did startle me," Sylvia cut in ruthlessly. "I am not accustomed to people sneaking up behind me. And besides, I am trying to work," she added, gesturing at the empty canvas, "and
interruptions are not welcome, let me tell you."

If that rebuff did not convey the message that his presence was
de trop, Sylvia was prepared to try something even more explicit.
Connan's sudden jerking movement distracted her, and Sylvia noticed that the scholar was clasping a modest bouquet of wildflow-
ers in his hands.

She stared at him, her frown dissolving, and he smiled nervously.

"They are for the countess," he mumbled, as though embar-
rassed at being caught in some shameful act. "She did so love
flowers, you know." He glanced down the hill towards the hut. "I
always bring her some when I can get away from the shop."

"How kind you are," Sylvia murmured, struggling to connect
this dry little man with such a grand romantic gesture.

"Oh, no, my lady," he stammered, embarrassment making his
cheeks pink. "It was all the poor countess's doing, you see. She
was so perfect in every way. We all adored her. Each in his own
way, of course." He paused, and his glance wandered again to the
stone hut in the distance. "But I was always her most loyal admirer. Her ladyship knew she might trust me with her most intimate thoughts, and she often did."

"Not everyone, Mr. Connan," Sylvia corrected him. "Someone
did not adore her quite as much as you seem to think, if local rumors have any validity at all."

Connan fixed his pale blue eyes on her, and Sylvia thought she
detected hostility in them. "If you are referring to the local belief
that Lord Longueville took matters into his own hands, my lady,"
he said stiffly, "I fear you are mistaken. He was the cause of her
unhappiness, that I cannot deny. The dear lady told me so herself.
And his lascivious friends from London—a more Godless group of
rogues it would be hard to imagine—only added to her despair, always fawning upon her, following her, importuning her with their
lewd suggestions. That I witnessed with my own eyes. Why, even
his lordship's brother, a young lad barely down from Oxford—it
was pitiful to watch him. And as for that precious cousin of his"—
Connan's face twisted into a moué of disgust—"I hope I never see
such unbridled debauchery again."

Sylvia listened to this litany of depravity with amazement. Connan's version differed so radically from the captain's cynical account of what had happened at the Castle that summer that she felt baffled. Was it possible, she wondered, for a female to be both goddess and witch? The young Countess of Longueville had certainly succeeded in dazzling the unsophisticated scholar into placing her on a pedestal, but had she been saint or sinner to the other gentlemen in the earl's house party?

Staring into Connan's pale, hostile eyes, Sylvia remembered her aunt's words as they drove over to the dowager's dinner party the other evening. *All that glitters is not gold,* Lady Marguerite had said, borrowing from Mrs. Rawson's endless store of folk wisdom. She could well believe that the scholar had been bewitched into believing what he wanted to believe about his ideal woman. For him she had glittered, an unobtainable star in a world where he did not belong. But for the others? Was it not possible that—to borrow another of Mrs. Rawson's sayings—*where there is smoke there is fire?*

Abruptly Connan ducked his head, pushed through the overgrown brushes, and marched off down the slope, his back rigid, presumably with disapproval of her lack of sympathy for the countess.

Sylvia sat down again at her easel, but her hands were idle. She watched Connan descend the shallow stone steps and approach the hut with a reverence that struck her as incongruous given the violence that had transpired there. The poor man was obviously obsessed, but could obsession lead to violence? she wondered. The kind of violence that had come to be associated with the countess in the minds of the locals. If one believed that obsession leads to madness, it was a possibility she had not considered before.

Recalling the hostility in Connan's washed-out blue eyes, Sylvia felt a sudden premonition that the mild-mannered scholar had not told her all he knew about the death of his idol.

An hour later, Sylvia had put these disturbing thoughts aside and was absorbed in her preliminary sketch of the new work when she was again interrupted by someone approaching through the copse. This time the intruder made no attempt to conceal his approach, so when the figure emerged from the shade of the trees, Sylvia had swiveled round to face him.

To her surprise, the new arrival was Tom Gates, the earl's agent. Gates came to an abrupt halt when he saw Lady Sylvia, and the startled expression on his face told her that he had not expected to find her there.

Not having had much opportunity over the years to exchange more than the barest civilities with Gates, Sylvia was immediately struck by the agent's manly bearing and rugged features. Unlike Connan's faded blue gaze, the agent's eyes were a deep, azure blue, and reflected an intelligence far beyond his station.

The fanciful notion flashed through Sylvia's mind that here was living proof of those improbable plots she had so often encountered in popular romantical novels in which the totty-headed heroine runs off with the under-gardener, or one of her father's footmen. She had always pooh-poohed such aberrations, but upon closer inspection, Thomas Gates caused her to reassess her opinion. In spite of his modest coat, homespun breeches, and muddied boots, the agent embodied all the masculine traits calculated to turn the heads of any fictional schoolroom chit with more hair than wit.

Sylvia felt the pull of his presence herself. Had she been ten years younger, she thought wryly, it was not inconceivable to think she might have done something incredibly stupid herself.

But that was beside the point. The point to remember was that the lovely countess *had* been ten years younger. Was it not possible—perhaps highly probable—that the impressionable lady had forgotten herself so far as to flirt with the handsome agent? Tom Gates did not strike Sylvia as the kind of man one would mock with impunity. And surely any hint of flirtation from his employer's wife would be considered a mockery of the worst kind.

"Good afternoon, my lady," the agent said, his voice low and respectful, yet hinting—at least to Sylvia's sensitized ears—at forbidden intimacies in the husky echoes that hung in the air between them.

"Good afternoon, Gates," she replied, ignoring the absurd fantasies that appeared to have taken over her brain. "I hope you do not intend to shoot that gun off around here," she added, noticing the shotgun slung over his shoulder. "I can guarantee that there are no rabbits within range. Rufus has seen to that."

"No, my lady." Again Sylvia was struck by the cultivated tone of the husky voice. Could the countess—evidently experienced in such things—fail to be impressed by the obvious masculinity of the handsome agent? Sylvia did not think so, but she balked at speculating on the outcome of such a confrontation.

"I come up here periodically to see that the lads from the village are not trespassing," the agent continued. "The cliffs here can be treacherous." He gestured vaguely in the direction of the stone hut.

"Well, no one has been up here all afternoon, except Mr. Connan," Sylvia remarked, settling herself once more before her easel.

"Connan was here, was he, now? Bringing his flowers, no doubt. As if the poor thing has any use for such trumpery wherever it is she is paying the price of her sinful ways."

Sylvia should not have been surprised that the agent knew of Connan's little tribute to the countess, but it was the edge of sarcasm in his voice that caught her attention. Gates's conviction that Lady Longueville had been a sinner placed him together with Captain Ransome in the opposite camp from Connan.

Interesting, Sylvia thought to herself, returning to her sketching after Gates had taken his leave. For a few moments she watched the agent's broad shoulders ripple under his coat as he strode purposefully down to the hut, following the identical path taken by his rival. Rival? The word had slipped into her consciousness quite innocuously. But its presence raised an intriguing question. Had these two men—so different in character and appearance—been rivals for the attention of the glittering female who had more than likely mocked both of them?

And if so—Sylvia finally dared pose the logical question—had one of these men turned to violence?

Idly she glanced at the hut, her pencil arrested in midair. Gates was descending the steps hewn in the rock. He walked over to the window ledge where Connan had deposited his floral offering, and Sylvia felt the agent's anger flowing up the hill to where she sat. Brusquely Gates snatched the modest bouquet and, clutching it roughly in one hand, disappeared round the corner of the hut.

For several minutes Sylvia sat there, her easel forgotten. What was the man about? she wondered, repressing the mad urge to rush down the hill and peer round that corner.

A stifled giggle jerked her back to sanity, and she whirled to find Timmy Collins standing behind her, barefoot, wearing a jacket too small for him and breeches several sizes too large, apparently salvaged from one of the sailors who periodically washed up on the Cornish coast.

The lad gestured at the hut, as the men before him had done. "Old Gates is at it again, is 'e?" At Sylvia's frown, he elaborated. "Always the same thing with those two, milady. Two dogs with the same bone, me brother Danny calls 'em." He paused to grin at her through the gaps in his teeth.

"What are you jabbering about, Timmy?" Sylvia demanded, although she thought she could guess.

"The countess," Timmy responded, his tone indicating that he found her wit severely impaired. "They were both of 'em after 'er, ye see, milady. But she laughed at 'em be'ind their backs, ye might say."

"What does Gates do with the flowers?" Sylvia demanded, ignoring the bluntness of the boy's speech.

Timmy looked at her with all the condescension of youth. "Throws 'em into the sea, 'e does, milady. Always 'as, since the very beginning, Danny says."

Sylvia sensed that she was on the brink of discovering part of the mystery. "And how does Danny know all this?" she inquired, holding her breath in anticipation.

Timmy waved a grimy hand nonchalantly. "'E used to come up 'ere that summer, that's 'ow. Sit 'ere and watch 'em come and go. Or climb one of the oaks in the Park overlooking the summer 'ouse, or climb into the bell tower in the chapel. One of 'er ladyship's favorite places, that chapel. Cool and dark it was." The lad let out another giggle. "Our Danny could tell ye stories to curl yer 'air, milady."

"I wish he would tell me those stories," she said impulsively, putting aside all prudence and modesty. If what Timmy said was true—and there was no reason to doubt him—Danny might know who was with the countess that last, fateful evening of her life.

Timmy blinked at her owlishly. "'Appens 'e might," he said slowly after a while.

"Will you ask him, Timmy?"

The lad's face took on the crafty expression Sylvia had encountered before. Many a shilling had she paid to induce the boy or one of his siblings to sit for her. It was a routine they all understood.

"A shilling?" Sylvia murmured, pretending disinterest in the transaction.

"Right-ho." Timmy leaped to his feet and dashed away towards the copse. At the edge of the trees, he turned.

"For another sillin'," he said with the sly grin she knew so well, "I might even persuade 'im to give you the letter."

Chapter Fifteen

~

A Second Wife

After spending a good part of the morning in his study with Tom Gates, discussing the cost of rethatching two of the tenants' cottages, the earl found his thoughts wandering from business to pleasure. He was mildly surprised that his afternoon sittings in Lady Sylvia's studio had acquired the status of pleasure in his mind, but he put his enthusiasm with that lady's company down to boredom and the dearth of eligible females in the vicinity.

His mother was right, he thought, rising from his leather chair and stretching his cramped muscles as the door closed behind the agent, it was high time they started entertaining again. Better that than the exodus to London in October as the dowager had planned. The thought of pulling up roots again so soon after returning home and jauntering off to join the crush of the autumn Season in London made Nicholas shudder. He had everything he needed right here in Cornwall. His mother, his favorite aunt, his best friend, his shipping interests just a short ride over in Falmouth. And he had Lady Sylvia.

The thought of Lady Sylvia made him smile. He did not yet have her, of course. The lady had proved to be more skittish than a female in her situation should be. But Nicholas did not expect her to hold out much longer. No sensible female could ignore indefinitely the advantages of the arrangement he had in mind. And she would be worth the wait. Nicholas was quite sure of that.

His smile broadened as he poured himself a glass of brandy at the sideboard and sipped it slowly. Oh, yes indeed, he thought, savoring both the French liquor and the delights that lay ahead of him. Lady Sylvia was a prize worth waiting for. A pity she was . . . He stopped short in mid-thought, alarmed at the direction of his musings. A mistress was one thing, he reminded himself. He had indulged himself with several over the years. A wife was quite another.

The prospect of taking a second wife appalled him, Nicholas suddenly realized, his stomach clenching into a knot of anxiety. After Angelica—and it had taken him years to admit the young Beauty had been a mistake, just as his mother had warned him—the fear of committing a similar error of judgment paralyzed him. Perhaps he should leave it in his mother's hands, as she never tired of suggesting. His gravest mistake had been losing his heart to the French Beauty, a mistake the dowager was unlikely to make.

The notion made him smile again. He could not imagine his mother growing sentimental over any female, no matter how refined and eligible, destined to take her place as Countess of Longueville. Yes, he thought, suddenly determined not to put off his duty any longer, he would ask his mother to scout out eligible candidates among her friends and acquaintances and invite them to one of the famous Longueville house parties.

The earl took his half-finished brandy over to the bow window and glanced out at his pristine Park, the pride of generations of Longuevilles. Not a blade of grass out of place; not a bush anything but perfectly trimmed; not a single tree in the long row of ancient limes that bordered the driveway out of line, by so much as a leaf—or so it seemed to the earl's suddenly critical eye—with its neighbors.

Then his glance shifted to the sparse flower beds, and his lips twisted into a wry quirk. There they were, in the same stiff row, like soldiers on parade, rigid and lifeless. His mother's rose-trees; pruned in identical round clusters on spindly stalks. All blood red—the color of the Longueville standard, the dowager claimed when questioned on her lack of variety.

Unbidden, a picture of the rose-garden at Whitecliffs flashed into his mind. Nicholas saw again the exuberant masses of pink blossoms reaching out their carefree arms in all directions, like tipsy butterflies. And through that world of riotous pink clouds drifted the enchanting presence of *The Lady in Gray,* a gentle smile on her lips, her hands outstretched in welcome.

Before Nicholas had made his unwelcome announcement that he intended to wed the daughter of an obscure French émigré eking out a dubious existence in Falmouth, the dowager had routinely invited two or three eligible young ladies with their parents to the Castle during the summer months.

It was time to renew that tradition.

Feeling a sudden uplifting of his spirits, the earl tugged the tapestried bell pull. He would enlist his mother's aid before he lost his nerve.

"Ask her ladyship if she will spare me a few minutes, Greenley," he said when the butler appeared at the door.

"Very well, my lord," Greenley responded, disappearing as silently he had come.

Ten minutes later, Nicholas joined the dowager and his aunt in the Yellow morning room and was relieved at the enthusiastic reception of his plans by both ladies.

"I am glad to hear you have come to your senses, Nicholas," the dowager remarked when she had heard him out. "Your aunt and I will start our list of eligible young ladies immediately after nuncheon."

At that moment the morning room door opened and Jason sauntered in.

"Finished with your dreary accounts, I see," the captain remarked. "Now do you understand why I prefer to purchase a frigate rather than property in some rural spot isolated from the rest of the world? I do not fancy spending my days tending cattle or tenants. Give me the wide-open sea any day."

"You will have to settle down and start your nursery sooner or later, Jason," Mrs. Hargate chided him gently. "And you may be in luck. Nicholas has just given instructions to resume the house parties that made Longueville so famous. Naturally, those plans will include a bevy of eligible girls that I am sure Nicholas will be willing to share."

Nicholas saw his friend glance at him in dismay, one ginger eyebrow raised inquiringly. "I see it will soon be time to take my congés," the captain drawled, a grimace of amusement on his face.

"Oh, no, you do not, my lad," Nicholas cut in with a grin. "I am depending on your support in this ordeal and—"

"Ordeal?" the dowager broke in sharply. "Since when is it an ordeal to take your pick of the choicest gels on the Marriage Mart, my boy? And believe me, Nicholas, they will be the most eligible candidates in England. Lydia and I will make quite sure of that. No more foreigners for this family, thank you."

In the awkward silence that followed this unfortunate remark, Nicholas heard his Aunt Lydia clear her throat.

"I hear the Ashfords have an American heiress staying with them," she said in her calm voice. "A distant cousin to the duke, I believe. She is reported to be a great Beauty, and very modest. Her father has no title, of course, being the youngest son, but he made a fortune in the railroads, and unless you consider the gel a foreigner, Dorothy—"

"Colonials are hardly foreigners, Lydia," the dowager broke in impatiently. "Especially if they are related to the Duke of Ashford."

Nicholas shot an amused glance at his friend, and noted that Jason was grinning at the dowager's incongruous remark.

"They are hardly colonials either," he drawled. "Particularly since they won the war and have established their own government. But you are right, Mama," he added, tongue in cheek, "a wealthy heiress from either side of the Atlantic must indubitably be on our list of candidates."

"If for no other reason than to give the selection a taste of the exotic," Jason added mendaciously. "Who knows? I may even take a fancy to the chit myself. Connections on the other side of the ocean might be good for the shipping business."

Before he could add his voice to Jason's, however, the door opened to admit Greenley, a note on his silver tray, which he presented to the earl.

A quick glance at the contents of the missive, written in a firm, elegant hand, cast an invisible cloud over his day. Although why Lady Sylvia's sudden canceling of his afternoon sitting should make the slightest difference to his mood, Nicholas was at a loss to understand.

"And exactly what do you hope to achieve by this mad notion of yours, Nick?" Jason demanded as the two gentlemen turned their horses towards Whitecliffs several hours later. "It strikes me that Lady Sylvia will view the purchase of that old nag as a deliberate attempt to thwart her creative design for your portrait. I fear she might be more than a little put out by your high-handed ways, old man."

"Nonsense!" Nicholas exclaimed, amused at the anticipation of the lady's wrath falling upon his head. "The lady is quite magnificent when she is angry. Besides, I consider the purchase of old

Hercules from Dudley a brilliant solution to this addle-pated notion of including the nag in my portrait. Now, if she had suggested adding Arion to the composition, I would not have resisted. Quite the contrary. Arion is as fine a piece of horseflesh as you will find anywhere. A fitting addition to a family portrait."

"Will you carry the news of this underhanded ploy to the lady yourself?" Jason wanted to know.

"Naturally," Nicholas admitted with a broad smile. "I shall look forward to doing so." For some reason he could not fathom, the idea of outwitting Lady Sylvia held a certain piquancy that tickled his fancy. Perhaps the lady would realize that the Earl of Longueville was not a man to trifle with.

When they rode through the gates of Dudley's farm, the old man greeted them with his usual heartiness. "Goodday t'ye, milord," he said, motioning to a scruffy youth to take the visitors' horses. "I trust ye 'ave come to tell me I'm to 'ave a new roof at last. This one"—he gestured towards the ancient sprawling farmhouse—"was put up by the old earl, your grandfather, and ain't goin' to last another winter, that's for sure.

The earl regarded the old farmer with real affection. He had known Dudley ever since he could remember. "I believe my grandfather would agree it is high time you had a new roof, Dudley," he said noncommittally. "I shall tell Gates to talk to the thatchers." He was reluctant to let the old man know that he had already authorized a new roof, at least until that ugly old nag Hercules was safely in his possession. "We are here on another matter."

Over a flagon of home-brewed ale served by Dudley's youngest granddaughter, and after the state of the crops, the price of barley, the weather, and sundry other topics dear to a farmer's heart had been exhausted, Nicholas made his tenant a generous offer for a horse that would have been better off underground long since. A ridiculously generous offer, he thought, watching Jason's blue eyes widen in surprise.

Dudley's expression remained impassive. Unless, Nicholas thought wryly, that was a flicker of unholy glee that flashed over the old farmer's weathered countenance and disappeared as rapidly as it had come.

"Yer lordship wishes to buy 'ercules?" Dudley asked, after a pause that severely taxed the earl's patience. This time he was sure, from the telltale quaver in Dudley's voice, that the old man was laughing at him. "Now, what would ye be wantin' with a fine 'oss like 'ercules, I wonder? Ain't there enough cattle in the Longueville stables to mount 'alf Wellington's army?"

Nicholas kept a tight rein on his temper. He had forgotten, after ten years away from Cornwall, just how irritatingly garrulous country-bred folk could be. He heard the captain stifle a chuckle and gritted his teeth.

"Perhaps not quite that many," he replied affably.

"So yer lordship wishes to add my 'ercules to yer stable, do yer, now?" Dudley repeated, unnecessarily, Nicholas thought. "And a right generous offer ye're making, to be sure, lad. I'm not sayin' ye ain't. Take after yer grandfather, ye do, and no mistake. But ye should know, milord, that old 'ercules 'as left 'is best days behind 'im, same as me. Ain't goin' to win ye any more races, 'e ain't, and that's a fact. Not that 'e wouldn't try if ye was to ask 'im. Grand old 'oss 'e is, even if I say so meself, who raised 'im from a colt nearly thirty years ago." He gazed off into the distance as though remembering his nag's past victories.

Nicholas shifted his feet impatiently. The sly old man was deliberately delaying his answer, but he knew better than to hurry a Cornwall man who had his crop still half full.

"Grand indeed," the captain remarked, interrupting the silence. "And I can well understand how reluctant you are to part with him, Dudley. But consider the savings. Why not let his lordship pay for the horse's oats and hay?"

The old man suddenly grinned, revealing a remarkable number of yellow teeth still firmly rooted in his gums. "Now, that's sound advice if ever I 'eard any, Captain," he said with a loud chuckle. "And I can just 'ear yer grandfather telling me I'd be balmy not to jump at it, milord," he added, his sharp eyes fixed on the earl.

"Then you will take my offer?" Nicholas interrupted, eager to conclude the sale.

"Well, I don't know that I can, milord," Dudley answered slowly. "Not that I'm complaining about yer offer, milord," he added, a definitely wicked gleam appearing in his eyes. "Right generous it is, to be sure."

"So you have told me already, Dudley," Nicholas interrupted again, his patience seriously frayed. "Now, tell if you will sell me that horse or not."

Even before Dudley replied, Nicholas had a premonition that something was wrong.

"Well, it's like this, milord," the old man replied ponderously. "And it's not as if I wouldn't sell ye the 'oss if I could. But 'appens that I can't, if you get my meanin'."

"No, I do not get your meaning at all, Dudley. Pray explain it to me."

"'Appens the 'oss ain't mine to sell, milord," the old man replied, looking the earl straight in the eye.

Nicholas returned the man's stare, his face stony. "Am I to understand you have sold the horse to another?" he demanded, knowing full well who that other must be.

"Aye, milord," Dudley admitted sheepishly. "But 'ad I known that yer lordship—"

"Who is this mysterious buyer?" Nicholas interrupted brusquely, exasperated at being outsmarted by a presumptuous red-haired female.

"Oh, it was 'er ladyship," the old man admitted with a wink. "Lady Sylvia, that is. Insisted on it, she did, milord. What was I to do, I ask ye? Quite set on it, she was, milord. Not a female a man would cross if 'e could 'elp it. Reminds me of that red-haired firebrand Lady Giselda, 'er as used to be mistress up at Whitecliffs when I was a lad. Folks around 'ere still tell stories of her ladyship riding around the moors on that big roan 'oss of hers, hair flying in the wind like some restless spirit from Hell."

"Looks to me that you are destined to go down in history astride a bone-setter of the worst sort," Jason remarked with ill-disguised amusement as they rode back down the lane. "But cheer up, old man. I daresay the lovely Sylvia would sell Hercules to you if she knew how much store you set on that horse."

"She is not about to know it," Nicholas snapped harshly. "And I forbid you to mention a word on the matter, Jason. Is that quite clear?"

"Very clear indeed, old man. But I should warn you that our Sylvia is not a lass to bamboozle with your high-handed games, Nicky. Heed Dudley's advice, I say, and do not cross the lady. You are bound to lose, you know."

Nicholas grunted something unintelligible, his mind torn between chagrin at being bested by the lady and delight in her ingenuity.

Chapter Sixteen

~

The Lost Letter

The slant of the sunlight on the stone hut warned Lady Sylvia that the afternoon was half over, but she could not seem to concentrate on her work. The sketch of the hut had progressed smoothly, taking on the sinister appearance of a gray toad squatting in the shallow indentation in the cliff wall. The stone chimney and slate roof were barely visible at ground level, but from her elevated position on the slope, Sylvia could clearly see the narrow front door facing the rough stairs cut into the rock wall.

It was the dark figure she had sketched in descending those stone steps that disturbed her. Broad shoulders hunched, as if attempting to conceal his presence, face half turned towards the sea, black hair ruffled by invisible fingers of wind, the man stood poised midway down the narrow stairs. Perhaps he had heard a noise, Sylvia thought. Perhaps he suspected the hut was empty. Or feared that his trip would be fruitless.

But no, Sylvia thought, as an almost palpable vision flashed through her mind, leaving her chilled and covered with goose bumps.

The door to the hut was ajar.

She blinked. That door had been closed in her previous painting of the hut; she was quite sure of it. The dark figure—added later—had been standing on the cliff looking down intently at the hut.

Today, her imagination had placed the figure halfway down the steps, hurrying to keep an assignation. He must know there was someone in the hut.

Sylvia glanced down at her canvas, and with a few quick strokes of her trembling fingers the door in the painting was suddenly ajar. From there it was but a leap of the imagination to brush in the shadowy figure—a woman's slim form—standing just inside the door. The ghostly face was indistinguishable in the shadow, but the hair stood out clearly, a pale golden mass hanging loosely about her shoulders.

Sylvia shuddered at the picture that had emerged from her imagination. Was she allowing it to run wild? she wondered. Or was there—as she firmly believed—more than a modicum of truth to her premonitions.

"Now, what deep cogitation has stilled our artist's pencil?"

The deep voice, coming from directly behind her, caused Lady Sylvia to jerk around, nearly toppling her chair. Had a strong hand not steadied her, she would have fallen to the ground.

"Oh, Captain," she gasped, looking up into startled blue eyes, "what a fright you gave me."

"I do beg your pardon, my lady," the captain said, his rugged face contrite. "You made such a charming picture sitting here at your easel that we could not resist the temptation of discovering the object of your attention."

At his words Sylvia noticed that the captain was not alone. She felt herself blush as her eyes met those of the gentleman who had occupied her thoughts most of the afternoon. The earl's expression was bleak, and Sylvia wished she could cover the sketch on her canvas, which was, she realized, far too revealing of her own suspicions regarding the countess's death. But it was too late for that; the earl stepped forward to stand beside her, and Sylvia could feel him stiffen as his eyes took in the shadowy figure at the open door of the hut.

After an uncomfortable pause, the earl asked the question Sylvia had been dreading:

"Who is that man?"

There was something about the cold, stilted tone that made Sylvia cringe. The question seemed rhetorical to her heightened sensibilities. She had the distinct impression that the earl had a very good idea of the dark stranger's identity. Or had he recognized himself? She wished she might ask, but that was clearly impossible.

"A figment of my imagination, my lord," Sylvia replied, which was nothing less than the truth, she reminded herself. The identity of that sinister figure on the cliff was unknown to her, although the vague feeling that she had seen him somewhere before nagged at the periphery of her mind.

"You have a very active imagination, my lady," the earl said dryly, his voice still cold. "Are you sure you did not have a specific gentleman in mind as a model?"

Sylvia stared at him. She found the question vaguely offensive. Had she not said the figure in the painting came from her imagination? On impulse she decided to counter the earl's question with one of her own.

"Do you, perchance, have a specific gentleman in mind, my lord, that you wish to accuse me of including without his knowledge?"

This daring rejoinder was followed by a heavy silence, during which Sylvia met the earl's thunderous gaze unflinchingly.

After several uncomfortable moments, the captain intervened. "At this distance, I admit the gentleman resembles any number of our acquaintances, Nicholas. But Lady Sylvia has established that he is imaginary. What more can we ask? I myself would hazard a guess that the man is a bit of a rogue. Why else would he be skulking about in the dusk?"

The earl said nothing, his eyes fixed on the half-finished sketch.

"You are quite correct, Captain," Sylvia said with a relieved smile. "He is indeed a rogue, and his mysterious air is only natural under the circumstances. After all, I am attempting to suggest a secret romantical encounter, and the gentleman cannot wish to be discovered."

"A romantical encounter?" the earl sneered. "Are we to assume that it is also adulterous?"

Startled by the bitterness in his voice, Sylvia glanced at the earl, and her heart contracted. He still loves her, she thought, pain slicing through her. In spite of everything she had heard about the countess's indiscretions, this man still loved his dead wife. Inexplicably, Sylvia experienced a deep sense of loss.

As quickly as it had come, the sharp pain left her, and the absurdity of her own emotions made her suddenly angry. Why should she care whether the earl was still infatuated with a woman long since in the grave?

"You may assume what you choose, of course, my lord," she answered coolly. "It is, after all, only an artist's representation of reality. An imaginary scene, an imaginary gentleman."

"And I presume you intend to convince me that the figure in the doorway is an imaginary lady?" His voice was strangely harsh, and Sylvia could only guess that the earl had convinced himself he was looking at his errant wife.

Lady Sylvia looked at her sketch. Was it some trick of light, she wondered, or had that female shape she had instinctively added to the scene gained an identity of its own? The blurred features stared out at her from behind the door, and Sylvia wondered if she had, all unwittingly, recreated a likeness of the unfortunate countess.

Sylvia searched her mind frantically for a suitable answer that would satisfy the earl she had not deliberately set out to stir up the past. She was thankful when the gentleman's attention was distracted by a sudden eruption of barking. Sylvia turned to see an excited Rufus bounding towards the trees where little Timmy Collins stood hesitantly watching her.

With a start, Sylvia realized that she had forgotten that Timmy had promised to bring her the mysterious letter found by his brother.

"Timmy," she called, noting that her dog's fierce reception of the boy was pure bluff. "Did you wish to see me?"

Timmy looked at her as though she had said something particularly stupid. Then he nodded.

"Aye, milady," he volunteered reluctantly. "I brung what ye asked fer." He pushed one hand into a voluminous pocket and produced a creased piece of paper. "Got it right 'ere."

Since he made no further motion, Sylvia walked up the slope to the trees, scarcely able to control her excitement. "Thank you, Timmy," she said, reaching for the paper.

The boy grinned slyly and instantly hid it behind his back. Without a word he held out his other hand.

Sylvia plucked a shilling from her pocket and placed it in the grubby palm. Still without a word, Timmy thrust the letter at her and disappeared into the trees at a dead run.

The world suddenly stood still, holding its breath. Lady Sylvia's feet seemed rooted to the leaf-covered ground, as if they had decided to take up residence there. The late afternoon breeze rustled the leaves of the aspen and scrubby pine trees, and her eye caught the flash of a squirrel under a thicket of brambles.

Sylvia looked down at the frayed paper in her trembling fingers. It was folded in four, the creases grubby with little boys' hands.

She unfolded the letter and stared at the bold, heavily slanted handwriting. A handwriting that was as well-known to her as her own.

My darling Angel.

The familiar salutation sprang from the page and froze her heart in mid-beat.

"No," she gasped. "Oh, *no,* this cannot be."

But it was. Her heart knew it long before her mind could bring itself to accept this indisputable evidence of a man's perfidy.

My darling Angel. An endearment she had heard so often from those same smiling lips. One she had imagined, in her misguided and love-struck innocence, hers alone.

The memories came surging up from the past to engulf her, and Sylvia felt herself losing control of her senses. Had she not known the telltale missive to come from Longueville a year before she had discovered the delights of love and passion in the arms of this same gentleman, Sylvia could have believed it to be one of the amorous billet-doux she had received at Weston Abbey. One of those tender, passionate notes that had induced her to ruin herself for the love of a gentleman who had, a few short months earlier, penned a similar love note—or perhaps many of them—to another woman—another *Angel.*

Sylvia was overcome by sudden dizziness. Reaching out blindly, she felt the smooth bark of an aspen under her fingers. She leaned her cheek against the cool, solid surface of the trunk and felt her strength ebbing away.

She was going to swoon, she thought fuzzily—she who had never swooned in her life. Not even when her father had burst into that poky little room in Dover minutes after that rogue had disappeared into the night, leaving his *darling Angel* to face a father's wrath alone.

No, it had taken those three incriminating words from the past—*My darling Angel*—addressed to another woman, another love, to make her heart acknowledge what her mind had known for years: she had been tricked and betrayed by a master scoundrel.

Hearing the rumble of male voices behind her, Sylvia tried to shake off the alarming weakness that was forcing her to lean more heavily against the tree. Her legs seemed unable to support her, and she felt herself slipping until she was kneeling on the cushion of leaves.

Before she collapsed any further, she felt two strong hands on her waist, lifting her back to her feet, which refused to support her.

Then she found her face against the rough cloth of a gentleman's hunting jacket, two arms bracing her against a solid chest.

She sighed and relaxed. The male voices were speaking again, but she could not make out what they said. All she heard was the rumble of sound from the chest of the man who held her. That and the uneven beat of his heart. The rhythm of it was comforting, as was the warmth of the arms that held her.

It had been a long, long time since Sylvia had been held in a gentleman's arms, she thought irrelevantly, far too long. She missed the safety and protection a man's arms provided—or had seemed to provide, in her case. It had all been an illusion, she remembered, a cruel illusion that had broken her heart. Perhaps this, too, was an illusion.

Her eyes felt heavy, too heavy to open. Or was she reluctant to identify the gentleman who held her? Sylvia wondered, fighting the waves of dizziness that threatened to engulf her. Part of her wanted nothing so much as to surrender to the warmth of those arms, to slip into unconsciousness secure in the knowledge that she would be safe there. Another part insisted that there was something she needed to do before she could rest. Something that would affect her and the man who held her in ways she dared not examine.

The letter! That was it, Sylvia remembered, suddenly aware that she still clutched that revealing missive in her cold fingers. She needed to prevent the earl from reading it, and more important, she wanted to avoid revealing any connection between herself and the man who had called her *Angel.*

If the perfidious writer of that note was known to the earl, as seemed all too likely. Or if he had been a guest at the Castle that summer, a distinct probability. Then her own sordid story would become common knowledge.

Sylvia shuddered convulsively and slipped into warm darkness.

Nicholas looked down at the unconscious woman in his arms. He had gathered her up instinctively when she collapsed against him, cradling her unresisting body against his chest as he would a child. The sweet scent of lavender rose from her hair as she nestled against his shoulder. He was overcome by a sharp desire to protect this helpless creature from whatever demons seemed to have distressed her.

It occurred to him that he had not felt protective towards any female for a long time, and as Nicholas gazed at Lady Sylvia's pale, still face, he began to understand the vague sense of dissatisfaction that had plagued him since his return from India. He had no woman to share his life, no one to protect, no one to . . . He allowed the thought to drift off, unwilling to put it into concrete terms.

Not since Angelica had he felt a sense of emotional completeness with a female, that comforting harmony that comes from sharing small secrets, that fierce protectiveness he had never suspected in himself.

And now it was all coming back to him, he realized with a tremor of alarm. As he gazed at this woman's calm face and felt the soft weight of her in his arms, Nicholas recognized the surge of longing he had felt all those years ago. The empty place in his heart suddenly felt like a cavern, full of darkness and vague memories of dreams unfulfilled.

Nicholas raised his eyes and saw Jason looking at him strangely. How much of his thoughts had been reflected in his face? he wondered. Suddenly he felt very vulnerable and tried to compensate with a burst of activity.

"Can you find a rug in the dog cart?" he said, carrying his burden down to where the easel still stood with its enigmatic scene of the secret assignation. "I think we should try to revive her ladyship if we can. If not, we should get her back to Whitecliffs. I have no experience with swooning females."

Minutes later, as he deposited the lady on a rug the captain produced from the trap, Nicholas was relieved to see Lady Sylvia's eyes flutter open. She smiled up at him with such sweetness that his heart flipped over.

"W-what happened?" she murmured in a voice that faltered. "I cannot b-believe I swooned, my lord. I n-never swoon." She struggled to sit up, but Nicholas pressed her down again, stripping off his coat to fashion a pillow, which he placed carefully under her head. Some of her hair pins had come loose, and her auburn curls lay in a tangle against the blue silk lining of his coat.

Nicholas thought she looked quite enchanting.

"I believe you received some distressing news," he said, twitching the folded note from her lax fingers. "A billet-doux perhaps?" he added lightly. "I can imagine no other missive that might cause a lady to swoon, do you, Jason? Although from the look of it, I would say this note is an old one." He examined the letter curiously. "Who is the scoundrel who caused you unhappiness, my dear? I shall knock his teeth down his throat for him."

"You cannot mean to read a lady's love letter, old man," Jason said incredulously. "Not done, you know. Very improper and all that."

Nicholas had not intended to open the letter, but at his friend's words he felt a burning desire to know who had dared to write a love letter—if indeed it was one—to the lady he wanted for himself.

"Please do not read it, my lord," Lady Sylvia pleaded in an agitated voice, which only reinforced his determination to do just that. "It was not meant for your eyes. How dare you even think of reading it?" She held out her hand, but Nicholas was struck by a disturbing thought.

"Perhaps you can explain to me, my dear, how young Timmy came to be in possession of this letter? I will not believe the lad is playing pander for someone in the village. Not that insipid fellow Connan, I trust."

"Oh, no," Lady Sylvia protested weakly. "That is not the case at all, my lord."

"Then tell us how the boy came by this grubby piece of paper whose contents caused you to swoon."

"Stop interrogating the poor girl, Sylvia," the captain exclaimed angrily. "It is none of our concern who sent that dashed letter."

Nicholas glared at his friend. "Oh, but it is, my friend. Very much my concern if it is addressed not to Lady Sylvia, as I suspect from the condition of the note, but to another lady whose actions affect me directly."

Jason looked grim. "Are you implying that Lady Sylvia is lying?"

Nicholas looked into his friend's angry blue eyes and knew he was behaving in an obnoxious manner quite unworthy of him. Dared he say that yes, he thought the lady was mistaken about the letter. It could not have been addressed to her. Its dilapidated condition suggested it had been exposed to the elements and to rough handling, perhaps read over many times, but not by Lady Sylvia. Her violent reaction to its contents confirmed to Nicholas that she had not seen it before.

Who, then, had been the recipient of the mysterious letter?

"I am merely suggesting that Lady Sylvia is mistaken, and that the letter was penned years ago and intended for quite another lady." He spoke deliberately, hoping Jason would understand his meaning.

If he were not mistaken, Nicholas thought, the love letter was meant for his wife, written by one of the many admirers who had flocked around her that summer. The most likely candidate, of course, was his Cousin Matt, who had admitted—although boasted might better describe the young man's attitude during that final bitter interview they are shared in the library after the funeral—to a liaison with Angelica.

Only if Lady Sylvia had known his worthless cousin, perhaps had a *tendre* for him, would Matt have written her a love note. He had undoubtedly written such notes to dozens of females in his time, but to discover the truth, Nicholas would have to read this particular letter.

He was strangely loath to do so. Perhaps he did not wish to know the identity of Lady Sylvia's admirer. Perhaps he could not bear the thought of her lavishing her attention on another man. Perhaps he could not stomach positive proof of Angelica's betrayal. Perhaps . . . Nicholas paused as another alternative occurred to him.

"Are you acquainted with my Cousin Matt, my lady?" he asked softly, conscious of Jason's grunt of surprise.

Lady Sylvia looked perplexed. "I do not believe so, my lord. What is the gentleman's name?"

Nicholas could not explain the relief he felt. She did not know the man he suspected of seducing his wife, the man who had been banished from the Castle ten years ago and told never to set foot there again. The man who would, unless Nicholas remarried and produced an heir, inherit everything he had.

"Farnaby," he said, "Matthew Farnaby."

There was a moment of complete silence, during which Nicholas saw Lady Sylvia's face drain of all color.

"Sir Matthew Farnaby is your cousin, my lord?" she whispered almost inaudibly, one hand clutching her throat as though she could no longer breathe.

"Yes," he answered, watching her gray eyes fill with dismay.

"Oh, no!" Her eyes fluttered shut as Lady Sylvia swooned for the second time that afternoon.

Nicholas stared at her, uneasy thoughts jostling in his mind. The most plausible explanation for the lady's distress was one he did not want to face. It was Jason, kneeling beside the stricken woman, rubbing her cold fingers, who voiced the earl's suspicions.

"I wager that bloody cousin of yours is the brute who ruined her," he growled.

Chapter Seventeen

~

In Flagrante Delicto

Longueville Castle, Cornwall
September 1804

The sun was still high in the cloudless sky when Nicholas dismounted and tossed Arion's reins to Josh, the youngest stable-lad at the Castle. It had always been a Longueville practice to provide employment for local lads and sons of tenants, and Nicholas was well pleased with this new addition to the staff. Josh was proving to be a cheerful and willing worker, but that afternoon he appeared less talkative than usual.

The fact that Angelica had deliberately lied to him about her visit to Grenville Hall and her presence on the cliffs had ceased to seem the serious crime it had two days ago. So she had not been where she had said she was, he thought, seeking an excuse to forgive and forget. Perhaps she had made an honest mistake? Perhaps Gates had mistaken the date he had seen the countess on the cliffs? Such mistakes happened all the time. He made them himself. The proper thing to do was to seek her out and break down that odious barrier of silence she had thrown up around herself, shutting him out while she smiled and flirted with every other gentleman guest.

"I see her ladyship is still out riding," he said, following Josh into the tack room, where the lad was removing Arion's saddle. "How long ago did she leave?"

"About an 'our ago, milord," Josh replied, keeping his eyes on his task.

"Did she say where she was going?"

The lad shook his head vigorously. "No, milord," he mumbled.

Josh appeared nervous, and Nicholas hated himself for his sudden suspicion that the lad was hiding something.

"Then tell me which direction her ladyship took," he said patiently. "And leave that saddle on, lad. I intend to go out again."

After several minutes of stern questioning, Nicholas discovered that his wife had bribed Josh not to reveal her destination. Once his silence was broken, however, the lad spilled everything in a rush of words.

"'er ladyship wished to be alone," he confided. "She wished to read a new book, she said, and there were too many guests at the Castle. Took a picnic with 'er, she did. Told me not to tell a soul. Tired of company, she was. Or so she said."

"And gave you a shilling to keep her little secret, did she, now?"

The lad's face brightened. "Aye, milord. 'ow did ye know?"

Nicholas ignored the impertinence and reached for Arion's reins. "Which way did her ladyship go, lad?" he demanded as he swung into the saddle.

"To Pirate's Cove."

Just like Angelica to defy him again, Nicholas thought disgustedly as he cantered down the lane and cut across towards Mullion and the stone hut in Pirate's Cove. His earlier euphoria had dissipated with Josh's confession of his wife's whereabouts. This further evidence of Angelica's perversity disconcerted him. According to his mother, a wife's first duty was obedience to her husband, a concept that his wife considered antiquated farradiddle, or so she was fond of telling him.

As Arion crested the hill and began the descent to the cove, Nicholas was relieved to see only his wife's mare tethered in a cluster of wind-bent pines some yards from the hut. At least she had told Josh the truth; she was alone.

Nicholas's mood mellowed slightly. He would surprise her, perhaps even make the apology he had planned. The lie still rankled, but he should not be so harsh with her. She was so French in her ways, so young, so beautiful, so willful, and he loved her as he had never imagined he could love a woman.

By the time he had tethered Arion beside the mare and descended the rough steps, he felt the tinglings of desire quite as though he were keeping a secret assignation with his beloved.

Heart beating with anticipation, he reached for the door latch and swung it open.

The dim interior was cool, and he realized the curtains had been drawn on the single window facing the sea. The light from the open door revealed the cramped little room, walls of bare stone, uneven floor, and tiny hearth built into the south wall. At first he thought the hut was empty, but a newly laid fire smoldered half-heartedly, and then a rustle of movement drew his eyes to a low settee covered with a brightly colored wool rug.

"What are you doing here, Nicholas?"

His wife's voice sounded shrill and breathless. He noticed that her eyes registered shock as he stepped into the room, and she shrank back against the cushions of the old settee.

Nicholas gazed down at her and marveled once again at the translucent beauty of his wife's perfect face. He had considered himself the luckiest man in England when Angelica DeJardin had accepted his offer of marriage. He would still be so blessed were beauty the sole criteria for happiness; but Nicholas had soon discovered that such radiant beauty as his wife's came with a price. Every other gentleman of his acquaintance wanted her, too. And although Nicholas tried not to show it, every flirtatious glance, every tinkling laugh Angelica shared with another, cut straight into his heart.

And she knew it; Nicholas was sure of it.

"I seem to recall," he began mildly, "asking you on numerous occasions not to ride about without the escort of a groom, my dear. Have you forgotten?"

She shrugged, and Nicholas wondered how he could make his apology if they continued to be at daggers drawn with each other.

"You are always asking me to do such monstrous silly things, Nicholas, it is not surprising I pay no attention to you." She spoke petulantly, but her mouth pouted so prettily that Nicholas felt himself stiffen at the thought of kissing it. Perhaps if he tumbled her back among the cushions, they might bridge this misunderstanding, as they had bridged so many others over the brief months of their marriage.

Before he could act on this notion, the countess waved impatiently, almost as though she had read his intention. "I do trust you have not come all the way down here to chide me for ignoring another of your nonsensical rules, Nicholas. I find it very tiresome, let me tell you." She gazed up at him from beneath fluttering lashes, and Nicholas felt his senses reel at this unexpected coquettishness. She was a mass of contradictions, this wife of his, and her moods all too often left him feeling gauche and inadequate, as he did now.

"As a matter of fact," the countess continued, "Jean-Claude had promised to accompany me today, but he was not back from Falmouth when I left. I assume my brother's protection would satisfy your unnatural insistence on propriety?"

"Had he indeed accompanied you, my dear," Nicholas replied, ignoring this obvious attempt to sidetrack the issue. "But he is not here, so I must assume you are alone, Angelica, and that I cannot like. Ladies do not sneak off to secluded places unless . . ." He paused, unwilling to accuse his wife openly of misconduct.

"Unless what?" she demanded. "I fail to see how you dare find fault with me in this case, Nicholas," she added, her voice sharp with annoyance. "I merely wanted a quiet place to read the latest Minerva Press novel that dear George obtained for me last week. It is impossible to find any peace at the Castle. Your mother has made it her business to instruct me on how to entertain houseguests at country estates. As if I had not been entertaining my father's guests since I left the schoolroom."

"It is dangerous to be alone in a place like this, Angelica," Nicholas pointed out, "and I have expressly forbidden it. Besides, it is your duty as my wife to entertain my guests. It will not be for much longer, my dear," he added placatingly, "since most of them will be leaving in a week or two. Then we may be comfortable again."

"Comfortable?" she cried. "I will be bored beyond bearing, let me tell you. Unless of course, you plan to take me up to London for the winter Season. I simply must have some new gowns," she added, a wheedling tone creeping into her voice.

Nicholas hesitated, knowing full well that if he denied her any hope of a stay in London, he might forget about a reconciliation with his wife. Yet he had no intention of taking Angelica to London. He wanted her all to himself here in Cornwall. The two of them together, as he had intended when she made her vows to him earlier that summer.

As he mulled over his response, he glanced around the stark little room, his gaze settling on the rustic table near the sluggish fire. He suddenly noticed the array of delicacies laid out on the plain blue and white tablecloth, and his earlier suspicions returned.

"Were you expecting someone?" he demanded, gesturing towards the table. "I hardly imagine you intended to eat all that."

He was watching his wife intently, but aside from a small quirk of her lovely mouth, Angelica showed no sign of guilt.

"I expected Jean-Claude to join me," she explained glibly, her eyes daring him to challenge her. "My brother mentioned that he might invite Matt to accompany us, and as you know, Matt likes his sweetmeats."

The thought of his wife shut up in that intimate setting with two notorious libertines turned Nicholas's blood cold. He had known for years of his cousin's addiction to the petticoat company, and reports from his contacts in Falmouth had confirmed his suspicion that Jean-Claude DeJardin was capable of any depravity that concerned money or women. Some old rumors—which Nicholas had dismissed as malicious gossip—even suggesting that the Frenchman's appetites did not stop short of debauching his own sister.

"And you have been left to cool your heels, my dear, while your two gallants dally in Falmouth, is that it?" Nicholas decided it was time for a little mockery of his own, and was rewarded with a dark frown. "Perhaps it is a good thing I am here after all."

Angelica's face brightened, and Nicholas could almost hear her mind working furiously. When she smiled and reached for his hand, he knew that he was being given the chance to make that apology he had planned.

For some odd reason he was no longer certain he wished to make it.

"You are such a tease, Nicky," his wife murmured, pulling him down beside her on the sagging settee and offering her lips for his kiss. "But I shall forgive you this time, and if you promise to be good, I shall invite you to join my picnic." She glanced at the gold timepiece pinned to her riding habit. "It is certainly time for a cup of tea."

Brushing away his hands, which attempted to prolong their embrace, Angelica jumped to her feet and pulled open the curtains. Then she went to the open door and looked out with studied casualness, or so it appeared to Nicholas.

Apparently satisfied, she returned to the table and filled the teapot from a sooty kettle that dangled over the fire.

"There," she said with all the enthusiasm of a child playing at housekeeping with her dolls, "everything is ready. As soon as the tea is set, we can enjoy a real tea-party together." She threw him a dazzling smile, and Nicholas marveled at his wife's ability to turn the tables on him.

She was a continual surprise to him, and the next moment she surprised him again by throwing herself into his lap and squirming into a comfortable position. His reaction was instantaneous, but even knowing that he was being deftly manipulated by a woman with something to hide, Nicholas was incapable of resisting the insidious pull of his wife's invitation.

Ten minutes later, he regained a modicum of control and raised his head from her open bodice. Now was the time to bring out his apology, he reasoned.

"My sweet Angelica," he began, gazing into the mesmerizing blue depths of her eyes. "I really came down here to apo—" He stopped abruptly, one ear cocked towards the door. Had he imagined it, or had that been the sound of footsteps he heard?

"What is the matter, Nicky?" Angelica murmured against his ear.

"I thought I heard someone outside."

He made a move to rise, but Angelica grasped him more tightly around the neck.

"Oh, Nicholas," she cried, "what a tease you are. You are dreaming, love. There is nobody here but you and I."

But Nicholas was certain he had heard a noise. Resolutely, he lifted a protesting Angelica from his lap and struggled to his feet.

"Nicholas!" his wife cried loudly, catching his arm and trying to drag him back to the settee. "What a heartless creature you are." She laughed hysterically. "There is no one out there, dearest. I swear it. Sit down and I will serve you a cup of tea."

With some difficulty Nicholas pried her clutching fingers from his sleeve and strode to the door.

Even as he flung it open, he knew he was too late. Either by accident or design, his wife had given the intruder time to make his getaway.

In the distance he clearly heard the sound of racing hooves. They were going in the direction of the Castle.

Without a backward glance, Nicholas took the stone steps two at a time and ran for his horse. Arion responded gamely, and in record time Nicholas reached the stable-yard and flung himself from the saddle.

"Josh!" he yelled, wondering why the lad was not there to take his horse. "Josh, where are you?"

A startled face peered at him from one of the stalls. "'ere, milord," Josh responded, his toffee-colored mop of hair falling forward over his face. He ran to take the earl's mount.

Nicholas strode down the aisle to peer into the stall in which Josh had been working. He could hear an animal panting heavily and saw the sweaty outline of the saddle the lad had recently removed from the chestnut's back. It was obvious that the rider had been in a tearing hurry and had not stopped to see his horse properly cared for.

Nicholas stood for several moments, staring at the blown horse. He would have to speak to his cousin about mistreating other people's cattle.

For there was no doubt who the abusive rider had been.

As there was no doubt that his Cousin Matt had been the stranger at the door of the stone hut at Pirate's Cove.

Chapter Eighteen

~

First Kiss

Cornwall
September 1814

After a restless night, Sylvia spent the morning up in her studio, putting the finishing touches to the portrait of her aunt and Giovanni in the rose-garden. Still dissatisfied with the results after several aborted attempts to capture the exact shade of pink she sought, she threw down her brush in disgust.

Her mind was too full of unsettling thoughts to concentrate on her work. Usually when she immersed herself in painting, all else faded into the background, but this morning she tried in vain to find that release from the riotous images that plagued her.

She glanced up at the two portraits on either side of the chimney. The pirate's charming smile cheered her, as it always did, and Sylvia felt the captain's comforting presence in the room with her. She truly missed his easygoing company and wry humor.

As usual, the captain's smile stirred memories of her brother, John, and a desperate longing for her twin's encouragement and practical advice caused her throat to tighten. It had been far too long since they had shared confidences, as they used to do before her disgrace, and her birthday—when John might reasonably be expected to make the long journey into Cornwall—was still weeks away.

Sylvia brushed at a suspicious dampness on her cheek. She refused to cry. That was for the pampered, naive schoolroom chit she had once been, who believed the world an enchanted place where her own personal fairy tale waited for her to step into it and live out her dreams in perfect harmony with the husband of her heart.

That dream had turned out to be a cruel joke, an illusion that had begun to wither ten years ago at the Blue Duck Inn in Dover, but had finally expired in a painful twist of fate the previous afternoon at Pirate's Cove. The insidious words *My darling Angel,* scrawled in Sir Matthew's careless hand, had killed the last vestiges of romantic foolishness in Sylvia's heart.

Her eyes strayed to the portrait on the other side of the hearth, and her heart skipped erratically. The tall, lean gentleman who stood in the shadow of the hedgerow, pistol in hand, eyes challenging, dark cloak flung casually about his broad shoulders, was nothing like her brother. His irregular features, hawklike nose, and sensuous mouth held promises of excitement no pirate could rival. His dark eyes held hers as inexorably as if he stood in the room before her, and Sylvia felt her cheeks grow warm at the immodest thoughts that flooded her mind.

Sylvia tore her gaze from the brooding dark eyes of *The Highwayman.* He might be beyond her reach, but she would carry the scent and touch of him with her for the rest of her life. She was sure of it. That and the warmth of his arms as he held her against him would be all she would permit herself.

Alarmed at the direction of her thoughts, Sylvia removed the smock she wore over her morning gown and ran downstairs and out into the garden. She made her way up a slope to a small folly that Giovanni had built in the early days of his residence at Whitecliffs. She often escaped from the house to sit on one of the marble benches he had placed overlooking the riot of roses growing in wild abandon on the slopes. The rose-bushes had been Sylvia's contribution to the landscape, and she found the perfume that floated in the air as restful as the hum of the bees raiding the flowers for their nectar.

An exquisite statue of Aphrodite, her arms holding an urn against her perfect bosom, dominated the vista in front of the folly. Sylvia had always considered it one of Giovanni's best pieces, and had begged him not to sell it. He had immediately gifted her with the statue, which Sylvia had placed where she could view it from her favorite bench in the folly.

Today, the perfection of the goddess's voluptuous body, draped around the hips with a cascading tunic, conjured up images of the Countess of Longueville. Sylvia had never seen a likeness of the

earl's young bride, but she imagined a fairy-like creature of dazzling beauty, petted and pampered by a doting husband until some
goddess, envious of such mortal perfection, reached down from
Olympus to destroy her.

Had she lived, Lady Longueville would have been close to
Sylvia's own age; they would have been neighbors, certainly acquaintances, even friends. They might have visited often, shared
confidences.

They would—if that letter revealed what she knew it must—
have shared lovers.

Sylvia shuddered, nauseated at the recurring image of Sir
Matthew coming straight from his mourning cousin's estate in
Cornwall to court naive, impressionable, wealthy Lady Sylvia
Sutherland in Sussex. Straight from the arms of the countess so
shortly after her death. Straight from adultery into betrayal.

Had the earl read Matthew's letter? she wondered. Sylvia regretted not demanding that he return it to her when the two gentlemen had delivered her to Whitecliffs yesterday. In her dazed
state, she remembered him grim-faced but oddly gentle as he carried her into the Italian Saloon and laid her on the green brocade
settee.

The memory of his arms around her stirred impossible yearn-
ings, which Sylvia ruthlessly suppressed. Or at least she tried to
suppress them, but the memory was too sweet, too enticing to re-
linquish entirely, and she slipped into a pleasant daydream. A deep
voice from close behind her broke into her reverie.

"Lady Marguerite told me I would find you here," Sylvia heard
the earl say. She jumped to her feet in confusion. How mortifying
that he should catch her thinking of him. Sylvia felt herself blush,
and quickly snatched up her floppy gray hat that she had abandoned beside her on the bench.

"Oh, my lord!" she blurted out. "What a surprise! I did not expect you until this afternoon. The portrait is so close to being com-
pleted that I—"

"I did not come about the portrait, Sylvia," he interrupted gently. "At least, not primarily. Ransome and I have been called to
Falmouth rather urgently to inspect a frigate I hope to purchase, so
I came to ask you to postpone our sittings for a week. It should not
take more than a week to come to a decision."

Sylvia regarded the earl warily. He might easily have sent a note
about the sittings. His presence disturbed her.

"What did you come for, then, my lord?"

"My cousin's letter."

Sylvia felt her heart jump into her throat. He had read it, then, she thought, searching about in her mind for something appropriate to say. She found nothing adequate enough to soothe the pain of betrayal, so she said nothing.

"I have read it," he said bluntly, confirming her fears. "Since the clandestine message concerned both my cousin and my wife, I felt I had the right, perhaps the duty, to do so. It was dated in late September, a week before my wife's death. A full month before my cousin went into Sussex and met you."

He paused, and Sylvia said nothing. Indeed, she could not have done so had she tried, her throat was so constricted.

"I am deeply sorry to distress you, my dear," she heard him murmur, and then somehow he was holding both her hands in his, pressed against the rough material of his hunting jacket. Even as she watched, the earl raised her fingers and kissed them lightly, lingeringly.

Sylvia felt as though she floated in the dream world of her girlhood, but the warmth of his hands was real, as was the compassion in the dark eyes fixed intently on her face.

"It is far worse that either of us expected."

Sylvia wondered what could possibly be worse than discovering your wife of three months had taken a lover. What could be worse than learning that the man you loved—and who swore loved you—had come to you still warm from the bed of another woman?

"What could be worse?" she heard herself say in a strangled voice.

She was so close to him that she caught the brief quirk of pain that twisted his lips. Evidently her own anguish was mirrored on her face, for without warning the earl bent his head and rested his lips on hers in the tenderest of kisses Sylvia had imagined possible.

"I forbid you to waste another moment of your life repining over that libertine," he whispered fiercely, inches from her tingling mouth. "He is not worth a single thought of yours, my dear, a single tear."

He looked into her eyes then, and Sylvia felt her world tilt crazily. Was she about to embarrass herself yet again by swooning? she wondered, clinging to the steadying warmth of his fingers.

"I brought the letter back to you," he said. "I should not have kept it, of course, since you were the one to discover it, but I had to know . . ."

His voice died, and Sylvia knew exactly what he meant. She, too, had been reluctant to read Matthew's letter, dreading to find out the extent of her betrothed's villainy. Yet simultaneously needing to know the whole so that she could banish him from her deepest memories forever.

"What did you find out from the letter that you did not know already, my lord?" Sylvia asked, wishing they might stay thus forever, hands clasped, lips inches apart, his warm breath brushing her cheek.

There was a long pause, and just when Sylvia thought the earl would not acknowledge her impertinent question, he answered it.

"I found out what my cousin apparently knew already," he said tersely, letting her hands fall and stepping back. "My wife was carrying a child when she died."

Arion was in fine fettle the following morning when the friends rose out of the Castle towards Falmouth, but Nicholas's mind was not on the glorious sunrise, the birdsong in the hedgerows, or the performance of his favorite mount.

"If you intend to spend the entire journey daydreaming, old man," Jason complained as they cantered past the iron gates to Whitecliffs, still closed for the night, "you might have let me sleep for another hour or two."

Nicholas had not failed to note the closed gates and found it oddly disturbing that Lady Sylvia had remained equally closed to him in spite of the kiss they had shared yesterday. He was exaggerating, of course; they had not shared that kiss. He had been the aggressor, and abruptly Nicholas wished he had taken advantage of the lady's vulnerability and kissed her the way he had longed to for days. But every time he had relived that intimate moment in the folly, no thought of taking more than she offered crossed his mind. In fact, he had not intended to kiss her at all. Neither could he honestly say the lady had offered anything. It had been the anguish in her eyes when she heard the contents of that bloody letter that had made it impossible for Nicholas not to kiss her.

He glanced at his friend and attempted a smile. "Actually, I thought you still were asleep," he replied. "If there was any scintillating conversation from you over the breakfast table, I must have missed it."

"You were too busy mooning over a certain lady, no doubt," Jason shot back. "Why, even last night after dinner, while we were speculating on how much the *Voyageur* might be knocked down to, your mind was not on it. I tell you, Nicky, you had best let me and Ned Barker do the bargaining on this one, or you will be fleeced before you can say Jack Robinson."

"I was certainly counting on your help in dealing with the Horton brothers, Jason," the earl said, sensing his friend's true concern. "Barker tells me they are honest enough but tight as a cork in a rum bottle when it comes to trading. If you can find something unseaworthy about the *Voyageur*—and if anyone can find it, you can—then we might stand a chance of knocking them down a couple of thousand pounds."

"From what I heard around Falmouth, the ship is in prime twig," Jason warned. "But if I find so much as a rivet loose, or a stitch in the sails unraveled, I shall certainly mention it."

"I hope you do," Nicholas replied. "And by the way, I was not mooning over Lady Sylvia, if that is what you meant with your snide remark."

"How did she take the news of Matt's infamy?"

"Are you referring to his secret affair with my wife," Nicholas remarked dryly, "or the possibility that he might well have fathered her child?"

"Or the equally unpalatable truth that he might have killed her?" Jason added slowly, after a lengthy pause.

Nicholas shook his head emphatically. He had been wrestling with this very question since reading the contents of his cousin's letter to Angelica, but the answers that had presented themselves—particularly the one the captain mentioned—had unnerved him.

"I would prefer not to think so, Jason," he confessed. "Surely there is a limit to his viciousness?"

The captain's laugh was full of cynicism. "If you believe that, my dear Nicholas, then you have been living in the Land of Cockaigne, where

the fences are sausage, the houses are cake,
and the fowl fly 'round roasted, all ready to take!

"Believe me, lad, there is no such pleasantness in Matt's world, although I would wager my last shilling he wishes there were. He has always been insanely jealous of you, Nick. Do you not recall the time Stephen fell off his pony and broke his arm? Had Matt not dared your brother to jump that hedge, Stevie would never have thought of it. And what about Luke's death that summer? I was certainly here then, and have always wondered why your precious cousin was the first one to find Luke at the bottom of the cliff."

Nicholas stared at his friend in dismay. "You cannot believe that Matt was responsible for his own brother's death," he demanded, appalled at hearing some of his own repressed fears stated so bluntly.

"Any why not? I can believe any villainy of that slimy little bastard. With Luke out of the way, the title fell to Matt, and you must remember those sanctimonious little remarks of his about the responsibilities he would be expected to assume when your uncle passed on."

"I trust you do not mean all of this, Jason," Nicholas said, unwilling to link his cousin's random sins into a sinister conspiracy as Jason had done. "I cannot believe it of Matt, and even if I did, why would he . . . ?" He paused and shook his head. "No, I will not believe that he had any hand in Angelica's death. What could she possibly have done to provoke him?"

Jason's laugh had lost none of its sarcasm. "Are you forgetting, my friend, that with Stephen and Luke out of the way, Matt became the heir apparent to the earldom? Still is unless you do something about it. And remember—as I wager your self-serving cousin did—that regardless of who fathered it, Angelica's son legally would have been your heir."

Chapter Nineteen

~

From the Past

"May I 'ave another bull's-eye, please?"

Sylvia glanced up from her canvas and smiled warmly at the little girl. She had to admit that Peggy had been one of her best sitters, and had earned another of the hard peppermint sweets Sylvia usually provided as inducement for the village children who sat for her. She had discovered long ago that the modest sums she paid to their parents for permission to include the children in her portraits were not nearly as effective in maintaining a child's attention as the large, sticky balls of peppermint to which they all seemed permanently addicted.

It had been old Mrs. Maltby who had passed on this gem of information. During her initial forays into the village in search of picturesque subjects, Sylvia had despaired of enticing the painfully shy children to sit still long enough for even preliminary sketches.

"Give 'em sweets, m'dear," the garrulous old woman had recommended one frustrating afternoon when Sylvia was about to pack up her brushes and return to Whitecliffs with little to show for three hours of work.

Sylvia had taken Mrs. Maltby's advice, and allowed herself to be guided by the old lady's superior knowledge of children. The results had been astonishing. Within the week Sylvia had become the most frequent customer of Maltby's Old-Fashioned Confectioner's Shoppe. She had also become a favorite with the village children, who discovered in less time than it took to set up her easel that the young lady from Whitecliffs carried a bag of sweets in her satchel.

"We are almost finished for the day, Peg," she replied to the little girl's polite reminder that it was high time for another dose of inducement. "Then you may have one. And tomorrow, after the painting is complete, we shall visit Mrs. Maltby together, and you may choose a tuppenny bag of any sweets you like."

Later that afternoon, eager to show her latest painting to her aunt, Sylvia delivered Puffin into the capable hands of a Whitecliffs groom and ran up the steps. After directing a footman to unload the trap and tidying her hair before the hall mirror, she went in search of her aunt and Giovanni.

She found them at the tea-table on the rear terrace amidst tubs of scarlet geraniums, sweet lavender, and tall blue delphiniums. A picture of domestic bliss, Sylvia thought enviously, deciding that such happiness deserved to be preserved on canvas.

"What a delightful picture you do make," Sylvia greeted them cheerfully. "I trust I am not too late for tea and tarts." She took a seat at the tea-table and allowed Lady Marguerite to pour her a cup of China tea and pass her the ravaged plate of Cook's gooseberry tarts. "I see Giovanni has been making inroads into the tarts," she remarked, glancing affectionately at the Italian sculptor, lounging at his ease in the rattan chair beside his inamorata.

Giovanni grinned at her. "I gather you had a productive afternoon, *cara mia,*" he said. "I hope you are going to show us your new masterpiece."

"A very modest masterpiece, I am afraid," Sylvia replied with a laugh, "but I am well pleased with it." She motioned to the footman who had carried her latest painting out of the house to prop it on an empty chair. "There," she said, indicating the picture, "what do you think?"

Neither her aunt nor Giovanni were accustomed to take a request for their opinion on art lightly, and it was some time later, after every aspect of the work had been examined and weighed and discussed at length, that they pronounced it a thoroughly charming and professional piece.

"You have come a long way from those little flower portraits you did so many of when you first came to Whitecliffs, my love," her aunt said, her gaze lingering on the small girl throwing handfuls of crumbs to a horde of greedy ducks. "A delightful composition. You have a definite flair with children, Sylvia. One might almost believe those eyes are looking straight at us. What will you call it?"

"I had thought of *Peggy's Friends*," she replied, thinking how pleased the little girl would be to have her name on a real picture, "although perhaps *Dinner Time* might be more appropriate. What do you think, Aunt?"

Sylvia never heard her aunt's reply, for at the moment Hobson appeared at her side and presented her with a letter on his silver salver.

"Thank you, Hobson," Sylvia murmured, picking up the letter. Her first thought was that perhaps Lord Longueville had been delayed in Falmouth and was unable to attend the Huntington ball as promised. But such an event would hardly require a letter to her, would it?

She glanced at her name scrawled in bold letters on the pristine cream vellum, and her heart stood still.

It was not the earl.

"Oh, no!" she gasped, her mind reeling as it refused to believe what her eyes were telling her.

Dizziness threatened to engulf her. Then her aunt's arm was about her shoulders and the strong odor of sal volatile in her nostrils.

"My darling child, whatever ails you?" Lady Marguerite's voice came to her from a great distance, and Sylvia felt her cheek pressed against her aunt's ample bosom. "It is not like you to swoon, Sylvia. What has upset you so, dearest?"

"It appeared to be the letter," she heard Giovanni say in his deep voice. The sculptor sounded as rattled as her aunt.

Yes, the letter, Sylvia thought, gathering her scattered wits. How could the rogue possibly dare to approach her? How could he *dare*?

But there could be no mistaking that bold, careless hand. She had seen a similar letter as recently as last week, addressed to another woman. A hand she had recognized instantly as Sir Matthew Farnaby's.

Before Sylvia had fully comprehended the audacity of that once beloved rogue from so long ago, another more frightening reality forced itself upon her consciousness. The letter was not franked. The sender must be in the neighborhood. Close to her. Too close for Sylvia's peace of mind.

That evening Sylvia pleaded a megrim and, after picking at her favorite dish of roast duckling and new potatoes, and declining to taste Cook's special lemon blancmange, left the dinner table and escaped to her studio upstairs.

Not twenty minutes later, she heard a soft tapping at her door, which opened to admit Lady Marguerite. When Sylvia turned from the window, where she had been staring out into the deepening twilight of the Park, she saw that her aunt's hazel eyes were filled with compassion. The time had come, she decided abruptly, to make a clean breast of everything. Aunt Marguerite would not be denied; furthermore, she deserved to know. Her aunt's first words confirmed Sylvia's suspicion:

"Giovanni is convinced that letter comes from that scurvy rogue who betrayed you years ago, darling," her aunt said, crossing the room with a determined step and clasping both Sylvia's hands in hers. "Gracious! Your hands are ice-cold, Sylvia," she exclaimed, rubbing them vigorously. "Come and sit over here and tell your old aunt all about it, dear," she added, indicating the old settee in front of the hearth, the only seat in the room not covered with paintings in various stages of completion.

Sylvia allowed herself to be led to the settee, but as her aunt fussed with cushions and arranged a rug over her knees, she felt tears gather in her eyes. Although Sylvia missed her own mother, she could not forgive Lady Weston for showing no such compassion ten years ago when her youngest daughter had sorely needed a mother's support. Lady Marguerite, on the other hand, was everything a mother should be, her niece had discovered soon after her arrival at Whitecliffs. She was warm, compassionate, generous, and endlessly patient with her heartbroken niece. No wonder Giovanni doted on her, Sylvia thought.

"I have asked Hobson to send up a tea-tray and some sandwiches," she said as soon as they were settled. "You barely ate a mouthful at dinner, love. And remember, no gentleman is worth starving yourself for."

"Not even Giovanni?" Sylvia asked in a choked voice.

"No, not even my precious Vannie," her aunt responded emphatically. "A prince among men, of course, and king of my heart now and forever, but definitely not worth red eyes and a runny nose, my dear."

Sylvia attempted a giggle, but her heart was not in it. "I am not really crying, Aunt. It was just such a shock, you see. I never expected to see him again. That is, I did not expect him to find me down here."

"By *him* I assume that Giovanni was right; it was that cowardly brute from the past, was it not? But that was all so long ago, darling. What could he possible do now to upset you? Surely you do not still harbor a *tendre* for the scoundrel. You cannot be so foolish; I simply will not permit it."

"Oh, no, Aunt," Sylvia assured her. "But you see . . . Well, everything is so complicated now. I thought that perhaps . . . But now it is utterly impossible." She made a hopeless gesture with one hand. "That wretch has ruined everything." She heard her voice catch. "I cannot believe that he has made me miserable all over again."

"I cannot and *will* not believe that things are as desperate as you paint them, dearest," Lady Marguerite said firmly. "Perhaps you had better tell me the whole, Sylvia. Who is this man who ruined you and now threatens your happiness all over again?"

Sylvia shuddered with sudden apprehension. What her aunt said was true. Her happiness—or at least the little she had enjoyed in a certain gentleman's company—would be damaged beyond repair if Sir Matthew moved back to the Castle.

"You will never guess, Aunt," she replied. "In truth, I could hardly believe it myself when I found out who he is related to and the extent of his iniquities. Here," she added, pulling the recent letter from her pocket and handing it to her aunt, "perhaps you had best read it for yourself. Then I will show you another, written ten years ago under very different circumstances. One that broke my heart afresh, if you must know the truth."

There was silence in the room as Lady Marguerite perused the baronet's letter. Sylvia held her breath. When her aunt had read the missive through for the second time, Sylvia realized that she had yet to make the connection between the writer of the letter and a man she must certainly have met years ago at the Castle.

"Matthew?" Lady Marguerite murmured half to herself. She looked at her niece with a puzzled frown. "Surely this Matthew cannot be . . ." She stopped abruptly, her eyes widening as comprehension dawned. "And I cannot believe he had the effrontery to approach you with another offer of marriage. *Marriage,* of all things! After the way he treated you, Sylvia. The man is beyond despicable."

Sylvia smiled grimly. "Oh, but he is, Aunt. The very same Matthew Farnaby whom you already know as cousin to the Earl of Longueville. And as for his renewed offer, the rogue's arrogance is such that I imagine he expects me to jump at the chance. I swear it must have been the purest coincidence that I never even heard his name mentioned in the village all these years."

"That is because he is persona non grata at the Castle, dear," her aunt responded. "He had a terrible set-to with the earl shortly after the poor countess's death, and was forbidden to set foot on the estate again. Nicholas forbade his cousin's name to be mentioned in these parts. Nobody—not even our loquacious busybody Mrs. Rawson—has ever been able to discover why."

"*I* know why," Sylvia admitted in a low voice, wishing she did not. Lady Marguerite stared at her as Sylvia showed her aunt the letter Danny Collins had been holding all these years, then revealed the earl's news about the unborn child.

"We must assume from this letter," said Aunt Marguerite in a shocked voice, "that she did betray her husband. How else would Sir Matthew know about the countess's condition? It is not something a woman would confide to a casual acquaintance. And who was the father of the poor wee mite?"

"That is something we will probably never know, Aunt," Sylvia replied, thinking that in the young countess Sir Matthew had found a woman as immoral as himself. "I do know, however, that the earl had no idea he was to be a father," she added, remembering the anguish in those dark eyes as he told her about his wife's condition.

"The poor boy!" her aunt exclaimed. "What a terrible shock it must have been to discover, all these years later, that the wife he adored—and you may take my word for it, Sylvia, Nicholas doted on the silly chit—was carrying a babe that quite possibly was not his."

Sylvia could find nothing adequate to say to this.

Suddenly, Lady Marguerite jumped to her feet and started pacing up and down before the hearth. Sylvia knew her aunt well enough to see that the lady's comfortable nature had been seriously unsettled.

"I do trust you will not even consider granting this monster the interview he seeks, Sylvia," Lady Marguerite said sternly. "I give you credit for more sense than to succumb to such a ploy. The wretch has no shame! He will not be received here, I can tell you that, love. I shall have Hobson throw him out if he so much as dares to knock on my door."

Sylvia smiled at the notion of their sedate, portly butler embroiled in fisticuffs with an unwelcome visitor. "I doubt he will call unless I answer his note," she remarked, "which I have no intention of doing, of course," she added hurriedly, seeing her aunt's angry retort trembling on her lips.

The arrival of the butler—blissfully unaware of the violence his mistress expected of him—bearing a carefully prepared tray of tempting delicacies and a pot of steaming tea caused Lady Marguerite to snap her mouth shut, but as soon as the door closed behind Hobson, she vented her indignation.

"I should hope not, indeed," she snapped, thoroughly worked up into a fury of indignation. She glanced down at the paper in her hand. "I gather he is racked up at the Pirate's Cove Inn in Helston. I can only guess at the rumors that must be flying around the village. That old gossip Mrs. Rawson must be in her element, reviving all those ancient accusations against Nicholas."

"I do not believe that the earl had anything to do with his wife's death," Sylvia said, aware that her intuition had not deserted her. "Is it not far more likely that his cousin had a hand in it?"

She heard her aunt let out a soft gasp.

"Are you suggesting that Farnaby was with the countess the night of her death?" Her aunt's voice was filled with dawning horror.

"I *know* he was there," Sylvia announced bluntly.

"Then you must believe he may have caused her accident?"

Sylvia drew a deep breath before she replied.

"Either that or her murder," she said slowly. "For whatever it was, the countess's death was certainly not suicide."

Chapter Twenty

~

The Ball

"I doubt you heard a word I said, Nick."

Startled out of his reverie by the note of exasperation in Jason's tone, Nicholas glanced across at his friend and grinned.

"You are off the mark there, old man," he drawled. "You have done nothing but talk trading routes, provisions, and crew ever since we left Falmouth. I heard every word. Several times, in fact," he added dryly.

"Then tell me what you really think about expanding our routes to include China. I realize that Indian spices and silks are in constant demand in London, and you have made a fortune with this merchandise, but now that we have a faster ship, I think we should—"

"Unless I am mistaken, my friend, you have acquired a comfortable fortune yourself over the years as master of the *Scavenger*, and now that you are part owner of the *Voyageur*, you are about to acquire considerably more. In a few years I expect to see you settling down on some tidy little estate surrounded by a horde of wild, red-haired rapscallions." He paused, then added in a different tone, "And perhaps a lovely red-haired wife to complete the picture."

Nicholas could not explain what prompted him to introduce this obvious reference to Lady Sylvia into the conversation. The last thing he wanted was to turn Jason Ransome's thoughts towards matrimony with that particular red-haired lady. But some inner compulsion drove him to probe his friend's intentions. Some urgency he did not fully understand—did not wish to admit—drew him to suspect the easy familiarity Jason shared with the lady might hide a deeper attachment.

Jason stared at him, and Nicholas noticed that his friend's eyes held a hint of laughter in them.

"Never fear, Nicky m'lad," the captain said, a grin breaking across his handsome face. "I am not yet ready to leave the seafaring life, so rest assured I have no thoughts of offering for any female, red-haired or otherwise. Besides," he added, his grin broadening, "I would not dare to trespass on your preserves, old boy."

For some inexplicable reason Jason's last remark made Nicholas uncomfortable. "You are mistaken if you think I have any special claim on Lady Sylvia," he said stiffly.

Jason looked surprised. "I beg your pardon, then," he responded. "I seem to remember that not too long ago you had some very specific plans for the lady."

"Then you remember wrong," the earl lied. "And I will thank you not to mention it again."

Jason laughed good-naturedly. "Ah, now I see what ails you, lad. The lady has refused your offer of protection, I take it?"

"Wrong again," Nicholas snapped. "No such offer was made."

After a short pause, Jason said in a more serious tone, "You cannot know how glad I am to hear you say so, Nicholas. As I have said before, I think the lady deserves much better from you. If I were a marrying man myself, I would not hesitate to step into parson's mouse trap, but I am a sailor at heart, and sailors make poor husbands."

They fell silent until their horses crested a rise and came upon the sight of Longueville Castle, perched on the cliffs overlooking the sea near the small fishing village of Mullion. As always, the sight of his ancestral home affected Nicholas deeply. He could understand how the original French invader, Baron Morlaix, must have felt upon getting his first glimpse of the fortress that had been bestowed upon him by the Conqueror.

Modified by generations of Morleys, the Castle had slowly acquired the appearance and comfort of a gentleman's residence on the inside, but from the outside, his home had lost none of that medieval grandeur and impregnability of a fortress. Nicholas felt humbled every time he gazed upon its eight-foot stone walls, turrets, fluttering pennants, and battlements still scarred by enemy arrows.

Jason's words rang in his ears as the two friends cantered under the huge stone arch that had once given access to the moat and wooden drawbridge that led into the fortress proper. The drawbridge was long gone, replaced by a stone one that arched elegantly over the still waters that—if the estate records were accurate—had in those harsh days of yore been filled with the bodies of French troops thrown futilely against the massive English stronghold.

All of a sudden the sight of the Castle brought Lady Sylvia to mind, and Nicholas had a vision of her standing regally on the threshold of his castle, dressed in green velvet, a golden chain around her slender waist, a veil covering her red hair.

Nicholas gave his head a shake. He must be hallucinating, he thought.

As a boy growing up in the midst of a rich tradition of historical events, Nicholas had spent many hours listening to his grandfather recount tales of heroism passed down—and doubtless embellished with the years—through generations of Morleys. Later he had himself pored through the ancient records, becoming so familiar with the accounts of the precarious daily life in the castle that it was but a step for his youthful imagination to fancy that he had been a part of those exciting times.

"Remember when we used to pretend we were knights in King Harold's service?" Jason cut in abruptly, as though he had read his host's thoughts. "You would lead us over the moors at breakneck speed, brandishing lances cut from old Dudley's ash trees. We could never keep up with you after your father gave you that roan pony for your twelfth birthday. Lionheart, I believe you called him. How we envied you that pony."

"Yes, old Lionheart," Nicholas added with a nostalgic laugh. "My trusty war horse. How grand he looked when Stephen borrowed one of those old tapestries from the South Hall to drape over him."

"I shall never forget the thrashing you got from your father when he found out about that little adventure. Something about wanton disregard for family heirlooms or such, I believe."

Nicholas well remembered that thrashing, one of several he received for failing to show proper respect for his heritage. It had been worth it, though. The thrill of leading his little troop at full gallop through the village, colorful tapestry flapping on Lionheart's rump, had gone down in history as one of his most triumphant moments.

"And remember the garter you carried on the end of your lance as a favor from a lady?" Jason added with a chuckle.

"How could I not," Nicholas responded. "One of the scullery wenches, was she not? Little Nelly Crofts. A jolly good sport, too. She married a tenant of Hazelworth's and moved up to Penryn, I believe. I wonder if she remembers lending us her garter?"

He had wanted to take one of his mother's, but at the last moment the probable repercussions of such a sacrilegious act had caused him to settle for Nelly's less flamboyant article instead.

"That I could not say," Jason remarked, "but I do recall the afternoon Matt threw Stephen into the moat, claiming he was a traitor to Harold's cause. We had to jump in ourselves to pull him out, remember, after the poor lad was chased by the swans. Your brother could have been drowned."

"Yes, he could have," Nicholas agreed, his amusement dissipating at the mention of his cousin's name. One more vicious act to chalk up to Matt's lengthy history of nastiness, he thought, although at the time it had seemed nothing more than a boyish prank. Now he was not so sure of anything anymore.

Nicholas found Tom Gates waiting for him at the foot of the staircase, cap in hand, an anxious expression on his weathered face.

"What is it, Gates? Nothing wrong, I trust?"

"That depends, milord," the agent replied in his terse way. "I thought you might like to know that your cousin is back, milord. Staying at the Pirate's Cove Inn at Helston, I hear."

Nicholas stopped dead in his tracks, a muttered oath on his lips. He had not seen his Cousin Matt since the day after Angelica's funeral, and had hoped never to set eyes on his wife's paramour again. Now that Matt's billet-doux had surfaced after all these years, reviving memories Nicholas had put behind him, the prospect of having to face Farnaby was less appealing than ever.

"When did he arrive?"

"Two days ago, milord, according to Bill Bates. Sent his youngest over with the news that Sir Farnaby was racked up at the Pirate's Cove. Tried to charge his reckoning to your lordship's account, he did, but Bates would have none of it without your permission, milord."

Nicholas heard Jason's snort of disgust at the agent's recital. Apparently, his cousin had not changed his ways, and what his Aunt Lydia had told him weeks ago must be true. Matt's pockets were to let again.

"He has not been here, I trust," he said sharply.

The agent looked apprehensive. "Aye, milord. Your cousin paid a morning visit yesterday, asking for Mrs. Hargate, but he was turned away. I trust we did the right thing, milord. Seeing as how you had given orders not to—"

"You did the right thing, Gates," the earl assured him. "At no time is Farnaby to enter my home. Under any pretext whatsoever. Understood?"

After the agent had taken his leave, Nicholas turned to the captain and found that his friend's eyes were sympathetic.

"This could become damned awkward, Nick," Jason warned him.

"Not if that bastard keeps out of my way," Nicholas growled.

Jason grinned humorlessly. "Matt was never one to keep out of the spotlight, Nick, as you well know."

Nicholas was all too familiar with his cousin's penchant for attention, but it was not Matt's visits to his mother or his perennial lack of funds that disturbed him. The suspicion that his cousin had a more sinister purpose in mind for revisiting the scene of his iniquity made the earl doubly wary. "I wonder if this sudden reappearance has anything to do with Lady Sylvia," he remarked, giving voice to his fears.

"We shall doubtless find out tonight at the Huntsvilles' Ball, old man."

"You cannot believe he will have the effrontery to show his face there," Nicholas exclaimed impatiently.

Jason's laugh held not a shred of humor. "If you doubt that, you are more of a nodcap than I thought, Nick, m'lad. So gird on your trusty sword and be prepared to defend the lady. It will be quite like old times. Matt always did dispute your right to be our leader, remember?"

Nicholas remembered. And the prospect of rescuing a real damsel in distress appealed to his sense of chivalry in ways he was still unwilling to admit. Even to himself.

Lady Sylvia gazed at her reflection in the beveled mirror on her dressing table and made a wry face. The silvery gray silk clinging to her slim figure revealed more than she liked of her bosom and outlined the curve of her hips rather daringly before falling in a shimmering line to the ruffled flounce at the hem.

Her abigail clucked her tongue approvingly. "That gown is stunning on you, milady. You will put every other lady in the shade." Molly stood beside her, holding the open jewelry box, waiting for her mistress to make a selection. "The pink diamonds would look wonderful, milady," she suggested, "although the opals are also lovely."

On impulse Sylvia selected the diamonds. In all the years she had attended, the Huntsvilles' Ball had never been one of those brilliant affairs she remembered from Weston Abbey, where diamonds were de rigueur and her mother's guests vied to outshine one another. A birthday gift from her brother, John, the pink diamonds were her favorite ornament, but one she never wore unless her twin was present.

As she bent her head to allow Molly to clasp the necklace, Sylvia smiled to herself. She might as well admit it, she thought. After her aborted infatuation with Sir Matthew, John had been a constant source of comfort and affection for her battered heart. His yearly birthday gifts kept her connected, however tenuously, to a family life she had forfeited forever. Sylvia treasured them accordingly, and the sight of the glittering jewels resting on her pale skin reminded her that in another week John would be with her again.

An hour later, it was with mixed emotions that Lady Sylvia descended the staircase to join her aunt and Giovanni in the hall below.

"*Brava!*" the Italian exclaimed as soon as he saw her. "I see you are prepared to slay every unsuspecting gentleman who dares cast his eyes upon you, *carissima*. You look utterly charming, my dear." He advanced to hand Sylvia down the last two steps, his face wreathed in smiles. "If I were but twenty years younger," he added with a theatrical sigh, "I would be at your feet myself, although I beg you not to say so to my sweet Marguerite, for she would cast me out, never doubt it."

Lady Marguerite, who stood behind him and had listened impassively to this flowery speech, chuckled. "Pay no attention to this Tenorio, my dear Sylvia, although I agree with him, you are stunning in that gown."

A short time later, as Sylvia followed her aunt up the stairs at

Huntsville Manor to greet their hosts, she wondered how well her stunning gown would hide the nervous fluttering of her heart. Her spirits revived somewhat when Lady Huntsville echoed her aunt's words.

No sooner had the Whitecliffs ladies taken a seat on one of the settees placed against the far wall than they were joined by Mrs. Rawson, out of breath and evidently bursting with gossip.

"Have you heard that the earl's cousin has returned to Helston, my lady?" she blurted out after the most perfunctory of greetings. "That handsome devil Sir Matthew Farnaby. Remember him? He was a guest at the Castle that dreadful summer the countess died," she explained, turning her shiny, stone-hard eyes upon Sylvia. "That would be before your time, my dear," she added. "Oh, but he was a handsome rogue if ever I saw one. The earl is nothing compared to his cousin. A veritable Adonis, I tell you. Not a girl in the neighborhood who did not cast lures out to him. Including the countess, they say," she added with a wink and a smirk. "And of course, our own dear Martha—Grenville as she was then— made a complete fool of herself over the lad."

"A gazetted fortune hunter, was he not?" Lady Marguerite put in, attempting to stem the tide of gossip that spewed from Mrs. Rawson's thin lips.

"Aye, yes, poor lad," the vicar's wife answered with a dismissive gesture. "All on account of his cousin's stinginess, Sir Matthew once confided to me. It appears the earl has control over Mrs. Hargate's fortune by her second husband, and refuses to open the purse strings to the dear boy."

"Possibly because your *poor boy* wasted his own inheritance— including his mother's portion, I hear—on dissolute living in London," Lady Marguerite interrupted sharply. Sylvia knew from experience that her aunt had little tolerance for gossips of Mrs. Rawson's ilk, but that lady appeared impervious to snubs.

"I daresay that is all a hum," she said lightly. "I cannot believe that a gentleman as polished and charming as Sir Matthew would leave his own mother destitute."

"Mrs. Hargate is not destitute, however," Lady Marguerite retorted. "Thanks in no small part to dear Nicholas, who refuses to allow her profligate son to squander the second fortune Mr. Hargate's left her."

"Be that as it may," Mrs. Rawson said huffily, "I consider it too bad of him to force his cousin to pin his hopes on a rich wife. Not that he would have any trouble attracting one, I imagine. Not with his looks."

Sylvia saw with disgust that the old Tabby was smirking again, quite as though she were personally responsible for her favorite's good looks.

"I pity the unfortunate female who is selected for that honor," she could not resist saying, ignoring a warning glance from her aunt.

The vicar's wife ignored this remark and favored Sylvia with a complacent smile. "No doubt the dear boy has already found his heiress and is settled down to a comfortable family life," she said. "I only wonder that he should wish to come back to the Castle when it is common knowledge that the top-lofty earl treated him abominably, cutting him off from the family—and from visiting his mother, I should add—after the countess died."

Incensed by this display of malicious speculation, Sylvia opened her mouth to retort, but a glance from her aunt silenced her. How she would have loved to inform this busybody that her dear boy had been thwarted in his search for a rich wife, but excelled at seduction and betrayal.

She was about to make her excuses and suggest to her aunt that they take a stroll around the room when she noticed Mrs. Rawson's plump cheeks flush with pleasure, and her smile widen until it threatened to crack her face in two. Her agate eyes, which had been darting about the room inquisitively, snapped open and riveted on the flock of guests making their way into the ballroom.

Against her better judgment, Sylvia followed the old lady's gaze and immediately wished she had not done so. She glanced away quickly, and saw that her aunt, who must have also noted the new arrival, wore a grim expression on her face.

"Can that be Mrs. Highgate from over in Penzance talking to Martha?" Lady Marguerite said with studied casualness. "I wonder how her mother is doing. Let us find out, shall we, Sylvia?"

Sylvia jumped to her feet, but before her aunt could follow her, Mrs. Rawson's shrill voice forced them to pause.

"There he is now!" she exclaimed, beside herself with excitement. "Do not rush off, my lady. I am sure the dear lad will want to renew his acquaintance with you."

Sylvia felt as though her heart had abruptly migrated to the soles of her pink dancing slippers. Now that the moment had finally arrived, she found herself singularly unprepared to face the man who had ruined that naive chit of eighteen she had once been.

It was too late to retreat, of course, and Sylvia straightened her shoulders. She was no longer that innocent girl, she reminded herself, and was more than equipped to depress the pretensions of fortune hunters and other such rogues.

She knew this to be true, but his voice, when it came, almost undid her.

"My dear Lady Marguerite," he drawled in that warm, caressing way she remembered so well, "what a delightful surprise. I swear you do not look a day older than the last time I saw you. At poor Angelica's funeral, was it not? Such a tragic loss for everyone who knew her." His voice dropped to a somber level, as if to remind them that he, too, had been touched by the countess's death.

Sylvia was appalled at the man's cynicism, and any thrill she had experienced at the sound of his voice dissipated like a puff of smoke. If that letter she had obtained from Timmy meant anything—and how could it not?—this villain knew more about the young woman's death than any of them, and may well have had a hand in it. How could he be so callous?

Curious to confirm whether the man she had once loved to distraction had indeed become so depraved as to seduce his own cousin's wife, Sylvia turned around.

The calculating look in Sir Matthew's Farnaby's pale blue eyes as they slowly raked her face, then slid down her body with barely concealed insolence, told her all she needed to know.

Chapter Twenty-one

~

The Threat

"What in blue blazes is keeping these women?"

Nicholas had been striding up and down before the enormous hearth in the Great Hall for the better part of twenty minutes, and his explosive outburst revealed the growing level of his impatience.

"Tut-tut, man," Jason said from his comfortable position on an old-fashioned settee, obviously designed to seat half a regiment. "The dowager will doubtless be down when she is ready."

"Do sit down, Nick," his friend said after another ten minutes had elapsed. "You are making me nervous, too. Lady Sylvia will still be at the ball whether we arrive late or not, and I am sure she will save a dance for you."

"I am more concerned about my cousin," the earl confessed reluctantly. "The more I think on it, the more I believe you may be right, Jason. That shameless wretch would not hesitate to present himself at Huntsville Hall if he got an invitation."

"Oh, he got one, you may be sure of that," Jason said with a cynical laugh. "Remember how Martha Grenville used to dote on him before she married Huntsville? All he would have to do is send one of those charming billets-doux he is so expert at writing, and dear little Martha will melt into a puddle of wax."

He had no time to respond, for at that moment the door was finally flung open, and the dowager sailed in, resplendent in plum-colored velvet and the Longueville rubies twinkling on her abundant bosom.

A half hour later, their coach drew up before the Hall, and

Nicholas handed his mother down, while Ransome escorted Mrs. Hargate, much less flamboyantly attired in dull green silk and a modest string of pearls.

The strains of the orchestra, brought expressly from Exeter for the occasion, wafted down to greet them as they mounted to the first floor. The receiving line had long since been discontinued, but their hosts—alerted by a footman of the dowager's arrival—were standing at the head of the stairs to accord her the reception and deference she expected.

"So good of you to come, my lady," their hostess murmured, acknowledging the dowager's rank with a shy curtsy.

The earl's attention was not on the social pleasantries their hosts poured on with practiced ease, however, and he chafed at the inanities that passed for acceptable conversation in such situations. His eyes constantly drifted towards the entrance to the ballroom, where couples could be glimpsed going through the movements of a lively cotillion.

He could not see the lady who had occupied his thoughts so consistently for the past week of his absence, and he wondered if Lady Sylvia was dancing, or whether she was sitting with the elderly ladies at the end of the hall. The thought that she might have taken refuge among those past the age of dancing disturbed him. She might soon be turning eight-and-twenty, he had recently discovered, but she was still in essence a young girl. At least she had always appeared so to him. She had the kind of beauty that, though not startling or extravagant as that possessed by some London Beauties, would carry her serenely through the years unblemished by the hand of time.

With sudden clarity Nicholas knew that he wanted nothing so intensely as to be there to watch those years pass by; to witness the ripening of that auburn beauty; to observe, day by day, the maturing of a fascinating woman; to uncover the intimate thoughts that made her what she was. And, of course, he wanted to make her his.

The dowager on his arm, the earl led the way towards the ballroom, his eyes seeking out that familiar red hair. When he found her, his heart gave a lurch. She was absolutely spectacular, much more so than he had expected. The silvery gown clung to her body in ways that caused his blood to surge and put him in grave danger of embarrassing himself.

"How very charming," Jason drawled from beside him, after the dowager and Aunt Lydia had been waylaid by a mountainous female in puce silk and feathered turban. "And utterly lovely, of course. I can understand your amazement, old boy, but do not broadcast your infatuation by standing there with mouth a-cock. Your mother will not be at all pleased, I can tell you."

Discovering that his mouth was indeed ajar, Nicholas shut it with a snap and glared at his friend. When his eyes slid back to Lady Sylvia, he noticed the man talking to her and his jaw clenched. "You *were* right, Jason," he muttered under his breath. "That damned shabster cousin of mine is here already."

"So I notice," Jason replied shortly. "But the lady does not appear to be paying him much heed."

"Why is she even talking to that rackety cockscomb?" Nicholas muttered with a peevishness that surprised him. "I want to smash the bastard's face in for him," he growled, loudly enough to cause a nearby matron to glance at him nervously, "for daring to approach her. Has he no shame at all?"

"Let me handle this," Jason said when the music stopped and couples milled around the floor. "The next is my dance, I believe, and I intend to claim it. And do remember where you are, Nicky, old chap. Lady Huntsville will hardly appreciate you turning her ballroom into Jackson's sparring ring."

As Nicholas watched, he saw the captain deftly remove Lady Sylvia from her companions and escort her to the dance floor, where sets were already forming for a country dance.

His devious cousin would welcome the chance to embarrass him, the earl knew. And to taunt him as well, unless Matt had changed considerably over the past ten years. This he doubted.

An ugly thought struck him. If Matt's pockets were again to let, as Aunt Lydia had claimed not long ago, and his luck with wealthy heiresses had run out, might his cousin not consider Lady Sylvia an easy victim? Perhaps his only chance of coming about. The more Nicholas pondered this possibility, the more likely it seemed that Matt was counting on sweeping Sylvia off her feet as he had done the first time. Why else would he return to Cornwall? Certainly not to see his mother, who heard from him only when he was in dire financial straights.

The thought of *his* Sylvia married to his cousin made Nicholas physically ill. Of course, the lady might consider such a step a belated reparation of her honor, but what about her happiness? Matt would not care a fig about her happiness. He needed her fortune.

And if he knew anything about his cousin, the earl knew that Matt would stop at nothing to get his way. Not even murder.

With a flash of insight, Nicholas saw what his course must be. If his cousin offered to repair the lady's reputation with marriage, surely an offer from the Earl of Longueville would more effectively restore Lady Sylvia to the social ranks from which she had fallen than anything Matt might offer. He, not his worthless cousin, would rescue the lady from disgrace.

Having made up his mind, Nicholas scanned the room, hoping for a glimpse of the first female in years who had made the prospect of a second nuptial anything more than a duty to his name. His heart contracted at the sight of her, smiling up at Ransome with a joyousness that made his breath catch in his throat. Nicholas was trying to imagine what it might be like to be the recipient of such a smile when a familiar insinuating voice interrupted these pleasant thoughts.

"My dear Nicholas," Sir Matthew Farnaby murmured softly, "what a delight to see you again. I trust you will not deny me the pleasure of your company after so many years of silence."

So, the earl thought cynically, his cousin was anxious not to be dismissed publicly by the relative he had—if evidence might be trusted—made a cuckold of. He turned slowly and found Matt standing beside him, his bland smile belied by the nervous flicker in his eyes.

After a lengthy pause, during which the earl was conscious of every eye in the room upon him, he nodded briefly but said nothing. He toyed with the idea of turning away and strolling across the room, but such deliberate rudeness was beyond him.

"What brings you to Cornwall?" he inquired after the silence became oppressive.

Farnaby relaxed instantly. "To see my dear mother," he offered with another bland smile. "However, to my dismay I found myself turned away from your door yesterday when I called. I told old Greenley he must be mistaken, but he had the impudence to call upon two stalwart footmen to stand ready to do me bodily harm if I did not leave instantly. His very words, mind you. I refuse to believe that you still harbor a grudge over that contretemps we had back then, Nicholas. I put all that behind me years ago."

The earl felt himself bristle at his cousin's casual dismissal of adultery as a contretemps. The wretch had the effrontery to grin, he noticed, wishing he had smashed that smirk off his face back when the shock of betrayal had been fresh upon him.

"I can well believe it," he said dryly. "That was ever your way of dealing with unpleasantness, was it not? After all, the lady is safely dead, is she not?"

Farnaby appeared somewhat taken aback by this direct attack, but he was not one to be troubled by remorse, so he brushed the earl's comment aside. "Callous as ever, Cousin?" His face broke into a grin, but Nicholas was not deceived. "My mother is not the only reason for my return, of course, although I do intend to make it up to the poor old thing. I know that if left to herself, she would give everything she has to ensure my happiness. But since you hold the purse strings, Cousin, I must rely on my own resources."

Revolted at the cynicism and selfishness of these remarks, Nicholas had to bite his tongue not to give this wretch a piece of his mind.

"Happy to hear you have finally come to your senses," was all he allowed himself to say.

"Oh, I knew you would approve, old man," Farnaby replied with a spurt of enthusiasm that sounded entirely false to the earl's ears. "And when you hear the rest of my plans, I wager you will applaud my good sense in finding a permanent solution to my troubles."

Nicholas felt his stomach muscles tense. So this was it, he thought wearily. This is where Sylvia enters the picture. A sacrificial lamb to save his cousin from ruin. Again the urge to smash his fist into Farnaby's smug face rose within him. He repressed it and merely returned his cousin's gaze impassively.

"I am to be married, Cousin," Matt said in a tone that grated on the earl's nerves. "The lady in question," he added complacently, "is wealthy and willing. I am primed to pose the question at any moment, perhaps even tonight, if I get the chance. And after that it will be smooth sailing. You will no longer need to worry about rescuing me from Debtors' Prison, Nicholas."

The earl let his eyes wander deliberately over the throng of guests in studied indifference to the baronet's announcement. Even though he had anticipated his cousin's designs on Lady Sylvia, hearing him admit it as though it were a fait accompli rattled him more than he liked. He suppressed a surge of jealousy at this cousin of his. Could it be that Matt had outsmarted him yet again? How could he be so sure of Sylvia's acceptance? Was there

something about the relationship between the two that he had overlooked? Did Sylvia still harbor a foolish *tendre* for the man who
had ruined her?

"Did you hear what I said, Nick? I am soon to be a married
man."

The earl turned to stare at him. "I heard you," he said nonchalantly. "I will believe it when I see it. I doubt the lady in question
will be so easily fooled as the first time, however."

His cousin's stunned reaction to this challenge was everything
Nicholas could have wished. Matt's mouth actually dropped open,
and his eyes flashed murderously before he could veil them.

After a considerable pause, Farnaby found his voice. "So you
know about Sylvia's little indiscretion?"

"Yes," was all the response Nicholas allowed himself.

"And may I know how you came upon this information?"

For the first time during the interview, Nicholas smiled faintly.
"The lady herself told me," he said coolly. Which at least was partially true.

"That I will not believe," the baronet replied angrily. "If I know
anything about the lady—and you can trust me on this—it is a
downright lie."

Nicholas shrugged and turned back to the dance floor, where the
country dance was coming to an end. "Suit yourself. Perhaps you
do not know the lady as well as you imagined. Now, if you will excuse me, I have a dance to claim."

Without a backward glance, Nicholas stepped down on the
dance floor and made his way to where Jason had just returned his
partner to her aunt.

The brilliant smile Lady Sylvia bestowed upon him as he joined
them went a long way to restoring the earl's spirits.

He hoped that smile had not been lost on Sir Matthew Farnaby.

When Captain Ransome led her back to her aunt after the country dance, Lady Sylvia was relieved to see that Sir Matthew was
no longer in sight. She devoutly hoped that he would not approach
her again, but set no store on his discretion. He had never been
known for caution, she recalled, and the knowing look he had
given her when their eyes first met suggested that he had been serious about renewing their betrothal.

She smiled up at the captain, who had just carried her gloved
fingers to his lips in a gallant gesture. "You have given the lie to

that old adage about sailors being unstable dancers, Captain," she teased. "I did not detect a single instance of tottering, swaying, or stumbling. You have restored my faith in seafaring men, let me tell you."

The captain laughed at her, his white teeth flashing in his tanned face. "I am relieved to hear it, my lady. Of course, I was on my best behavior. I doubt I could acquit myself so well had our dance been a waltz."

"Fiddle!" Sylvia exclaimed. "You are teasing me again, sir." And in truth, she loved him for it. The captain's easy laugh and friendly banter had steadied her nerves after that first encounter with Sir Matthew.

Ransome let out a crack of laughter that made several heads turn in their direction. Sylvia relaxed and flashed him a brilliant smile in return.

"Now, I wonder what idle flattery you are pouring into the lady's lovely ears to win such a charming smile from her."

Sylvia had not noticed the earl's approach, but the sound of his voice flushed all thoughts of other suitors from her mind. She met his dark eyes over the captain's shoulder, and her heart lifted at the sight of him.

"You are off the mark, Nicholas," the captain replied dryly. "I have just been called a heartless rogue, so you have nothing to fear on that score."

It seemed to Sylvia that the two men had just exchanged some secret message, but before she could demand an explanation, the orchestra struck up a waltz, and the earl led her onto the floor.

Sylvia sighed softly. The moment she had anticipated all week had finally arrived. Here she was in his arms again, her body attuned to every movement of his, responsive to his slightest touch, melting in the warmth of his hand on her waist. If only his eyes had not appeared so withdrawn when she glanced up into them, she would have been ecstatic.

The earl was clearly uneasy, and Sylvia suspected it was directly related to the return of his cousin. His first remark, after they had circled the room twice in complete silence, confirmed her suspicions.

"I trust Farnaby is not making a nuisance of himself."

Sylvia looked up and found herself being scrutinized by those dark eyes that seemed to see into her very soul. She felt a wild urge to tell this man the truth, to seek his advice and protection. Yes, she would admit, Farnaby was being a nuisance, frighteningly so. His letter proposing they resume their betrothal had been couched in vaguely threatening terms, but Sylvia was at a loss to understand why an offer of marriage could be a threat.

"I can see that he has," the earl said tersely when Sylvia did not respond immediately. "I should have known it." He smiled grimly. "Only say the word, my dear, and I shall send him away."

Sylvia was so surprised by this offer that she stumbled. "Oh, no!" she exclaimed, alarmed at what Sir Matthew might do if he learned she was in any way responsible for a second banishment. "That is to say," she added hastily when his expression darkened, "I d-do not b-believe that will b-be necessary, my lord."

She could say no more, for the music had stopped and guests moved towards the open doors to enjoy the cooler air. Several couples went out onto the broad balcony and wandered down the stone stairs to the garden below, brilliantly illuminated and dotted with chairs. The illuminated garden was one of Lady Huntsville's hobbies, which she delighted in throwing open to her guests when the occasion arose.

Sylvia found her fingers tucked into the crook of the earl's arm as he steered her onto the balcony.

"Allow me to take you strolling in the gardens," the earl murmured in her ear, causing Sylvia to feel a sudden tremor of excitement at the implications of such an invitation. "We must talk, Sylvia, and there is no privacy here."

As they reached the bottom of the stairs and the earl guided her along one of the many lighted paths that followed the flower beds and branched off under the trees, Sylvia glanced back and caught sight of Sir Matthew leaning over the balustrade watching them closely. She shuddered.

"Cold?" the earl inquired solicitously, pausing beside a laburnum bush heavy with blooms. "Shall I send for your shawl?"

Sylvia shook her head. "Tell me what you wish to talk about, my lord," she urged, her curiosity thoroughly piqued.

The earl did not answer until they reached a cluster of rosebushes arching over a stone bench half-hidden from the path. He led her into the small clearing, but when Sylvia attempted to sit, he turned her around to face him, both hands firmly clasping her arms.

He drew a deep, shuddering breath.

Sylvia stood passively in his embrace, her thoughts riotous with conflicting emotions. From such an intimate situation something definitive had to emerge. If it turned out to be only an offer of carte blanche, at least she would know that he did not care for her enough to make her happy. She could put all romantic notions regarding Nicholas Morley out of her head and carry on with her life.

"My cousin tells me he is about to be married."

Sylvia had expected anything but this. She answered before considering the consequences:

"Yes, that is what he says."

"And the name of this unfortunate lady is?"

Sylvia gasped in surprise and annoyance. Were they to waste these precious moments of privacy in discussing Matthew's ill-conceived plans for forcing her into a second betrothal?

"I fail to see what concern this lady is of yours, my lord," she said stiffly.

In the faint light from one of the lanterns on the path, Sylvia saw the earl's lips twitch into a smile.

"She is very much my concern, my dear Sylvia."

"I do not understand—"

"Here," he said, his voice suddenly gruff with emotion, "let me show you."

Before Sylvia could divine his intentions, he had pulled her unceremoniously into his arms and covered her mouth with his in a kiss that even in her most erotic fantasies—and there had been many of them of late—she had not imagined possible.

With a small sigh she surrendered, feeling her knees give way as she leaned against his chest, held firmly upright by two arms whose comforting strength she had felt before.

If this was the way a gentleman went about making an offer of *carte blanche*, she thought dizzily, there was no reason why she should not derive as much pleasure from him as possible. There was no telling when she would be kissed like this again. Perhaps never. The depressing thought caused her to press herself more urgently against the male form already plastered intimately to her own. The earl's response was a deep groan and a tightening of his already vice-like hold on her person.

Casting aside all pretense of decorum, Sylvia opened her mouth and traced his lips with her tongue.

Chapter Twenty-two

~

The Debt

Nicholas stood on the steps of Huntsville Hall, watching the Sutherland carriage disappear into the night. The swaying light of the carriage lantern became an intermittent flicker in the darkness, then disappeared entirely round the bend in the driveway. After the sounds of the chaise had died away, the earl turned to mount the stairs in search of his own party.

Sir Matthew Farnaby stood at the top of the steps, a singularly unpleasant smirk on his face.

Nicholas hesitated briefly. He would have preferred to avoid a confrontation with his cousin, but after what had occurred in the illuminated garden with Sylvia, he knew this to be impossible. That smirk told its own story. Nicholas had seen it often in the past, always as a harbinger of one of his cousin's vicious tantrums.

Even as a child Matt had been subject to uncontrollable rages when he was crossed. The earl could remember countless instances of unpleasantness and violent outbursts orchestrated— Nicholas did not doubt it—to ensure that his cousin got what he wanted. On those occasions when tantrums did not work, the object Matt had coveted invariably turned up broken. Not merely broken, but shattered into a thousand pieces, as if it had been hurled with deliberate force and malice.

Or it turned up dead.

In a vivid flash from the past, Nicholas remembered the first puppy his father had given him. There were plenty of other dogs on the estate, but they had belonged to his father: a noisy hunting pack, shaggy sheepdogs, and a testy old wolfhound called Nestor.

Major had been special, his own personal puppy. Brought down from Scotland after one of the former earl's fishing holidays with an old Oxford crony, the young mastiff had appealed to Nicholas's sense of adventure. Here was a dog worthy of a medieval knight. A dog who would wear a spiked collar and run beside his master's destrier when he rode into battle.

Only Major never lived long enough to do any of these things.

As the earl trod up the stone steps, his eyes riveted on his cousin's smirking face, he remembered with a pang of bitterness that the puppy had been found one morning floating in an abandoned well. That was the first time Nicholas recalled noticing Matt's smirk.

Deliberately, he put the memory aside. If he remembered too many of those apparent accidents that seemed to follow Matt around, Nicholas thought, he would give in to rage and do something he would regret.

If the earl had hoped to avoid unpleasantness, his cousin's first words dispelled any such hope.

"Well, well," the baronet sneered, his voice harsh and flat. "I never thought to see the high and mighty Earl of Longueville sniffing around the skirts of one of my castoffs. I wonder what Mrs. Rawson would make of that tasty piece of information." He snickered as though he had uttered a witticism.

Nicholas muttered an oath and clenched his fists, his resolution to avoid a dust-up with his cousin evaporating at this insult. Before he could carry out his intention, Sir Matthew stepped back, one hand raised in protest.

"Always ready to salvage a maiden's honor, I see." His cynical laugh grated on the earl's ears. "In this case you have arrived too late, old man. I shall be the one to rescue Sylvia from the consequences of her own folly. And when we are wed, she will no longer be anybody's castoff, now, will she? And you had better not lay a hand on her, my dear fellow. This woman is *mine*. You may consider yourself fortunate that I do not call you out for dragging the poor lass into the garden tonight. What did you do to her? Steal a kiss or two? There was hardly time for anything more . . . shall we say, incriminating. I trust she slapped your face for you, Cousin."

Rigid with rage, the earl listened to Farnaby's litany of insults and falsehoods with growing consternation. These were the wild ramblings of a madman, he thought. Could it be that his cousin's long-standing envy of everyone more fortunate than himself had affected his mind?

"What? The cat got your tongue, Cousin?" Matthew jeered. "Or your courage fail you, is that it?"

Before Nicholas could reply, he heard voices and saw his mother and Mrs. Hargate descending from the first floor, accompanied by Ransome. His Aunt Lydia stopped to take leave of her son, who had—the earl had witnessed it himself—spent a part of the evening charming his mother out of what little funds she carried in her reticule. The dowager swept past her disgraced nephew without so much as a glance, attaching herself imperiously to her son's arm.

As the Longueville carriage drew away from the Hall, the earl glanced back and saw his cousin still standing at the top of the stairs, feet apart, arms akimbo, defiance in every line of his body.

There was something openly threatening about Farnaby's posture that caused a tingle of apprehension to run down the earl's spine.

Nothing good would come out of tonight's tangled events. Of that he had no doubt at all.

Although she had not retired until very late the previous evening, Sylvia awoke at her usual early hour the day after the Huntsvilles' Ball. Her sleep had not been peaceful, and she detected the beginnings of a megrim as her abigail plumped the pillows and fussed over arranging the covers.

"Here is yer chocolate, milady. Nice and hot just as ye like it."

Sylvia watched as Molly poured the steaming liquid from the silver pot into the thick blue Staffordshire cup she had used every morning since she came to stay at Whitecliffs. It was a ritual of sorts, and unlike her aunt, who was a creature of impulse, Sylvia felt comfortable with rituals. They provided a sense of continuity, a pattern for living, the kind of predictable events out of which traditions were born.

She sipped the rich chocolate and debated the wisdom of attempting to get a few more hours of sleep.

"What is the weather like, Molly?" she demanded at length, knowing that if the sun was shining, she could not lie abed like some pampered London matron after an evening at the opera.

The abigail tugged on the thick velvet curtains. They parted in a soft rush to reveal the kind of cloudless blue sky that made

Sylvia's fingers itch to be at her palette. Discarding any further thoughts of sleep, she slid out of bed and sat down at her dressing table. Her jewelry box was still sitting there, and she lifted the nacre-encrusted lid. Her brother's pink diamonds lay on top where she had put them last night after the ball.

It dawned on her that John's imminent visit and her birthday had been relegated to the back of her mind by the excitement of last night's events. The shock of seeing her former betrothed and hearing his cajoling voice insisting that they might—if she were willing—relive that happiest period of her young life had left her unsettled and confused rather than overjoyed, as Sir Matthew seemed to expect. He had not been pleased at her refusal to grant him the dance he had requested, and the predatory look in his eyes had frightened her.

On the other hand, the earl's kiss had delighted her, reminding her of the joys of intimacy with a gentleman that had been denied her all these years. The memory of her immodest response to that embrace brought a tinge of color to her cheeks, and she shuddered.

"Not taking a chill, are ye, milady?" Molly demanded, a worried frown on her rosy face. "We cannot have ye taking sick, now, can we? Not with the viscount, yer brother, arriving any day now."

"Of course I am not sick, Molly, so do not go alarming the whole household with your silly rumors."

This was patently untrue, of course, Sylvia admitted reluctantly. She *was* sick, as sick as any moonstruck schoolroom chit over her first infatuation with some unattainable gentleman glimpsed tooling his sporting curricle in Hyde Park. But she would get over it, she told herself prosaically. She had got over Sir Matthew, had she not? And things had not gone nearly that far with the earl as they had with Matthew. At least not yet.

Sylvia suddenly wished they had. Then she would *know*, she told herself with unaccustomed recklessness. She would know again the dizzy delight of a man's intimate touch, of Nicholas's touch. She felt herself grow warm at the thought. Last night among the roses he had revealed a side of himself that had surprised and thrilled her. He had always been so reserved towards her, so cautious, as though he disapproved of displays of emotion. As cautious as that first tender kiss he had given her in the folly. But now she knew that beneath that enigmatic exterior lurked a man who could—and doubtless would if she gave him the slightest encouragement—delight her with a passion that matched her own.

Sylvia sighed and reached for her hairbrush. She had taken but two or three strokes when she heard a scratching at the door.

"Hobson heard you were up and about, milady. He thought you would wish to have these two letters, both delivered early this morning, he says."

Sylvia stared with a touch of alarm at the two pieces of folded vellum on the silver salver. She recognized both handwritings, one the insolent flourish of Sir Matthew, the other the neat, precise script of Nicholas Morley.

After a brief hesitation she picked up the earl's missive. Would she ride with him that afternoon? he wanted to know. He had something of vital importance to discuss with her. Of course she would, Sylvia thought, her spirits rising. She would go anywhere, do anything with him. Had she not made that abundantly clear last night with her response to his kiss?

She went over to her little escritoire and wrote a short reply, which she gave to Molly to take down to Hobson. Only after that was taken care of did she pick up Matthew's missive.

The second message was equally short but not nearly so pleasant. Sylvia's lips thinned at the peremptory tone of the baronet's note. Meet him at Pirate's Cove that afternoon, he commanded, or he would be forced to satisfy the curiosity of a certain vicar's wife whose penchant for gossip would spread the tale of Sylvia's disgrace the length and breadth of Cornwall.

And what about *his* disgrace? Sylvia thought rebelliously. How unfair that a man could do the most dastardly deeds—both she and the unfortunate countess could testify to that—and the world would look the other way. But if a female so much as looked askance, or dared to set her foot outside the prescribed path, she was damned forever.

Sylvia felt a sudden surge of compassion for the young countess. Whatever she had done, whatever mistakes she had made, she had not deserved to die for them, almost before her life had begun. Particularly not if she was carrying a child at the time. Nicholas's child perhaps.

This was a sobering thought, and Sylvia knew she must make a push to stop the man who might well have brought about the countess's downfall.

She must tell the earl. He had promised to send Matthew away if he bothered her. Well, he was bothering her, and it was time to fight back.

*   *   *

Nicholas read the letter again, then glanced up at the distraught face of his Aunt Lydia. A fresh wave of anger enveloped him, but he let none of his feelings show. It was characteristically callous of his cousin to use others for his own selfish ends; he had done so all his life, and Nicholas had little hope of his changing now.

He had fallen under the spell of Matt's charming persuasion himself any number of times, but he had never been reduced to the point of tears by his cousin's gifted rhetoric. The letter he held in his hand was a prime example of Matt's talent for exaggeration and falsehood. Not only was Debtors' Prison mentioned twice, but also gruesome examples of the penury and hardship endured by its unfortunate inmates. No wonder poor Aunt Lydia's face was tear-stained and anxious.

Nicholas could have strangled his cousin at that moment with the greatest pleasure. What kind of a son would deliberately put his mother through this kind of distress? The wretch knew him far too well, Nicholas thought disgustedly. Matt's repeated pleas for funds he could ignore, but his Aunt Lydia's tears touched his heart.

"How much do these debts add up to, Aunt?" he said finally, debating whether or not he should relent and pay off his cousin's notes if only to see his beloved aunt happy again. "Matt does not say."

"He was afraid you would be angry, Nicholas," Mrs. Hargate said in a shaky voice. "You know how upset the poor boy gets when he is crossed, dear."

Nicholas knew only too well how opposition affected his cousin. Unfortunately, he could not tell his aunt the more lurid details of her son's responses to being thwarted. He loved her too much to inflict that burden upon her.

"How much?" he repeated gently.

His aunt hesitated, twisting her hands nervously. "It is not as though I did not have the money, dear. Poor George left me more than well provided for."

"Yes, he certainly did," the earl replied grimly. "But so did Sir John, Matt's father. And I do not need to remind you, my dear Aunt, that your precious Matt wasted it all, including your portion, two years after my uncle died. Had I not stepped in, the estate would have been sold off."

He stopped abruptly, cursing himself for distressing his aunt by bringing all this up again. His cousin's sins were better left buried.

His past ones, that is. Nicholas was far more troubled by those his infamous cousin might commit in the future—and commit them he undoubtedly would.

"Oh, I know you are right, my dear Nicholas," his aunt said in a quavery voice. "There was certainly no love lost between my late husband and Matthew. But my poor boy was hurt when George named you executor of his will. He always felt left out, you know. As though George did not trust him."

"He was right," Nicholas could not help pointing out. "If he had, we would not be having this conversation. There would be no fortune left. Now tell me," he said in a gentler tone, "how much does your son need to give him a fresh start in life—to quote his own words," he added, glancing again at the paper in his hand.

"Twenty thousand pounds."

"Twenty thousand pounds?" Nicholas repeated, astonished in spite of himself at the enormity of his cousin's irresponsibility.

"Yes, dear. That is the sum he mentioned at the ball last night. He is desperate, poor boy. Terrified of Debtors' Prison, as you can see. He is depending on me to save him."

With an effort Nicholas kept his expression from revealing his contempt. How could he tell this woman that she was being used by a master deceiver? He himself felt the insidious tentacles of his cousin's machinations. This letter he held in his hand had been carefully constructed to play upon the earl's deep love for his aunt.

"And it is not as if this sum would be anything more than a loan," his aunt continued in a more cheerful voice. "Matthew swears he will repay me just as soon as he is married. He intends to move back to Farnaby Hall and set up his nursery, you see. I have been begging him to do so for years, of course, but he cannot be comfortable with this terrible debt hanging over his head, poor dear."

Nicholas was thunderstruck. "Married?" he repeated, stunned at his cousin's audacity. How could Matt dare to spread rumors of a match with a lady who, if last night's kisses were any indication, had no intention of renewing her aborted betrothal with the man who had betrayed her? But then again, a small voice reminded him, the Earl of Longueville was far from infallible in his selection of females.

Could he have made another mistake in Lady Sylvia?

"Am I to understand that my cousin has found a wealthy bride?"

His aunt brightened perceptibly. "Oh, yes, dear. Of course, it is still a secret, and Matthew warned me to tell no one but you, Nicholas, but he is to wed Lady Sylvia Sutherland. A charming girl, as you know."

Mrs. Hargate chattered on excitedly, but the earl heard none of it. A knot of anger grew in his stomach as he began to understand the full extent of his cousin's perfidy. Tell no one but him? How Matt must have enjoyed putting this piece of advice into his mother's willing ear, knowing that she would come straight to the earl with it. How ingenious, he thought. Matt had exceeded himself in vicious intrigue. He was cleverer, and far more dangerous, than Nicholas had imagined possible.

"Has the betrothal been formalized?" Nicholas hardly recognized his own voice as he asked this vital question.

"If you mean, has the announcement been sent to the *Gazette*, no, not yet, dear," his aunt replied, seemingly unaware of the chaos her revelations had created in her nephew. "But Matthew tells me she has accepted him," she added, a smile chasing away her former anxiety. "All the poor dear needs is your assurance that he may start his married life free of debt."

Nicholas felt as though a stake had been driven through his heart. Could any of this be true? he wondered, his mind struggling with the ugly suspicions planted there by his cousin's clever manipulations. There was only one way to find out. He must confront Sylvia herself this afternoon during their ride together. He could not afford to put his suspicions aside until after he was irrevocably tied to her, as he had done with Angelica.

The irony of the situation was not lost on Nicholas, as he was sure his devious cousin had intended. Here he was on the brink of selecting a second countess, and the very man who had come between the earl and his first countess appeared to be repeating his despicable performance with the second.

Nicholas felt the tentacles of his cousin's malice, vindictiveness, and spite tightening around him. The air fairly crackled with a sense of danger. The earl's skin crawled with apprehension, and he felt chilled, as though he had witnessed an aberration so horrendous he could not name it.

Jason's dire warnings flooded back to him, and for the first time Nicholas believed them. He himself might—nay, he *must* if Matt's plans to step into his shoes were to bear fruit—be the next victim.

Abruptly, Nicholas folded his cousin's letter and stuffed it into his pocket. "Allow me to keep this, Aunt," he said in response to her startled glance. "I will speak to Matthew myself and see what can be done. In the meantime, do not worry your head on the matter. I know my mother is counting on your help with her guest list for the house party she is planning. Leave this matter to me."

He watched his aunt's solid figure trip off down the hall, and felt the overwhelming need to protect this beloved woman from the machinations of her own son.

And Sylvia, too, he thought, turning to go upstairs to change into his riding clothes. He would save her from the consequences of her own folly, if indeed she had done the unthinkable and accepted the man who wanted her for all the wrong reasons.

How could he be so sure that his own reasons were the right ones? he found himself asking an hour later as he mounted and turned Arion's head towards Whitecliffs. The question made Nicholas smile for the first time since he had read his cousin's letter.

He knew the answer lay in his heart, and he was determined that Sylvia would know it, too, before the day was over.

Chapter Twenty-three

~

Kidnapped

The sky was no longer cloudless, nor the sun so brilliant when Lady Sylvia descended to the front hall shortly after nuncheon, dressed in her slate gray riding habit. She paused before the portrait of *The Lady in Gray,* as she often did, and gazed up at the radiant happiness reflected in the painted face. This was how she would appear if her aunt were to paint her portrait again today, Sylvia thought, conscious of the glow of joy that made her heart sing.

"You look very pleased with yourself this afternoon, my dear." A melodious voice broke into her reverie, and Sylvia turned to see her aunt coming out of the library. "I trust his lordship does not plan to ride too far, Sylvia. The weather is changing, and Hobson says that we may get some rain."

"We shall be back long before that, Aunt," Sylvia replied, adjusting her little gray beaver more firmly on her head, so the pink feather curled seductively against her cheek. "I expect Longueville will want to stay for tea. You know how much he enjoys Cook's tarts."

Lady Marguerite merely smiled enigmatically and swept down the hall towards the back of the house. Sylvia suspected her aunt entertained some romantic notion of a match between the unsuspecting earl and her niece. Vain daydreaming, of course, but since she shared the same fantasy, Sylvia could hardly accuse her aunt of foolishness.

Dick, the undergroom, was holding Greyboy for her at the bottom of the front steps when Hobson opened the door. The gelding was restless, and Sylvia felt guilty for not taking him out more often.

"Morning, milady," the boy said cheerily. "Old Greyboy is feeling 'is oats, 'e is. Fair itching for a gallop."

"So I see," Lady Sylvia replied, running her gloved hand down the gelding's sleek neck. "We shall have to do something about that, old boy." The horse turned his head and nibbled at the sleeve of her riding jacket with velvety lips.

Hobson, who had come down to stand beside her, looked up at the scudding clouds and shook his head. "Looks like rain, milady," he said lugubriously. "Old Jake has been saying so since yesterday. Gardeners always know these things, and Jake is hardly ever wrong."

From her seat on the tall horse, Sylvia looked down on her aunt's ancient butler and smiled brightly. No threat of rain was going to keep her from riding out today. Nicholas had invited her. He had something of importance to discuss with her, his note had said. Something of importance? Of *vital* importance were his actual words, and Sylvia could not wait.

"I shall return long before it rains, Hobson," she promised. And with that she was gone, cantering down the driveway, past Giovanni's statue of the naked Diana beside her lily pond, under the shady arch of the ancient lime trees that must have witnessed the passage of Lady Giselda on her wild moonlit sorties, past the fierce stone lions with their gray eyes fixed on the cliffs in the distance, eyes that had seen more than their share of Sutherland history.

She turned left towards Mullion and pulled Greyboy down to a sedate trot. It was still early, and Sylvia did not wish to appear too anxious, too eager to see *him* again. Although the very fact that she was out on the public road at all, instead of waiting in the drawing room, as a proper lady should, would have damned her in the eyes of London's Beau Monde. But this was not London, Sylvia reminded herself. This was the tip of Cornwall, as far away from the Metropolis as one could get short of stepping into the Channel. Here she could escape from prying eyes, from censure, from tedious restrictions. Here she was safe.

Except for . . . Sylvia jerked her thoughts away from the one flaw in her happiness. But surely Sir Matthew could not harm her here? So close to home? And so close to Nicholas, who had kissed her last night as she had dreamed he would, and who had promised to protect her from his cousin.

Above her the sky seemed to be clearing, and a weak sun glinted through the gray clouds. Sylvia's first impulse was to take this as a good omen, but a familiar prickling of premonition made her uneasy.

Then suddenly she saw him, a solitary rider cresting a rise ahead, and all caution evaporated. He was early, too, she thought, elated at the notion that the man she loved was as impatient as she. Greyboy must have detected her excitement, for he nickered and broke into a canter, ears pointed towards the approaching horseman.

Too late, Sylvia saw that the rider, whose horse had also quickened its pace, was not the Earl of Longueville.

"Well met, my love," Sir Matthew drawled softly, his eyes roving over her lazily. "It pleases me immeasurably to see you so anxious for my company that you venture out alone, Sylvia."

He pulled up beside her, his knee brushing hers. "But then, you always were a reckless chit, my dear. I remember it well. A trait that I found most endearing. And convenient, too, of course." He laughed gently, as though at some private joke, and Sylvia shivered at the sound of it.

Sylvia tried to move away from the touch of his knee, but the baronet's hand shot out and grasped Greyboy's bridle. "No need for alarm, my love. After all, there is nothing I can do to your sweet self that I have not done before, now, is there?" He sniggered then, and Sylvia felt a tremor of panic. "I am quite looking forward to renewing our amorous games," he added with a suggestive wink that made Sylvia's blood run cold. "You were such a willing pupil, my dear. One of the best. I was devastated when your father snatched you away from me. Heartless of him, you must agree, love. What did he hope to achieve, after all? You were quite, quite ruined by then, of course. Why not allow us to marry? I could have used the blunt, let me tell you. Pockets to let and the bailiffs breathing down my neck. I expected you to convince the old fool to countenance the match, Sylvia, but when I received no word from you, I realized you had cast me aside. Broke my heart it did, love. Almost put me off women for good, I swear."

Sylvia listened with growing consternation to this litany of lies. She was appalled at the cast he had put upon an experience that had meant the world to her, and broken her heart into a thousand pieces when he had not come to claim her. He made it seem all her fault, she thought indignantly. She wondered if the rogue had been able to explain away his affair with the countess as easily.

"If you will excuse me, my lord," she said stiffly, "I am expected at the Castle." She pulled on the gelding's reins, but Farnaby merely grinned and edged his horse closer.

"That is another bone of contention, my love," he drawled, leaning over until Sylvia felt his breath on her face. "I cannot have my betrothed disappearing behind the bushes with other men, now, can I? Particularly not one who is showing all the signs of a man in love. Or, not to put too fine a point to it, a man who is hot for you, sweetheart. I cannot have my future wife spreading her charms about indiscriminately. No, sir, I can overlook any past indiscretions, of course, and knowing what a shameless little chit you were at eighteen, Sylvia, I can believe there must have been several."

"There you are off the mark, sir," Sylvia interrupted, her anger aroused. "I am not your betrothed. And you had better release me at once, or—"

"Or what?" Farnaby laughed, and Sylvia did not like the sound of it. "You will run to tell my cousin? Has the white knight promised to save you from the dragon? Is that it? Perhaps he has even offered to wed you, my dear. How unkind of him to deceive you. Our starched-up Nicholas is not a man to take other men's leavings, I should warn you, dearest."

He seemed to find this terribly amusing, for he let out a wild crack of laughter. The humor did not reach his eyes, however, and Sylvia felt a sudden chill, as though the gentleman she had thought she knew so well had turned into a total stranger. A dangerous stranger.

"So you can forget about becoming a countess, Sylvia, my pet."

"His lordship has never given any indication of such a possibility," Sylvia replied coldly. And unfortunately that was true. Except for that revealing kiss last night, the earl had been cautious in his dealings with her.

"That I can well believe," Sir Matthew said with a smirk. "Our dear old Nick has no intention of offering you anything honorable, Sylvia, so put that out of your pretty head. Much better to take my offer and become Lady Farnaby, my dear girl. And who knows? If some accident should befall our Nicholas—and one can never be sure when accidents will happen, as Angelica found out—" He paused abruptly and sneered, as though deciding not to reveal his thoughts on the matter.

Farnaby stared at her for several moments, during which Sylvia felt her skin crawl. The look in Matthew's eyes was not entirely sane, she thought, wondering what he could hope to achieve by detaining her against her will.

"I really must go, Matthew," she said, fighting to keep her voice from trembling. "I am on an errand for my aunt," she lied, hoping to persuade him to let her go.

"Are you, now?" he said sarcastically. "I wonder why I do not believe you, Sylvia. I suspect you are off to a secret rendezvous with my esteemed cousin." He paused and stared at her with hard, cold eyes. "You are wasting your time, my love, and making me very angry with you. And believe me, love, you do not want to make me angry with you. I may do something I will regret, and you will most certainly regret it."

Sylvia glanced down the lane in the direction of Longueville Castle, but no horseman—no white knight, as Matthew had called him—came riding over the hill to rescue her.

Farnaby laughed, and the sound grated on her ears. "He will not come, my love. So why not be reasonable? Give me the answer I wish to hear from your sweet lips. Say you will marry me and all will be well."

"I shall never consent to wed you, Matthew," she said coldly. "You are a fool if you believe that I could care for the man who betrayed me. So release me this instant, or I shall complain to your cousin."

Too late Sylvia saw that her rejection had been too harsh for the baronet's patience. Or perhaps it had been unwise of her to mention the earl. Whatever the cause, Sir Matthew's face turned an ugly shade of purple, and his grip on Greyboy's bridle tightened until the horse jerked his head in fright.

"So," he snarled in a tone Sylvia had never heard him use before, "you have set your heart on being a countess, have you? Well, let me warn you that will never happen. Only look what happened to that slut Angelica when she chose to be a countess instead of a baroness. She might have been alive today had she chosen wisely. But no, nothing I said could convince her that we might live well enough at Farnaby Hall with her dowry and the rents from the estate."

Appalled at what she was hearing, Sylvia shrank back from the ugliness Matthew hurled at her.

"You mean, you were b-betrothed to Angelica?" she murmured disjointedly, not quite believing her ears.

Farnaby glowered at her. "What do you think I mean?" he snarled. "Until that cousin of mine came along and filled her head with dreams of being a pampered countess, Angelica was mine. Nicholas took her away from me. But he did not enjoy her for long, you know. I saw to that."

Sylvia shuddered at the implications of Farnaby's admission. Her alarm must have been apparent, for the baronet grimaced at her. "I am not a man to trifle with, my love," he said in a gentler voice. "But do not try my patience too far, Sylvia, or you will come to the same fate. I will not be thwarted a second time by that pompous fool. I shall make sure that he does not interfere this time."

Before Sylvia realized what he was about, she felt the reins jerked out of her hands, and found herself a prisoner led along helplessly beside the baronet.

"Where are you taking me?" she demanded, with as much force as she could muster, as they turned back towards Helston.

"You will know soon enough, my dear," he replied with another ugly laugh.

Premonitions of disaster flooded Sylvia's consciousness, and she saw in her mind's eye where Matthew was taking her. Of course, she thought, her heart cringing inside her. Where else but Pirate's Cove and that sinister stone hut?

Frantically, Sylvia glanced around, hoping for the sight of someone, anyone who would dare to confront Sir Matthew and put an end to this nightmare. But there was no one in sight.

And then she saw a movement in a clump of brambles. Inexplicably, for there was no breeze. Had she imagined it, or had there been a face peering at her through the leaves? Hastily, she withdrew her gaze, fearful of alerting Matthew to the presence of a witness.

When she glanced again, she was sure of it. Little Timmy Collins was staring at her with round eyes jumping out of his face.

Sylvia relaxed infinitesimally. She might yet be saved.

"Steady, boy. Steady."

Nicholas let out a muttered oath as Arion shied violently, almost unseating him. Once he had controlled the horse, the earl glanced around to see what had startled the big bay.

A small, grubby lad stood barefoot on the grassy verge, huge eyes staring up at him. He appeared to be out of breath, for his thin chest heaved and his mouth hung open. After a brief pause Nicholas recognized the urchin as the son of one of his tenants, one of the Collins boys from the village who had posed in several of Lady Sylvia's paintings. What was the child doing so far from home? he wondered.

"Trying to break my neck, lad?" he growled, keeping a firm hand on the reins. Once aroused, Arion appeared to be toying with the idea of bolting. The big horse sidled nervously, tossing his head up and down.

"Oh, no, m'lord," the lad said in his reed-like voice, one child-ish hand touching his forelock. "But you must come, m'lord. 'Tis urgent."

Now that Nicholas had recovered from the shock of almost coming a cropper, he remembered where he had last seen the boy. "You are the lad who brought that old letter to Lady Sylvia over at Pirate's Cove, are you not?" he demanded, a coil of fear unwind-ing in his stomach.

"Aye, m'lord. Me name is Timmy. But that ain't what I come fer. 'Er ladyship sent me. Or no, she dinna send me exactly. But she wanted me to come, I saw it plain-like. She would 'ave said it, m'lord. She did say it, with 'er peepers, that is. 'Er ladyship couldna speak, yer see. But I known at once she wanted me to come fer you, m'lord. So I run all the way."

Breathing heavily and obviously exhausted by his long speech, Timmy stared at the earl expectantly.

Nicholas listened to this garbled speech with growing appre-hension. "Are you telling me that Lady Sylvia is in danger?" he de-manded sharply, unwilling to believe the lad's jumbled message. "Did she send you to find me?"

The lad looked at Nicholas disgustedly, and the earl felt as though he had not lived up to the lad's expectations.

"Aye, m'lord," was all he said, however.

"And she needs my help?"

"Aye," the lad repeated patiently, and the earl knew he had been labeled a slow-top by a twelve-year-old. "I couldna do it meself, yer see. The gent was too big, and as mean as old Dudley's prize boar—"

"What gent is this?" Nicholas interrupted, his premonition of danger growing.

"The one as nabbed 'er ladyship."

Nicholas felt his jaw drop. "Nabbed her?"

"Aye. Nabbed 'er. Loped off with 'er. I couldna do nothin' to stop 'im. I only had me slingshot, ye see." Timmy reached into his back pocket and pulled out the crude weapon. "No good against a big blighter like that."

The earl felt his blood run cold. "Are you saying that someone kidnapped Lady Sylvia?" A flicker of impatience in the boy's eyes caused Nicholas to add, "Where did he take her?"

"Pirate's Cove," came the terse reply. "Ye'd best 'urry, m'lord. Said 'e'd kill 'er, same as the other lady, if she gave 'im any trouble.'

Convinced that the lad was not making up a Canterbury tale, the earl was about to clap heels to his mount when he remembered something.

"Do you know Captain Ransome, lad?"

Timmy grinned. "Everybody knows the captain, m'lord."

Nicholas tossed him a shilling, which the lad caught and slipped into his pocket. "Find him for me and tell him what you have just told me, Timmy. Tell him to come to Pirate's Cove as soon as he can."

And then the earl gave Arion his head. Sylvia needed him. He was well aware who that other gent was who had kidnapped his love. What his cousin's motive could be for taking her to Pirate's Cove, Nicholas could only guess. But he did not for a moment believe Matt's intentions were honest.

Timmy's ominous words rang in his head as he raced along the Helston Road. *Said 'e'd kill 'er, same as the other lady, if she gave 'im any trouble.* That *other lady* could be none other than Angelica, Nicholas realized as the truth of his cousin's threat sank in. He had been right—he was dealing with a madman.

The past was repeating itself in more ways than one, and his Cousin Matt, confident in winning this test of wills, as he had won so many times before, was about to taste defeat.

Nicholas had promised to protect Sylvia from his cousin, a promise he intended to keep.

Chapter Twenty-four

~

Pirate's Cove Revisited

Far too soon for Lady Sylvia's peace of mind, they came in sight of the mysterious stone hut where so many of the dramatic events leading up to her present predicament had played themselves out. As Sir Matthew dismounted and tied the two horses to a wind-battered grove of maritime pines, Sylvia glanced furtively about for a means of escape. She found none, so was forced to submit to being pulled roughly from Grayboy's back. The possessive touch of her captor's hands on her waist frightened her, but she refused to show it.

"Well, love," Sir Matthew murmured close to her ear as he guided her, one arm firmly wrapped around her, towards the narrow stone steps, "here we are. An ideal spot for an amorous rendezvous, do you not agree? I always found it so. The locals rarely if ever come near the place because they believe it inhabited by ghosts of dead women." He paused, then let out a cynical chuckle. "They may well be right. So do not look for help in that quarter, my sweet." He threw back his head and laughed again, a high-pitched, raucous sound that rang eerily in the still, darkening afternoon.

"You surely do not mean to force me to wed you against my will, Matthew," she said, forcing herself to keep her panic at bay. "I never took you to be cruel. Careless perhaps, but never deliberately hurtful."

They reached the steps, and Sir Matthew drew her closer to his side as they descended the narrow steps together. "No, my sweet love," he whispered as they stepped onto the uneven rock floor around the hut, "never hurtful, especially to those I love. And as for you, Sylvia, I intend to show you just how much I adore you, sweetheart. Always provided you do not cross me," he added in a sinister tone. "I cannot answer for my actions if you cross me."

"If you truly loved me, as you say, Matthew, you would let me go," she said, grasping at any straw.

"Come, Sylvia, no more questions. You must believe that what I do is for the best." So saying, he dragged her towards the door of the hut, pushed it open, and pulled her inside.

The interior of the hut, which Sylvia had never dared enter before, was dim, and she had to wait a moment for her eyes to adjust. She glanced curiously about her. The room was smaller than she had imagined, but had a cozy though unkempt air about it, as though it had not been used since the countess's death ten years earlier.

Sylvia could not suppress a shudder as the charged atmosphere of the hut began to work on her sensibilities. Call it foolishness, she thought, but her senses were picking up the vibrations of an invisible presence in the tiny room. It was all in her imagination, of course, she reminded herself, having experienced similar sensations many times before during her painting sessions, when she had been able to *see* shapes and colors that were not there. At least not visibly there.

Her premonitions were rarely mistaken. Even now Sylvia caught the heavy scent of flowers, a heady perfume that she found too provocative for her own taste. A woman's perfume here in this desolate place?

A movement at the door reminded her that she was wasting precious time. Instead of trying to commune with ghosts, she should be looking about for a means of escape. Glancing over her shoulder, Sylvia saw that Matthew still stood on the threshold, his gaze fixed on the scattered clumps of pine, scraggly junipers, and an occasional larch through which they had just ridden. Did he fear pursuit? she wondered. Her thoughts flew to Timmy, and she offered up a small prayer that the bright lad had understood the frantic message in her eyes, and was even now at the Castle, urging the earl to come to her rescue.

In the meantime, her practical self reminded her, she had best fend for herself. But by what means?

It was then her darting gaze fell upon the flowers, and she smiled as the mystery of the perfume resolved itself. They sat on the narrow mantel, in a squat jelly-jar, a modest posy of wild lupines, two or three tall blue delphiniums from someone's garden, and a single white rose, arranged with apparent care.

Sylvia's thoughts flashed back to the afternoon she had seen George Connan, the Helston bookseller, place a similar modest bouquet on the window ledge of the hut. The same bouquet the Longueville agent had thrown over the cliff into the sea. Well, here was one bouquet Tom Gates had not found, she thought, absurdly pleased that the countess had enjoyed at least one of poor Mr. Connan's tributes.

Suddenly, Sylvia heard the door slam behind her and whirled to see Matthew standing there, a calculating smile on his handsome face.

"What? No weeping and swooning and calling for hartshorn?" he asked in a mocking tone. "I am glad to see you have sense enough not to send me into the boughs with futile female farradiddle, my dear. Never could abide those Cheltenham tragedies. Angelica was addicted to such nonsensical displays of temper, and I warned her often enough that she would rue the day she riled me beyond bearing. And I was right, of course. Little enough good her hysterics did her in the end."

An uncomfortable silence followed this revealing remark, which Sylvia did her best to ignore. It would do her as little good as it had done the poor countess to dissolve into hysterics now, she thought. Far better to pretend that this was a normal conversation, a rendezvous between lovers. Anything but what it might well turn into. A repetition of an act of violence that had shocked the neighborhood and left the master of Longueville without a wife.

The baronet smiled at her then, and Sylvia braced herself, dredging up a weak smile in response.

"Let us see how reasonable you can be, my love," he murmured in a low voice, so like the seductive tones of their first encounters that for a giddy moment Sylvia imagined herself back at the Blue Duck Inn in Dover with a younger, more charming, gentler Matthew whose kisses she had craved and whose hands had guided her into womanhood.

He walked over to stand before her, gazing deeply into her eyes until Sylvia felt mesmerized. He trailed a finger down her face, then raised her chin and lowered his mouth to hers.

Determined not to provoke the baronet by resisting his advances, Sylvia remained passive, hoping against hope that he would demand no more of her. She realized that she had misjudged him when his arms enveloped her and he jerked her against him roughly.

"Show a little enthusiasm when your future husband kisses you, my girl, or I shall have to give you graphic lessons on how to keep a gentleman happy."

Gingerly, Sylvia slid one arm up his sleeve and round his neck. This appeared to satisfy him momentarily, for he lowered his head to nuzzle her neck and bosom. It was all she could do to suppress her distaste for his hot breath burning her skin, but when she felt evidence of his desire pressing against her, she was unable to stand this repulsive invasion any longer.

"I do not remember you being such a bully, Matthew," she protested as mildly as she could. "You have changed far more than I thought possible over the years. I had such fond memories of our short time together," she continued, instilling a hint of nostalgia into her voice. This at least was true, of course. Her memories of their short-lived *marriage* were pleasant if hazy and centered on a laughing, teasing Matthew who was a far cry from the moody, violent man who now held her prisoner in his arms.

"You are mistaken, my dear," he said, pulling back to gaze hotly into her eyes. "I am no bully, and when you are my wife, you will find me the gentlest of husbands, I swear."

Before Sylvia could think up a suitable reply to this outrageous lie, she sensed the earl's approach moments before she actually heard the racing of his horse's hooves. How she knew it was the earl, she did not stop to ponder. Her whole attention was focused on keeping the baronet distracted long enough for her rescuer to arrive.

She returned Matthew's gaze with a smile and lowered her lashes provocatively. "I do believe you, Matthew," she began, but was cut short when the baronet released her abruptly and swore a string of oaths as he jerked the door open and peered out.

"Your white knight has arrived, my dear," he sneered at her over his shoulder. "But never fear. I am more than a match for him."

Sylvia saw a lathered Arion pulled to an abrupt halt amid a scattering of loose stones, and the earl fling himself from the saddle and race down the steps, two at a time.

Matthew slammed the door and glanced around for the wooden bar that held it shut. "Hand me that bar," he growled, pointing to a short length of wood lying beside the hearth. "Quickly!"

Sylvia made no move to obey.

The baronet's face turned an ugly red. "Do as I tell you, bitch," he shouted, bracing his shoulder against the door, which buckled visibly under the assault from outside. "Or I shall teach you a lesson you will never forget. The bar, quickly!"

Moving with deliberate slowness, Sylvia picked up the piece of thick wood.

The baronet held out his hand for the bar, but Sylvia continued to ignore him. Without it whoever was outside trying to get in— and she gloried in the knowledge that it was Nicholas—would eventually break the door wide open.

And he would save her, she thought, making no move to approach her captor. She wondered if she had the strength to raise the wooden brace and hit him with it. Appalled at the violent thoughts this man had generated in her, Sylvia gripped the bar with both hands and remained rigid, staring with growing anxiety as the door buckled more under each blow from outside.

Without warning, Matthew stepped back, and the door slammed open. The earl came flying in, carried by the impulse of his own blows. Tripping on the uneven stones, he was thrown spread-eagled onto the dilapidated settee, covered with an old wool rug in a faded red and blue tartan. The ancient settee, weakened by years of ravaging by rodents, collapsed with a loud crack and overturned in a cloud of dust, landing the earl on the stone floor.

When he groaned but made no move to rise, Sylvia took a step towards the inert form, but felt herself violently jerked back.

"Oh, no, you do not, you sneaky little bitch," Matthew snarled. "You will never belong to *him,* I can promise you that."

With that, the baronet picked her up and strode outside. When he rounded the seaward corner of the hut, Sylvia gasped in terror. Was she about to be tossed over the cliff to her certain death? Exactly as the young countess—Sylvia saw the scene clearly in a flash of intuition—had been flung over the edge by a man driven mad by thwarted passion?

Without warning he put her down, and she found herself standing on the edge of the cliff, the dark green sea swirling against the rocks fifty feet below.

Nicholas opened his eyes and blinked. He lay flat on his face on a stone floor, and it took him a second or two to remember how he got there. When the events came flooding back, he staggered to his feet, wincing at his aching shoulder, which he had used to throw himself against the door of the hut. A single glance around the tiny room told him that his quarry had fled. With a groan he ran out. Matt was capable of anything, and in his cousin's present crazed state, Nicholas feared for Sylvia's safety.

The sound of a strident, angry voice drew him round the corner of the hut at a run. What he saw brought him to an abrupt halt, his heart in his mouth.

His cousin stood at the edge of the cliff, legs spread and hair tousled by the breeze coming from the sea. At first glance Nicholas thought Matt was alone, and his world tilted sickeningly as the image of Sylvia crushed and broken on the rocks below flashed through his mind. Then his cousin moved and there she was, standing perilously close to the precipice, her face pale and drawn. Nicholas drew a great, shuddering breath of relief.

But there was no time to lose. Matt held Lady Sylvia by one arm and was shouting at her. Every now and then he shook her viciously, and to the earl's horrified gaze it appeared as though his beloved was in imminent danger of falling backwards over the cliff.

As Nicholas racked his brain feverishly for a means of preventing the disaster that enfolded before his eyes, snatches of his cousin's words reached him.

". . . lied to me, she did. Thought she could keep me at her beck and call, the little slut."

Matt shook her again, and Nicholas's heart stood still as Sylvia swayed over the edge. She uttered a little shriek, and Nicholas braced to fling himself upon his cousin. But at the last moment he paused, knowing that any false move on his part would precipitate disaster rather than prevent it. His cousin was sure to thrust her over the edge at the first sign of interference.

"Reject me, would you?" he screamed in a voice that reminded Nicholas of his cousin's childhood tantrums. "No woman rejects Matthew Farnaby and lives to boast of it, let me tell you. I warned you ten years ago, but you would not listen, you lying little tramp."

"You are confused, Matthew," Sylvia cried, struggling to free herself. "I never rejected you ten years ago; we were to be married, remember? You loved me or so you—"

"Married?" His cousin's voice rose hysterically. "Of course we were to be married, you two-faced strumpet. But you jilted me when that cousin of mine came sniffing around."

"I never knew your cousin then, Matthew," Sylvia pleaded. "Please be reasonable."

"Reasonable? How can you ask me to be reasonable when I am surrounded by conniving, deceitful females? Heartless sluts every one of you. You deceived me once, Angelica, and now you want to do so again, do you? Well, let me tell you something, Angel, I know what to do with deceitful chits like—"

"I am *not* Angelica," Sylvia interrupted, her voice rising with frustration.

The baronet lifted her bodily from the ground and shook her violently, sending her hat with its saucy pink feather flying over the cliff and spilling a cascade of auburn curls down her back. Nicholas clenched his fists, but dared not make a move. How could he live with himself if by some careless act, the woman he loved was thrown to her death by a madman?

"Are you not?" Farnaby snarled, holding her aloft for an interminable instant before putting her down again. "Then I should not be surprised to hear you deny you are carrying my child, I suppose. If you can lie about that, Angel, you can lie about anything."

"Of course I am not carrying your child, Matthew. You are being quite ridic—"

"You swore you were, and now you say you are not. What kind of a harpy are you, Angelica, to mock a man by promising him a son and then snatching that joy away?"

"I never promised you a son, Matthew," Sylvia insisted, and Nicholas could tell from the quaver in her voice that she was becoming increasingly frightened at Matt's wild accusations. "And I am not Angelica. I am Sylvia. Look at me, Matthew. Have you forgotten the Blue Duck Inn at Dover, where my father caught up with us? Remember the gilded music box you gave me that played 'Greensleeves'? You got so tired of hearing it you threatened to throw it out of the window?"

"Of course I remember that infernal noise," Farnaby growled. "But it was your brother who tossed the damned thing into the street, Angelica, not I."

"My brother? But you never met John. He was away in Scotland at the time. It was you who—"

"Cease this infernal bickering, Angelica," the baronet shouted, giving Sylvia another shake that made Nicholas catch his breath. "It was Jean-Claude who agreed we had heard quite enough of that maudlin ditty. And the box was not gilded, it was lacquered rosewood. I remember it distinctly."

"Jean-Claude? Surely you are mistaken, Matthew; my brother's name is John. And the box you gave me was *not* rosewood. I, too, remember it clearly, unless . . ." She paused, and Nicholas saw the puzzled expression on her face.

"What are you jabbering about now?" his cousin demanded harshly.

"Unless you gave her a music box, too," Nicholas heard Sylvia say in a choked voice. "Did you? Oh, Matthew! How *could* you?"

Her voice was so full of anguish that for a wrenching moment Nicholas felt his heart plummet. Was it possible that Lady Sylvia harbored a *tendre* for the man who had betrayed her?

"You said you adored it, Angelica," he snapped impatiently. "Now, where is that damned brother of yours? He was supposed to meet us here to help plan our escape."

"Plan our escape?" Sylvia repeated hesitantly. "What escape are you talking about, Matthew?"

"I forbid you to play your bird-witted games with me, Angelica," Matt warned. "Do not mistake me for that idiot husband of yours, my love. I am not to be hoodwinked by your pretty face and provocative smiles."

"But, Matthew, I truly do not know what you mean—"

"You did not imagine that I would allow Longueville to raise my son, did you?"

"There is no son, Matthew, have I not told you so?"

"That was another of your lies, Angelica," Nicholas heard his cousin say. "I know how you delight in tormenting me. But when we run off together, Nicholas will be branded as a cuckold before the entire *ton*. He is bound to divorce you, my love, and then we can be married, as we should have been months ago before he turned your silly head with his title and wealth."

Nicholas listened to this with growing apprehension and no little revulsion at the depths of his cousin's iniquity. And of Angelica's. He had been taken in by the tangled web of deceit and lies his wife had woven, and it appeared from his cousin's ravings that Matt had been as neatly duped by the countess's selfish games as he had himself.

But Angelica and her sins, which Nicholas had ceased to deny since reading that long-lost letter from Matt to his wife, lay in the past. She no longer had the power to hurt him, and he realized with a start of surprise that his heart no longer ached at the memory of her betrayal. It ached to hold Sylvia safe in his arms, to save her from the monster who had her in his power. From the cousin he had known all his life as unstable, selfish, and vindictive, but who had now blossomed before his eyes into a full-blown bedlamite.

The earl's musing were interrupted by the sound of a horse approaching at breakneck speed. He heard Jason's shout and glanced over his shoulder as his friend flung himself from the lathered horse and stood poised at the top of the steps, taking in the spectacle on the cliff.

When he looked back, his gaze clashed with his cousin's startled face. He saw Matt's expression turn thunderous and heard his voice grate across the space that separated them.

"Welcome, Cousin," the baronet drawled at his most cynical. "You and your friend are just in time to congratulate us on our betrothal. As you see, Nicky, I have won the day and stolen this lovely lady from you. Meet my affianced bride, gentlemen. Is that not so, my sweet?"

He transferred his grasp from Sylvia's arm to her hand, which he raised to his lips with an exaggerated courtly movement. "Tell them you are mine, Angelica," he commanded.

Nicholas detected Lady Sylvia's intention in her eyes, but before he could warn against taking foolish chances, she had ripped her hand from his cousin's grasp and stumbled across the space that separated them, falling into his arms with a moan of sheer relief. From the corner of his eye Nicholas saw a pale-faced lad step from the shelter of the hut wall, slingshot poised.

Taken by surprise, Sir Matthew uttered a coarse oath and whirled to follow Sylvia. Before he had taken even one step, however, he paused abruptly and rocked back on his heels, one hand flying to his temple. Then he tottered, and before Nicholas could fully comprehend what was happening, he saw his cousin sway backwards, dangerously close to the edge.

And then he was gone. The cliff where moments before his cousin and Sylvia had stood arguing was empty.

Nicholas braced himself, and then he heard it. A thin wail of indescribable terror keening up the face of the cliff and spilling over the rim for a second before being cut off abruptly by a dull thud.

The silence that followed was the loudest sound Nicholas had ever heard in his life.

Chapter Twenty-five

~

A Birthday Surprise

Lady Sylvia stood at the bow window in the Italian Saloon, watching the rain beat its monotonous tattoo against the glass. It had rained fitfully all week, ever since that harrowing afternoon at Pirate's Cove, when the darkening sky had seemed to presage the dire events that followed.

The desolate Cornish countryside lay soggy and uninviting around Whitecliffs, and even the garden was beginning to shed its summer colors. The roses sagged on their long stems, dropping their pink petals one by one under the persistent onslaught of water.

Sylvia sighed as another gust of wind scattered a cloud of petals across the grass. She knew how the roses must be feeling, for she felt much the same way herself, wilted and spiritless. Almost as though some vital element had been lost from her life. This mawkishness was unlike her, but she seemed unable to shake off the chill that had enveloped her that afternoon on the cliff when she had realized that she was in the hands of a madman.

"Do come and sit down, Sylvia," her aunt called from behind her. "Missing your tea will not bring your brother here any quicker, my dear, I can assure you. The roads must be appalling after all this rain, and John is probably bogged down somewhere between Shaftesbury and Exeter."

"I had pictured him already past Launceston," Sylvia replied without turning from her perusal of the rain, "perhaps even stopping for a bite to eat at the Stag and Horn there. You know how much he praised their roast duckling last time he visited us."

Reluctantly, Sylvia turned away from the window and made her way across the luxuriant Axminster to take her place on the elegant brocade sofa beside Lady Marguerite. She could not very well confess to her aunt that it was not John who had occupied her thoughts as she stood by the window. Her eagerness to see her brother had been eclipsed by the anxiety she felt over the Earl of Longueville's prolonged absence from the Castle.

What could be keeping him? she asked herself for perhaps the fifth time that day, absently stirring a lump of sugar into the tea her aunt had just handed her. Did he not guess how much he was missed here? How much she needed him?

"My dearest Sylvia." Giovanni replied, "do not fret yourself to ribbons over that gentleman I fancy you are thinking of. He will come back before you know it, and then you can be happy again."

The following morning Sylvia was to hear similar advice from her brother, who arrived in time to join the family in the dining room for nuncheon.

"Although I should caution you, my dear Sylvia," John warned her after hearing a full and uninhibited account of his sister's interest in the Earl of Longueville, "that the *ton* is bound to frown on such a match. Besides which the Morleys are traditionally pretty well starched up in their adherence to social conventions. Frankly, I have a hard time seeing Morley flying in the face of tradition. If he should do so, however, you may be sure he is well and truly at your feet, Sylvia."

Her brother was standing before the small hearth in Sylvia's studio, gazing admiringly at the portraits of the two gentlemen she had recently executed. Using the new paintings as an excuse, Sylvia had whisked John upstairs as soon as nuncheon was over. She was in sore need of counsel, and knew she could count on her brother to deflate any romantical notions he thought might cause her grief. He would tell her the truth without roundaboutation but with compassion and understanding.

Sylvia had always regretted not waiting to seek John's advice before her aborted elopement with Sir Matthew. If she had, she might never have met her betrayer again, but on the other hand, she would never have met Nicholas Morley either. She would not have known the joy of falling in love again. Or perhaps she would; it was impossible to predict the future. But the truth of the matter was, she had confessed to John, she wanted no other man but Nicholas.

"Now, this other fellow looks like an excellent candidate," she heard her brother say in a tone she recognized as his conciliatory voice, "and he already has the Sutherland hair. Who is he?"

"That is Captain Jason Ransome, youngest son to the Marquess of Milford. He has recently become partners with Longueville in a new shipping venture. And yes," she added in response to her brother's raised eyebrow, "I like him well enough. In fact, I consider him a good friend, but that is all."

"He has not shown signs of anything more?"

Sylvia hesitated. Had the captain shown more than friendship towards her? she wondered. At times she suspected that had she been more encouraging . . . but no, the captain was wedded to the sea and to his ships; there was no room for a wife in his life.

"Jason is a seafaring man," she replied slowly. "If he had other thoughts, he said nothing to me. Besides," she added with a rueful laugh, "he is far too much like you, John. Do you not see the resemblance? I am very comfortable with him, almost as though he really were my brother."

"And you are not comfortable with Longueville?"

Sylvia laughed. The trouble with John was that he knew her too well. Not for nothing were they identical twins. Talking to him was almost like talking to herself, except that she suspected her brother was far wiser in dealings of the heart.

"Have you never been in love, John?" she countered.

It was John's turn to smile. "You know I have not, you minx. You would have been the first to know had I been daft enough to throw my heart away. All I recall is a couple of passing infatuations with heartless chits who made me miserable for a week or two but left no lasting scars."

"Well, when you do find the right female—and believe me, you will know it when it happens—one you feel you *must* spend the rest of your life with if living is to have any meaning at all, then you will find out that love can be very uncomfortable indeed. So to answer your question, yes, I am uncomfortable with Nicholas. It is not what he says that makes me anxious, but what he does not say. It is not what he does, either, for when he kissed me, it felt as though he really meant it, if you know what I mean."

"Then I daresay he did mean it," John remarked, his eyes returning to the highwayman in the tattered cloak and tricorne hat on the wall. "Of course, he does not belong to my set, and that long sojourn in India may have changed him in ways we cannot tell, but if he is a true Morley, I am willing to wager he will make you an offer. But you must be patient, Sylvia. After all, the man has just buried his cousin—"

"Oh, John, I know that," Sylvia broke in, her voice quavering, "and I am willing to be patient, but I fear he may decide to run away to India again. He did so when his countess died, you know. Cornwall holds such painful memories for him, and he has that new ship of his sitting in Falmouth ready to sail at a moment's notice." She paused for a moment and then added in a choked voice, "I simply cannot bear the thought of being abandoned a second time."

Her brother turned away from the portrait of the earl and came across the room to put an arm around her. Sylvia laid her head on his shoulder and sighed. "I am so glad you are here, John," she said in a muffled voice.

Tired, and wet, and splattered with mud, Nicholas cantered under the stone arch that for centuries had guarded the entrance to his estate. He had ridden down from Bath in record time, pushing on in spite of the intermittent rain, stopping only to quench his thirst and rest his horse.

The austere fortress that was his home appeared almost benign in the pale sunlight that had begun to filter through the dark clouds as he rode through Helston. The rain had finally broken, and by the time he cantered across the stone bridge and into the cobbled courtyard of the Castle, Nicholas felt a rush of intense joy at being home again. He was no longer the stalwart warrior of his childhood dreams, returning with the spoils of war after an arduous campaign on the battlefields, and there was no lady in green and gold awaiting him in the Great Hall. But a battle had certainly been fought and won, a battle that would determine—if the last remaining skirmish went his way—his future and the future of his line.

Love and war should not belong in the same arena, but he had recorded evidence in the annals of Morley history that they did. The old baron's eldest son had, according to the story, stolen his bride from a neighboring castle and then fought the lady's chosen suitor for the right to keep her. The young Morley—or Morais as he had been then—had won that battle, conducted, it was also recorded, in full medieval armor and mounted on war horses.

Nicholas felt the fierce joy of that barbaric victory sing in his own veins even as he tried to repress it. In light of the past week's events, it seemed almost sacrilegious to be overcome with joy. And with thoughts of love.

For at that moment Nicholas had discovered he could love again. He finally understood what had driven that warrior ancestor to stake his life on love. Nicholas could only be thankful he had not himself caused his rival's death, although he could not forget that his ancestor had had no such qualms.

He threw his gloves on the hall table and allowed Greenley to take his damp cloak. The past week had been trying in more ways than one, and Nicholas had been glad to leave the dowager and his aunt in Jason's capable hands and come home. His mother had refused to leave Aunt Lydia by herself in that old house, emptied now of all its menfolk. In an ironic twist of fate, Matt's desperate action had changed the course of their family forever, but in ways his cousin had not anticipated. Instead of stealing a wealthy wife from under his cousin's nose, and eventually inheriting his title, Matt's death had brought Farnaby Hall to the earl, Matt's only heir.

And as for the lady, he thought, turning towards the elegant marble staircase that had replaced the wooden one sometime in the fourteenth century, that issue must still be settled, and the sooner the better.

"Send Digby up to me will you, Greenley? I shall need a bath and change of clothes. Then you may order my curricle around."

He almost added, *for I have business at Whitecliffs, business that will affect us all,* but he did not wish to set tongues wagging before he was sure he had won the fair lady. And wag they certainly would when—and providing Sylvia was willing—it was bruited about that the Earl of Longueville was to take a second countess so soon after his cousin's *accident.*

And there was no doubt in Nicholas's mind that he wanted that second countess in his home and in his bed as quickly as it could be arranged. His mother—whom the earl had felt obligated to inform of his intentions to replace as mistress of Longueville Castle—protested less than he had anticipated.

"Take care you do not repeat the mistakes of the past, my dear," she told him. "A gentleman cannot be too careful in the choice of a wife and mother of his children."

Mother of his children! The words rang in the earl's head as he climbed into his curricle an hour later and turned his horses' heads towards Whitecliffs.

This time, he told himself with a satisfying sense of conviction, there would be no doubt as to the identity of the father of his wife's children.

Chapter Twenty-six

~

The Second Countess

"Hobson was right, the sun really is coming out," Sylvia announced from her position at the window. "We are to have a sunny day for our birthday after all, John. Do you think it is a good omen?"

"If it means that we can have tea served in the garden tomorrow, then I would say that yes, it is a good omen, my dear."

Viscount Brandon left his place on the settee next to their aunt and strolled over to stand beside her at the window. Casually, he threw an arm around her shoulders and squeezed her affectionately.

"I forbid you to wear that long face again, Sylvia," he teased. "Perhaps the sun is a lucky omen and will bring Longueville back to the Castle. Hobson tells me that as of last night, however, they had no news of the earl." He paused, then added, "Does he know your birthday is tomorrow, love?"

"Oh, yes," Sylvia replied with a shaky laugh, "Aunt Marguerite made quite sure of that by inviting both Longueville and the captain to dine with us. A small family affair, she told them, to celebrate your birthday visit. Oh, dearest John," she added impulsively, slipping an arm round the viscount's waist, "I am so very pleased you are here. Marguerite has been wonderful, of course, and Giovanni, too, but I do miss you, John. I wish you had not been away in Scotland when . . ."

"No sense moping over what might have been, love," the viscount said bracingly. "I want you to concentrate on the ride you promised me if it is fine tomorrow. And I cannot wait to see that famous horse you have acquired. I understand the animal is something of a legend in these parts. Am I to see you put him through his paces?"

"Oh, no, I do not think so." Sylvia giggled at the thought of putting a saddle on old Hercules' bony back and trotting around the countryside. "He is rather past his prime, I fear, besides being sadly temperamental. I have the suspicion that he would rather see me flat on *my* back in the mud than on *his* back."

"Perhaps if I were to mount the brute, he might be more tractable?" her brother remarked. "He does not appear old and decrepit in the painting of the highwayman."

Sylvia felt herself blush. "That is because I did not reproduce Hercules in all his hip-shot, sway-backed glory. I meant to, of course, but at the last moment I relented. Longueville protested vociferously when he learned my intent, and I wished to show him that even earls do not dictate to artists. But when it came to the sticking point . . ."

"You could not put your white knight on a broken-down horse, I gather. I trust Longueville appreciates the extent of your devotion, Sylvia. I am quite looking forward to meeting the man who has brought color back to your cheeks, and a shine to those beautiful eyes of yours."

"You are a sad tease, John," Sylvia injected with a smile. "I hope—"

Sylvia never did say what it was she hoped, for at that moment Hobson opened the door of the Italian Saloon to announce a visitor.

"His lordship, the Earl of Longueville," the butler intoned expressionlessly, the twitching of his shaggy eyebrows the only sign of a more than cursory interest in the visitor.

"Well, do not keep his lordship kicking his heels in the hall, Hobson," Lady Marguerite exclaimed sharply. "Show him up immediately."

"Oh, John, he came," Sylvia exclaimed breathlessly, feeling the color recede from her cheeks. She took a step towards the door, then turned, an enigmatic smile on her lips. "On second thought, perhaps I should receive him in my studio, Hobson." The time had come, she thought as she swept out of the room, to find out if John was correct about the earl. Was he about to behave like a true Morley after all?

Chapter Twenty-seven

~

Love Conquers All

The sound of the studio door opening behind her made Lady Sylvia flinch, but she did not turn. She remained standing before the portrait she had called *The Highwayman,* admiring the strong, sun-bronzed features of the man who stood, pistol in hand, under an ancient oak beside a lonely stretch of road. Although she suspected the earl would have the name changed as soon as she delivered the painting to him, Sylvia would always think of it—of him—as *The Highwayman.* The gentleman thief who had stolen her heart when least she had expected it.

Head poised critically to one side, Sylvia gazed up into the brooding eyes of the man in the portrait.

How she would love to keep this man for herself. He would hang in her bedroom, she decided in a flash of daring. Opposite her bed, so that *The Highwayman* would be the last thing she saw before going to sleep, the first thing to greet her in the morning.

She sighed.

"Handsome fellow, is he not?"

The low, vibrant voice came from directly behind her, so close that the warm breath teased the curl that had escaped its pins to flutter beside her cheek. Sylvia's heart leaped up into her throat, and she whirled round to face the man who had fueled such foolish, romantical notions a moment ago.

"My lord," she stammered, mortified to be caught like some brainless schoolroom miss daydreaming over her French dancing master. "You s-startled me."

He smiled, and Sylvia felt her heart flutter wildly. "So I see," he drawled, his voice caressing her skin like warm honey. "But why so surprised, my dear? Surely you knew I would come?"

He was so close that Sylvia could detect the clean smell of starch on his shirt, the scent of his Holland water. Her head reeled with the intoxication of his presence. She wanted to step back, but her feet seemed to be rooted in the worn rug. Then she had the urge to sway forward, against his chest, which seemed extraordinarily broad and inviting. And so close. How easy it would be, she thought, to give in to temptation. Surely she must be the only female in the world who would resist the lure of such a man.

Towering over her and exuding an animal magnetism that awakened all her dormant female instincts, the earl seemed to be daring her to let herself go. To immolate herself on the irrevocable fires of passion. Sylvia knew the sensation all too well, having trodden down that path once before. Even after ten long years, she remembered the pull of the senses, the tingling of the body, the furious palpitating of the pulses, the blessed ecstasy of surrender.

He had yet to touch her. Sylvia knew that when he did—and she never doubted for an instant that he would—she would crumble like a child's sand castle before the relentless onslaught of the surf.

Unless she managed to rally her strength to resist the almost irresistible.

"How c-could I possibly know such a thing?" she protested, taking refuge in banter. "I am not a mind reader or fortune teller. If you must know, my lord, I rather thought you might be on your way back to India by now."

She finally dared to raise her eyes to his, and was startled to see that she had wounded him.

"You consider me the sort of paltry fellow who would run off and leave things unsettled between us?"

Sylvia had but a hazy notion what this ambiguous remark might signify. She searched his face for a clue as to his meaning and noticed, for the first time, that his eyes were not unrelieved black as she had thought, but flecked with shades of gray. She marveled that she had not noted this as she painted *The Highwayman*. An unforgivable omission for an artist.

"I see I did not quite capture the color of your eyes, my lord," she said in her cool, professional voice, glad of the excuse to fall back to a less emotional level. "I must remedy that before I can deliver the portrait to you."

"The devil fly away with the portrait," he responded impatiently. "I did not come here to talk about painting, my girl. Now, will you answer my question?"

Sylvia opened her eyes in mock surprise. "You do not like it, my lord? I was afraid you would not, so I am quite prepared to do another—"

"I never said I did not like it—"

"It does not surprise me in the least, my lord," Sylvia continued brightly, as if he had not spoken. "I realize it is not quite the way an earl would wish to be remembered by his grandchildren."

"I have no grandchildren."

Sylvia smiled condescendingly, thankful to have regained control of this ridiculous conversation. "Oh, but you will, my lord, just as soon as the Dowager Countess finds a suitable candidate for you."

"My mother has decided not to return to Cornwall," he said bluntly. "She has washed her hands of me, so to speak, and accepted my aunt's invitation to make her home in Bath."

Sylvia paused for a moment, disconcerted by this unexpected development. "Oh, dear me," she exclaimed, striving to maintain a light tone. "Then you will just have to find a suitable candidate yourself, my lord. That should not be difficult given your—"

"I already have," he interpolated, and Sylvia could swear the rogue had leaned forward an inch or two to reduce the space between them. She felt suddenly unbearably hot and flustered, and wished fervently that she could regain control of her feet, which still refused to obey her frantic commands to uproot themselves from the carpet and flee this looming danger.

"In that case, you will undoubtedly have any number of grandchildren," she pointed out breathlessly. "May I wish you happy, my lord?" she forced herself to ask, although her entire being rebelled against the notion of this man belonging to another woman.

"No, you may not, you naughty little tease," he muttered. "And I stand not a tinker's chance of having any grandchildren at all unless you answer my question, Sylvia."

He glared at her with such ferocity that Sylvia quailed. "Oh," she exclaimed, suddenly recalling the odd question she had tried her best not to answer. "You are referring to the comment about you being a paltry fellow or something of that nature, my lord?"

"Something of that nature," he assented, his lips curling into a dangerously wicked smile.

Averting her eyes quickly, Sylvia took a deep breath before

launching into another diversion. "I would hardly call you *paltry*, my lord. Indeed, you are substantially larger than my brother. Have you met my brother, Viscount Brandon? You will like him, I am sure."

Sylvia distinctly heard the earl utter a low growl of frustration. "I have not yet met Brandon, but I will do my best to find him agreeable since we are soon to be related."

"You are?" Sylvia gasped as the implications of this remark sank in.

"Exactly, my dear. And believe me, Sylvia, I have no intention of reverting to the barbaric practices of my ancestors, particularly Sir Roderick the Ax, best known for snatching his bride from the altar as she was exchanging her vows with another."

"Was Sir Roderick happy with his stolen bride?" Sylvia murmured from among the folds of a rapidly wilting cravat. "He did wed her, I hope."

"Of course, he wed her, you pea-goose." He cupped her chin and disentangled her face from his cravat. "And the records say they were very happy together. Had eight children and lived to a ripe old age." He paused to trail warm kisses over her closed lids and down her cheek to the curve of her neck. "Her name was Blanche, by the way," he added, after allowing his lips to meander across the tops of her breasts until Sylvia felt delirious with joy.

"A lovely name," she agreed breathlessly, wondering where all this would lead.

"I have always thought so," she heard him murmur against the tender spot at the base of her throat. "I would like to call our daughter Blanche if you have no objection, my love. If our first offspring is a boy . . . hmm, you taste so sweet . . . he could be Roderick. I rather like the idea of another Roderick . . . hmm, simply heavenly, my pet . . . as the master of Longueville Castle. Would you not agree, love?"

Sylvia had reached a point of delirium where she was ready to agree to anything. All she craved was the taste of his mouth on hers. This talk of children was reassuring in its own way, but she needed to hear this man speak of love.

"Are you listening to me, Sylvia?" He had raised his head and although her eyes were still closed, she knew he was gazing at her.

"Of course, my lord," she murmured meekly. "You have just informed me that I am to produce a boy and a girl, to be named Roderick and Blanche."

"My name is Nicholas," he remarked gently, "and we will not stop at two, my girl. Roderick had eight according to the records, but I would be willing to settle for six. That is if you agree, Sylvia. Do you?"

She smiled encouragingly and snuggled back into the cravat. "The production of six offspring will take some time, my lord," she pointed out. "When do you intend to start?"

"You are a delight, my love," he murmured. "If I leave now, I can obtain a special license in Falmouth and be back tonight. Your birthday—and no, I had not forgotten that, my dear—could be your wedding day. If you will have me, that is."

Of course she would have him, she thought, watching the doubt flicker in his eyes again. How silly men could be upon occasion. But if this was his idea of an honorable offer, she mused, still not entirely satisfied, she would have to pry those magic words out of him some other way.

"Is that why you came to Pirate's Cove?"

Sylvia looked at him for a moment, the recent events at Pirate's Cove dissolving and reassembling in her mind in a sequence not unlike that which had played itself out centuries ago between the impulsive Sir Roderick and another thwarted bridegroom.

"Young Timmy told me you were in danger, my love," he whispered, increasing the pressure of his arms until Sylvia could feel every curve and hollow of his body pressed against hers.

Sylvia sighed against his lips, which were moving lazily over hers. "Is that the only reason you came?"

He gazed at her in surprise. "Oh, I see," he added after a moment's pause, "Perhaps you need to know that I discovered I could not live without you, my love."

While this was not the whole of it, Sylvia smiled brightly. "You were worried about all those grandchildren, no doubt?"

From his puzzled expression Sylvia knew that future generations of Morleys had played no direct part in his decision to come to her rescue. Then she saw, with no little relief, a flicker of comprehension in those dark eyes.

Suddenly, he picked her up and carried her over to the settee. Settling her firmly in his lap, he brushed an errant red curl from her forehead and smiled down at her with so much love in his eyes that Sylvia knew her fondest dreams were about to come true.

"I can see I have been going about this in all the wrong way," she heard him murmur. "I should have donned one of Roderick's suits of armor and come charging over here, pennants flying, and simply snatched you away from your brother. Would you have liked that, my love?"

Sylvia giggled. "That might have worked for Roderick and Blanche five centuries ago, but in 1814 a female likes to hear some plain speaking if you please, my lord."

"Oh, so what if I told you I came to Pirate's Cove that afternoon because I love you, Sylvia." His voice dropped lower. "So much that I cannot conceive of spending my life without you, love. Will you marry me, my dear?"

Sylvia knew she was smiling foolishly, but could not control herself. She nodded vigorously, not trusting herself to utter a single word for fear of releasing the tears of joy that were building up inside her.

Unlike his chosen bride, the earl did not appear to need plain speaking to understand his lady's response.

PENGUIN PUTNAM

online

Your Internet gateway to a virtual environ-
ment with hundreds of entertaining and
enlightening books from Penguin Putnam Inc.

*While you're there, get the latest buzz on
the best authors and books around—*

Tom Clancy, Patricia Cornwell, W.E.B. Grif-
fin, Nora Roberts, William Gibson, Robin Cook,
Brian Jacques, Catherine Coulter, Stephen King,
Jacquelyn Mitchard, and many more!

Penguin Putnam Online is located at
http://www.penguinputnam.com

PENGUIN PUTNAM
NEWS

Every month you'll get an inside look at our
upcoming books and new features on our
site. This is an ongoing effort to provide you
with the most interesting and up-to-date
information about our books and authors.

Subscribe to Penguin Putnam News at
http://www.penguinputnam.com/ClubPPI